STRIVERS ROW

During the 1920s and 1930s, around the time of the Harlem Renaissance, more than a quarter of a million African-Americans settled in Harlem, creating what was described at the time as "a cosmopolitan Negro capital which exert[ed] an influence over Negroes everywhere."

Nowhere was this more evident than on West 138th and 139th Streets between what are now Adam Clayton Powell, Jr., and Frederick Douglass Boulevards, two blocks that came to be known as Strivers Row. These blocks attracted many of Harlem's African-American doctors, lawyers, and entertainers, among them Eubie Blake, Noble Sissle, and W. C. Handy, who were themselves striving to achieve America's middle-class dream.

With its mission of publishing quality African-American literature, Strivers Row emulates those "strivers," capturing that same spirit of hope, creativity, and promise.

D1166821

Also by Nichelle D. Tramble
The Dying Ground

The Last King

The Last King

A Maceo Redfield Novel

Nichelle D. Tramble

Strivers Row / One World

Ballantine Books • New York

Strivers Row
An Imprint of One World
Published by The Random House Publishing Group

Copyright © 2004 by Nichelle D. Tramble
Reader's guide copyright © 2004 by Random House, Inc.

www.striversrowbooks.com

Library of Congress Cataloging-in-Publication Data

Tramble, Nichelle D.
    The last king: a Maceo Redfield novel / Nichelle D. Tramble.
        p.   cm.
    ISBN 0-375-75882-8
    1. Oakland (Calif.)—Fiction.   2. African American men—Fiction.
  3. Basketball players—Fiction.   4. Male friendship—Fiction.   5. Rape—
Fiction.   I. Title.
PS3570.R334L37 2004
813'.6—dc22   2004043720

Text design by Mercedes Everett

Manufactured in the United States of America

10 9 8 7 6 5 4 3 2 1

First Edition: April 2004

For Malcolm Spellman

Fort comme la mort
Doux comme l'amour

"We are forlorn like children,
and experienced like old men,
We are crude and sorrowful
and superficial—
I believe we are lost."

—Erich Maria Remarque,
All Quiet on the Western Front

The Last King

Prologue

The first time I saw Cotton play ball I was nine years old. He was shoeless on a scorching basketball court in the middle of July, dominating a game made up of men twice his age. His T-shirt was ragged around the collar where out of habit he had chewed through the fabric. The material, worn thin from poverty, hung loose from his bony frame like a second skin, and his hand-me-down shorts were so tight they revealed in two places that he wasn't wearing underwear. His eyes were bloodshot and wary, and his ill-fitting clothes looked as if he wore them for both waking and sleep.

Whenever he passed in front of me I was able to see the pink ringworm patterns in his scalp and smell the sweet, pungent odor of stale urine that escaped from his body. So could his teammate, who nudged him away when he got too close.

"Damn, man, you smell like you been wiping your ass with your clothes."

Cotton didn't acknowledge the insult or the snickers of the crowd, and we didn't notice, until the game was nearly over, that the court was peppered with his blood.

His feet were bleeding.

The crowd, mesmerized by the skill of his hands, hadn't noticed that he was barefoot, hadn't noticed his oily Converse tennis shoes discarded near the fence, the laces and tongue missing from the left foot. His bare feet were littered with cuts from the debris on the ground, blistered and red from the puckered asphalt, but he had played the entire game without complaint.

It was the first and only time many of us would ever witness talent so pure that it transcended the physical. While Cotton played basketball he was not aware of his pain, his surroundings, or the poverty that existed so drastically in his life. Instead, for the forty-eight minutes of the pickup he awed the crowd with his abilities. At a mere fourteen years old, a gangly five foot ten and sprouting, he commanded the court. He was focused in a way that made his opponents invisible, his teammates mere appendages to his body, and his drive a force so singular it could not be named. It kept us from ridiculing his appearance. It killed the snickers, made us stomach his foul smell and the sores on his scalp.

At least while he played.

After the game, as Cotton stood there accepting the congratulatory nods of the other players, his world came back into focus. A girl, too young to understand the power of what she'd witnessed, too poor and unhappy herself to really care, laughed and pointed at his feet.

He looked down, and just that quick, the rare moment we'd all experienced disappeared. The high of the court, the illusion of being someone and someplace else, crashed down around him to be replaced by mismatched, ragged clothes, a malnourished body, ashy feet, and dirt embedded in his toenails and fingernails, and in the creases of his elbows and knees.

The snickers and jokes found their mark and that's when the second thing he came to be most famous for as an adult flashed forward. His anger, like his talent, was so pure we had to step back in awe. It seemed to boil up from the ground, an entity all its own that traveled up through his body to take possession. Before anyone could step in to stop or alter the course of his actions, Cotton reached out to strike, punching the girl with incredible force. She fell backward, her eye swelled, and Cotton disappeared into a battalion of neighborhood kids itching to protect one of their own. He tried to defend himself, and his height worked in his favor, but he was outnumbered.

At that same moment I registered the wicked smiles of my two best friends, Jonathan "Holly" Ford and Billy Crane. Without giving it a second thought or exchanging a word between them they jumped into the fray to help even Cotton's odds. They heeded the call of the underdog for reasons of their own, but Holly, before he took his first swing, turned to shove me backward into the crowd. I was a star in my own right, my pitching arm just short of being minted in gold, and Holly thought to protect it.

The three of them—Holly, Billy, and Cornelius "Cotton" Knox—worked like plowers, each taking a separate row and chopping forward to the chain-link fence. Though Holly and Billy's friendship would one day lead to tragedy, that day they worked blindly, side by side, backing their foes into a corner without displaying an ounce of mercy. In the confusion the girl was forgotten. She stood to the side, crying, a bruise developing beneath her eye. Cotton hadn't hesitated at all when he hit her, hadn't allowed his anger to distinguish between boy or girl. She ran off toward the adjacent projects with the other kids right behind her.

As they scattered, Coach Elliott and a group of parents hurried over to see what damage had been done. The fight was exactly what they'd all feared when the Cougars, a team made up of kids from the roughest housing project in East Oakland, were added to our schedule. But those kids hadn't stood a chance because Holly was cut from the same cloth, and despite two years of living under my grandparents' protective roof, he quickly reverted back to the boy who sprang from the same soil as Cotton.

I knew without being told that Holly saw him as a kindred spirit. He also saw the dirt, neglect, and hunger that had existed for him before my grandparents opened their home. As he fought to help Cotton, he also fought against the part of himself that wouldn't be denied. The part that woke him from deep sleeps to remind him that the other boy—the real boy—wasn't far away. He recognized Cotton's anger and desperation and in that moment a lifelong partnership was formed.

"Hey! Hey, now, break it up!" The last of the kids ran off as Coach Elliott arrived with the parents hot on his tail. The adults all talked at once while Holly, Billy, and Cotton struggled to catch their breath.

"We told you they didn't need to play in this park," Delores Crane shouted. She was protective of Billy, her only child, and oblivious to the traits that would later make him a drug lord.

"We shoulda canceled this game," another parent shouted. "These rough-ass kids don't know how to act."

"Where are your shoes?"

It was the voice of my grandmother, cutting through the shouting with her soft Creole accent. "Where your shoes, *bébé*?" she asked Cotton a second time. He blinked hard, his bloodshot eyes wild with panic, not trusting the concern she offered.

"It's alright." She reached out to touch an elbow caked with blood. He backed away with a flinch. In his world, the touch of an adult represented at least three different kinds of trouble.

Gra'mère dropped her arms to her sides. "Alright, alright now, *chér.*" The French endearment calmed him. "It's okay." She called to my grandfather, using his last name. "Redfield! Redfield, hand me a towel."

Gra'mère, founder of the Celestine Home for Young Ladies in West Oakland, knew her way around wounded children, so she stepped lightly around Cotton's fear. She took the towel handed to her by Daddy Al and approached Cotton for a third time. He hesitated only a second before deciding to take the risk and trust her kindness. She wiped the blood from his mouth and stroked his shoulder.

He grabbed hold of her hand, pulled the towel away, and pressed her palm to his cheek as the tears flowed hard down his face. Holly, Billy, and I, uncomfortable with his crying, walked away, heads down, and went back to being nine-year-old boys on the way to permanently distancing ourselves from tears and signs of weakness.

Gra'mère, aware of the scrutiny, led Cotton toward the clubhouse. As they walked I saw him slip the collar of his T-shirt into his mouth. The tension left his body at the familiar feel of the fabric. It served the same purpose as a pacifier.

It was a habit he would never break.

Years later, the fans who followed his career from Castlemont High School to UNLV and finally to the Anaheim Vanguards would grow used to him storming the court with the edge of his jersey dangling from his lips.

His chewing during a game, we'd hear from a million different sportscasters, meant he was in a zone—the kill zone—a place where he had no equal, the place with the same name as the East Oakland neighborhood he called home.

ONE

The sky above the Bay Bridge was a gunmetal gray, and in the distance I could hear the low rumble of freight trains that ran along the Eastshore Highway. I loved the sound, and hadn't realized how much I missed it until it echoed down the early morning streets. The wheels on the tracks, the whistle of the train, the foghorns on the Bay were all part of the soundtrack of my life in Oakland; sounds, like smells, that gave me definition.

It wasn't just the streets and people that claimed me, but the city itself. As I took it all in I realized just how much I was stamped by the place that I'd fled after Billy's murder in 1989. I was only hours back—a newborn—having rolled in with the mist off the Bay, quiet, and under the cover of night. I hadn't planned to come back, but an ominous phone call triggered my speedy return. During my travels I found that the open road suited me so I stayed away as long as I could. I grew accustomed to living a nomad's existence, and I found kinship rather than family with men and women who were not at all interested in who I claimed to be.

I liked being a person without a name; I relished the blank looks I got when I introduced myself as Maceo Albert Bouchaund Redfield. At home any one of those names would have elicited some sort of response, but on the road it hadn't meant shit. Not a single thing. So I convinced myself that the disinterest translated into freedom.

The delusion worked until a single phone call from my aunt Cissy shattered the fragile sense of peace I'd built for myself. The plea on the other end of the phone line was riddled with urgency—*Holly's in trouble, Maceo*—and it meant my days of wandering were done.

It was time to make amends.

After two years of drifting I finally knew there was only one place that could offer me a shot at peace, and that was my hometown. The city was my crossroads, the crooked man with the slanted grin, my temptation, and I wanted to beat it. I wanted to win, and yet I still had expectations, because when the Oakland skyline came into focus, a part of me expected to see grave dust hanging above the city, or a mourner's shroud of black clouds, to acknowledge all that had been lost with Billy's death.

Yet the world hadn't stopped, neither had I, and I'd learned the truest, if not the hardest, lesson of my friend's murder.

Life goes on.

———

The wind was high as the sun broke over the bay, bending trees and fences and moving the chilly fog of early January out into the Bay. Nature had conspired to give her wayward son a fitting welcome-home party, and the theatrics matched my dark mood.

Looking for a reprieve I turned up the heater in my car, then scanned the boulevard until my eyes landed on a Flight Athletic billboard towering over the intersection. During my travels from South Texas through New Mexico and finally California, my way had been shadowed by billboards that featured Cotton, and now a new one loomed above me, barely visible in the mist that blanketed San Pablo Avenue. It featured a bare-chested Cotton, hawking his gray-and-white basketball shoes with his full name— Cornelius Knox—written above his head. His matching Anaheim Vanguards shorts were pulled down low enough to reveal the elastic band of his underwear and the stitching that read: LET ME FLY. The shoes were christened Fort Knox in his honor, with the famous taglines GUARD 'EM WITH YOUR LIFE and WORTH THEIR WEIGHT IN GOLD scattered along the edge.

He looked like a king, and I wasn't the only one who thought so. In pure Oakland style, a fan had climbed the scaffolding to add what they thought was missing from the picture. The tagger had used black spray paint to draw a crown above Cotton's head, then red to give him a long, flowing robe. Beneath the additions in bold, block letters the piece was finished with the rallying cry from *Scarface:* THE WORLD IS MINE.

I had to smile. It made me proud. I understood the fan worship and I knew where it came from. Cotton was a warrior-king to the brigade of lost boys who littered the Oakland streets. The raw aggression he used on the court was an emotion they recognized, and they loved him for that. Loved him because he hadn't been spit-shined into respectability or polished to the point of forgetting who he was, and more important, forgetting who they were.

The friends of his youth remained his friends, and Vanguard games were often filled with guests of the superstar who had rap sheets longer than his stats for college and pro combined. He'd said more than once that he didn't consider the other players to be a part of his family. His teammates were coworkers. The only family he had was in Oakland.

The management's frustration with Cotton's stance was obvious in their vaguely coded public comments about "synergy" and "team dynamics," but they couldn't fault his play. He might not smile and clown for the camera or refer to his coach as a "second father," but he delivered on the court by averaging twenty-nine points a game and making the All-Star team three years in a row. At the end of the day it didn't matter that he was quick with his fists or barely contained his contempt for authority, because he filled seats, which filled the pockets of the people in the front office. The phrase *role model* was never used to describe him, but he was featured in three different commercials promoting a soft drink, his athletic shoes, and a sporting-goods chain.

I was proud of Cotton's triumphs, and I cheered his success from the sidelines, but I also knew that the campaign was a façade, and now, because of recent events, so did the rest of the world. While the advertisement celebrated all that was golden in the ballplayer's life, the discarded *USA Today* on my car seat exposed the darker side to his tale. The newspaper also filled in the details Cissy left out, and more simply, it clarified the reasons for my return.

Shooting Guard Questioned in Murder Investigation

San Francisco (AP)—Jan. 14, 1992—
A woman was found bludgeoned to death in a San Francisco hotel room

registered to Anaheim Vanguard star Cornelius "Cotton" Knox. The former Oakland resident missed Tuesday's game against the Sacramento Kings in Anaheim after he was detained by the San Francisco District Attorney's Office for questioning. Police are seeking information about an unidentified man seen fleeing the hotel room on the night of the murder.

Cotton.

A dead body.

An unidentified man.

The words flashed at me like Morse code.

Since the first year Cotton had entered the league, he'd spent every NBA All-Pro weekend with his boys from Oakland, a gangsta's ball in whichever city hosted the game; Houston, Philly, Denver, and finally Oakland in 1992. Sometimes his guest list for the All-Pro included as many as twenty people, expanding and deflating from year to year to allow for arrests, marriages, illnesses, and murders. But no matter how many people came and went, there was always one name that never changed.

Holly.

TWO

As I sat in my car contemplating my best friend's involvement in the murder, I lit a second cigarette and threw the newspaper behind my car seat. The usually soothing smell of sulfur from the struck match did nothing to calm my nerves, but I inhaled the smoke anyway. In addition to the cigarette jones I'd picked up on the road, I'd acquired two other things while traveling: a scar that ran from the corner of my right eye down into the crease of my mouth, and a three-year-old jet-black 125-pound Cane Corso named Kiros, who sat beside me in the car. I'd heard once in a psych class at UC Berkeley that pets often represented their owner's inner psyche, but I couldn't figure out what the big, slobbering dog said about me.

Outside the car the storefronts along San Pablo Avenue were dark. It was just after seven o'clock in the morning, and the sidewalks were nearly empty, but I'd come back to the area with one destination in mind: Crowning Glory. The barbershop was the site of three separate gangland shootings, and a place Holly considered to be the birthplace of bad luck, but it was also the first outpost on Oakland's bush telegraph. Cutty, the barber, was a compatriot of my grandfather's from his days in Louisiana, and a man steeped in local happenings. He always had the sort of information that never made the newspapers, the bits and pieces that were closest to the truth.

I cut the engine and jumped out of the car. As I approached the shop, I noticed that even though it was mid-January, the window was still covered in fake snow from the holidays and the cheerless direction to HAVE A MERRY CHRISTMAS AND A HAPPY NEW YEAR.

Inside, the barbershop was furnished with discarded church pews—an attempt by Cutty to stave off a string of bad luck—and when I entered I saw him sitting in the last row with his back to the door. He was talking with a tall man who looked to be in his twenties. The stranger wore a white smock with the barbershop's signature gold scissors and an elaborate CROWNING GLORY stitched on the sleeve. Cutty had stressed for years that he would never hire anyone under fifty to work his chairs so I was surprised to see the young recruit.

I closed the door with force and the bells nailed above the doorjamb crashed to the floor. I smiled when Cutty turned around to investigate the noise.

"What the hell?" At first he looked startled when he saw me, then a wild smile broke out on his face.

"Hey there, old man," I said.

"Hot damn! Maceo, is that you?" He moved quickly across the room to grab me in a bear hug. "Gotdamn, boy, what you doing sneaking up on people? I thought I was seeing a ghost up in here!"

"It's just me."

I slipped from his grasp and looked to the walls above the mirror. It was an old habit. The space was filled with photographs of local sports figures, and for years had included a Little League photo of me, Holly, and Billy. It broke my heart to see that it was missing, but I didn't ask about it. I didn't care to know the reasons why the three of us were no longer relevant.

"Don't you owe me a haircut?" I said instead. The last time I'd seen Cutty, the news of Billy's death had driven me from his shop before I'd even made it into his chair.

"I just might, Youngblood, I just might. What you need?"

"Clean it up."

"Be glad to. You know I been trying to get you to wear a bald head for years." He motioned toward the two old men reading papers in the corner. "You remember Lester and Greavy."

I didn't but I said hello anyway.

He grabbed a towel to wrap around my neck, and pulled a folded white drape from a box on the floor. "When you get back?"

"Just got here."

"You come all the way back just to get a haircut? Or to show me you got a little taller?" He gave me a weak smile. At twenty-five I was still only five feet five inches tall and my height, or lack of it, had been a source of ridicule my entire life.

"Two years ago, you were, what, maybe three feet high?" The insult was mild, devoid of the usual venom that classified Cutty's communication style, which showed me just how much I was missed.

"Just the same old me."

"Naw, boy, something's different. Something's changed."

He was right. There were changes, the most obvious registered in the newfound bulk of my arms, legs, and chest. I'd always been in top shape, even when my baseball career started to fade, but the muscles of the last two years were earned the blue-collar way of construction: heavy lifting and hauling, an occasional fight, or the grueling exercise of looking off into the distance of my own regret.

"What you need, Maceo?" This time Cutty's question was not about my hair.

"I need to find Holly. You heard anything?"

"I heard the police are looking at him for this murder, and that's killing your granddaddy."

I snickered, and the pointed sound chased away the easy, back-and-forth banter of my homecoming. "If I remember right, Daddy Al didn't want anything to do with Holly when I left." *Or me,* but I kept that thought to myself.

"You think he meant that, after the smoke settled and all his sons were gone? He was mad, and he had every right to be mad, but he still loves both of you." He caught my skeptical look in the mirror and frowned. "I guess part of being young is being hard-headed, huh? Your granddaddy missed you, that's all you need to believe. You been gone too long, boy."

It was the second time he'd called me that in less than five minutes. I wanted to laugh, not at the sentiment, because I knew he meant it, but at the nickname. Boy? Had I ever been that? I was convinced my soul had been recycled, handed to me already injured and used.

"If you hadn't left, you would know that. If you'd stayed and talked to your granddaddy . . ."

"There wasn't anything to say."

"There was plenty to say. You and Holly fucked up, you made some bad choices, but Albert loves you both."

"Bad choices? That's one way to put it."

"Well, what would you call it, then? You must've spent the past two years coming up with something. If you didn't you woulda blew your brains out by now."

Cutty wasn't one to mince words so I took a minute to answer him with the same clarity. I ran over all the conversations I'd had with myself on the road, all the taunts I'd heard from my father, and it kept coming back, stalling on the same thing. Oakland. To me the city was a way station for lost souls, a holding station for the damaged hordes of lost boys roaming the city. I said as much to Cutty.

"Maceo," he cut me off, "you don't believe that shit, do you?"

"What you mean?"

"I can tell that you halfway believe what you're saying, but I know you ain't that stupid."

My temper flared. "When did you ever lead a perfect life?"

"The twelfth of never, but I own what I've done. Nowadays everybody got a dramatic reason for why they act a fool."

"Well, sometimes the reasons get complicated."

Cutty plugged the clippers into the wall and tightened the drape around my neck. "You can lie to me if you want to, Maceo, long as you tell yourself the truth."

"What's the truth?"

"The truth is that you boys killed this city, and each other, because you were greedy and lazy."

"Knowing Cotton, knowing Holly, knowing me, you believe that?"

"Knowing your granddaddy I believe every word. Y'all took

the easy way out and now you want to cry foul after trapping yourselves in bullshit."

He spun my chair around and I faced the intense gazes of Lester and Greavy. The two old men obviously agreed with his assessment.

Cutty's hand came down on my shoulder, maybe to straighten me in the chair, possibly to take the sting out of his words. "But I'm glad you're back either way."

I grunted.

"But I guess it's too much to hope that you were in a Farm League somewhere, prepping to play some major league ball."

Cutty asked the question but he knew, like I did, that baseball was so far in my past that it didn't even exist in the same dimension.

I held up my pitching arm and shook my head. "Never healed right."

"That's a gotdamn shame." He looked away. It would have been easier for him to digest the information if I admitted to losing out to bigger talents, but to hear it was gone because of the beating I suffered was too much for the man who'd once sponsored my Little League teams.

It was a bigger shame, I wanted to tell him, that I had lost my drive years before Smokey Baines eliminated the possibility of my success by dislocating my shoulder, spraining my wrist, and bruising my ribs. Gutsier players had come back from lesser injuries but I didn't belong in that category. Never had. Even at my zenith on the mound there was a part of me that always knew my success existed only in that moment.

"I learned to live with it."

"Then you should go on out there and give lessons, Youngblood. Make yourself a fortune 'cause, far as I know, most people ain't got what it takes to deal with *accidentally* throwing a winning lottery ticket in the garbage."

"That's the way it reads to you, huh?"

"That's the way it reads to anybody that ever saw you pitch."

Lester and Greavy nodded in agreement. I had been a minor celebrity in local sports since the days of Pee Wee League baseball, and there were people all over the city who knew my face from the *Oakland Tribune*. At the age of nine I developed a pitching style with a long, drawn-out prep that earned me the infamous nickname "the Watch Dog," as well as a legion of fans from all over the Bay. Those same fans encapsulated the thornbush of coming home. There would always be people to remind me of what was and could have been about my life. So home held the same pitfalls as looking into a funhouse mirror; at first I could laugh and enjoy the spectacle but then I'd recoil from the accuracy of the image.

THREE

"I knew I recognized your face when you came in here." The new guy strode over from the shampoo bowls. "I just couldn't place it, even after I heard your name. I always knew you as the Watch Dog." He looked around. "There was a picture of you in here when I first started. Anyway, I'm Andre Morehouse."

I gave him a pound, the closed-fist greeting I preferred to handshakes.

"You help out Cutty and Oliver?"

Andre glanced at Cutty. "Uh, no, Oliver died about a year and a half ago."

"I'm sorry to hear that." I was taken aback by the news. Oliver was healthy the last time I'd seen him, younger than both Cutty and my grandfather.

"Yeah, I came in about six months after that." Cutty walked away and Andre nodded after him. "He still can't talk about it. Oliver was my uncle, but he was a brother to Cutty. Cancer. He was weak toward the end so I came in to help him out, then I stayed on once he died."

"A lot has changed since I've been gone."

"Yeah, it has. You heard about Cotton?"

"A little. You know anything about the girl that died?"

"Figured she was a Nightingale."

"Nightingale? What's that?"

"You know, the Pussy Posse, a call girl or some such."

I didn't know, and just that fast my two-year absence felt like ten. In my old life I would've known every detail.

He continued. "There's a ring of 'em out of San Francisco that go to all the parties with athletes and famous people."

"Serious?"

"Man, where you been? Some guy touched down a couple years ago with a crew of badass chicks. They come out in force for big parties."

"Who's the guy?"

"Can't think of his name but he came to town ballin', throwing money and girls around like confetti."

"So, you think it was one of his girls?"

"I'd bet my bottom dollar."

I considered that before I asked the next question. "You know a guy named Holly Ford?"

Andre caught my eye in the mirror. "I know *of* him and that's the best way to keep it. He a friend of yours?"

"In another life."

"You know Cotton, too?"

"In a life before the first one."

Cutty came back to interrupt. "Ya'll talking about Cotton?"

"What else is there to talk about?" Greavy answered.

"You think he did it?" I asked the old man.

"Who knows," Greavy shrugged, "all I know is we've had back-to-back minstrel shows the past couple months. Clarence Thomas and Anita Hill playing the clowns on national television, the circus over Tyson losing the last two blue marbles rolling around in that big head of his, and now Cotton. Can you imagine shit getting any worse than this?"

Lester folded his paper. "'Course it's gonna get worse than this. Black people ain't got no pride and the NBA is a coon show, the new chitlin circuit." He hit Greavy's shoulder to get his attention. "Hear what I said, 'chitlin circuit'?"

"I heard," he laughed with Lester, "and I do see some similarities."

Cutty rolled his eyes. "Maceo," he cut through the laughter, "you seen your granddaddy yet?"

"Not yet. Just got here." He tried to hold my gaze but I looked away.

"I heard he went to L.A. yesterday for Cotton's press conference."

"What conference?"

Cutty motioned for Andre to turn on the television. "They suppose to run it this morning. Something happened last night and they blacked it out."

"Are they cutting him from the team?"

"We'll see," he answered.

Andre flipped through the channels until he spotted the legend CORNELIUS KNOX, ANAHEIM flashing below the face of a sports anchor on channel four. He turned up the volume as a long shot of Vanguard Stadium came into view on-screen.

The parking lot outside the arena was filled with press vans and scores of fans who dubbed themselves the Cotton Nation. They were rowdier than the followers of the Raiders, and took pride in the fact that they'd been fans of Cotton since his early days in Oakland. They showed it by wearing green and yellow, the colors Cotton wore at Castlemont High School, instead of the gray and white of the Vanguards.

Inside one of the press rooms a row of microphones were set up at a long banquet table with a podium in the middle. The Vanguards banner hung above it all, as well as pictures of the team and a large portrait of team owner Harper Coolidge. Coolidge, an oil man, had lost a bid to bring another basketball team into his home state of Texas, and the city of Anaheim helped ease the slight by luring him and his money to Southern California. They built him a showpiece of a stadium complete with state-of-the-art press boxes, two restaurants, VIP lounges, and a luxurious press room built to mollify even the most ornery journalists, but a quick scan revealed that neither Coolidge nor coach Jeremiah Healey were present to support their star player.

In short, Cotton was on his own. Moments later, he came through a metal door with his wife, Allaina, at his side. Daddy Al followed behind the two of them wearing a black suit and his favorite Stetson—black, trimmed with silver—which added to his height. He looked older around the eyes, but not in body or spirit. To me my seventy-five-year-old grandfather would only be powerless in death and not a minute before. I watched as he took his place against the wall, leaving three chairs empty for the lawyers.

My response to seeing him after so much time was so strong I had to drop my head. Cutty, before he turned up the volume on the television, squeezed my shoulder.

Another man came through the door after Daddy Al. He was tall, dark like Cotton, and bald, with sunglasses shielding his eyes. He looked familiar to me but I couldn't think of his name. A battalion of lawyers filed in after that. Once they were seated the photographers jumped to attention. Flashbulbs went off in unison, and Allaina threw up a hand to block the glare.

Lester whistled at the rock on her finger, and the ones around her wrist. "Look at that there."

"You whistling at that ring or that woman?" Greavy asked, laughing.

A legitimate question.

Allaina was fine. Beautiful. Tall like her husband, she wore her long, silky black hair in a dramatic wave that fell over her right eye. She was shirtless beneath a blinding white suit with a vicious V-neck that appeared to dip down to her navel. A diamond necklace rested on her collarbone. When she removed her sunglasses they revealed smoky green eyes that were a sharp contrast to her dark skin.

Lester whistled again. "Boy, that fella better keep his job if he wants to keep that woman."

Cutty shook his head. "You ain't never lied. That is not the wife of a poor man."

While the five of us took in the couple, Cotton leaned in close to Allaina and whispered in her ear. She placed her hands on both sides of his face and kissed his forehead. They smiled at each other and the room went quiet. When he stood to walk to the podium she held on to his fingers. He squeezed, then let go to read the piece of paper in his hand.

"That boy stay clean, don't he?" Cutty asked.

"That boy wear some beautiful suits, I ain't gonna deny

that," Greavy answered, "but I ain't never liked that plantation hairstyle of his."

Cotton, sharp as usual, wore his hair in neat, intricate corn-rows that hung loose at his collar. His six-foot-five frame was en-cased in a dove-gray suit that did nothing to hide the East Oakland swagger he still wore like armor. He looked good, with a diamond sparkling in each ear, but he exhibited none of the ease and grace he was known for on the basketball court. Instead he was awkward and stiff, rolling with a program that wasn't his, casting war-torn eyes on the people in the room. He gave them all a moment to take him in, then without preamble or a lengthy introduction he read a prepared statement in a steady, emotion-less voice.

"Thank you for coming." He inhaled deep before continu-ing. "In light of recent events I have informed Coach Healey, and the Vanguards organization, that I will sit out the remainder of the season in order to protect the integrity of the team. It should be apparent to anyone who has ever seen me play that my love for the game is foremost in my mind, and that is the one and only reason I've made this decision."

I took note of the fact that he conveyed a love for the game and not for his teammates or for the Vanguards organization.

"I don't want the events in my personal life to distract my teammates from their quest for the championship, so I will cheer them on from the sidelines. I will also show my support by aiding the police in their investigation of the recent murder," he stum-bled over the word but kept going, "and by allowing my team-mates to remain focused on their goals for the current season."

He looked at his lawyer, who gave him a slight nod in return. His chin hit the microphone when he leaned back in to deliver his final words. "At this time I would like to thank you for coming. I would also like to ask that you respect my wife and son in regards to this story. Thank you for your time."

The same lawyer stepped forward to take Cotton's place at the mic but before he had a chance to speak a reporter jumped up to introduce himself.

"David Starr. *Sports Syndicate*." At the sound of the man's name a collective groan went up around the barbershop.

"Starr and his cronies been waiting to crucify Cotton for years."

Greavy was right. When Cotton first hit the league in '88 he represented the West Coast in the hardest way possible, by wearing cornrows and braids, until then a California style seen mostly on gangstas and prisoners. He furthered the image by aggressively shit-talking his way up and down basketball courts, with a scowl plastered firmly in place. He had a tattoo of Oakland on his forearm and the cryptic message FLY OR DIE calligraphed across his back. In a national column, Starr bemoaned Cotton's presence in the NBA at least once a month during the regular season.

"Mr. Knox, in truth, weren't you *suspended* from the team? And don't you now face complete expulsion from the league?"

Cotton leaned into the mic. "Not true."

The room waited for him to elaborate but he clasped his hands together and remained silent. Everything in his demeanor conveyed that he did not want to be there, that he did not want to be in the back room of the stadium giving up his career, even for a short time. As the reporters looked on he rotated his wedding ring in counter-circles until Allaina reached out to still his hands.

The lawyer stepped up again.

"Mr. Knox *volunteered* to sit out the remainder of the season.

His first thought, after his family, was for the team. It's not his intent to cast shame on the Vanguards or the National Basketball Association."

"And consorting with murderers? How does that fit in?"

"Mr. Starr, you must be privy to information that neither this legal team nor the San Francisco District Attorney's Office has. Mr. Knox has agreed to help in any way he can but at this point, no one knows the identity of the murderer."

"Does Mr. Knox know the identity of the unidentified man seen leaving the hotel room?"

The lawyer didn't miss a beat, but behind him Cotton looked at Allaina. For a moment he lost his game face, and the reporters picked up the scent of blood. Daddy Al clamped a reassuring hand on Cotton's shoulder.

"Neither myself nor my client can comment on the specifics of the investigation."

"Are you aware that there's footage of the man leaving the room where the murder took place?"

"That information is unsubstantiated at this time. Any other questions?"

"Just one. Cotton stated he didn't want to *shame* the Vanguards organization. Does that courtesy extend to his wife?"

"Excuse me?" Cotton glared at Starr with dead eyes. He was trussed up for the cameras but at the end of the day he was still a man who'd come up hard on the Oakland streets. He had a ferocious nature on the court, and the reporter was about two seconds away from seeing it firsthand.

Starr continued undeterred. "Maybe Allaina could answer the question herself."

"Allaina?" Cotton's smirk was deadly. "You think you know my wife well enough to call her by her first name?"

Starr flashed a smirk of his own. "Forgive me, Mrs. Knox." Even on-screen I could feel the tension building in the room. "Were you aware your husband was having an affair with the deceased?"

"What'd you say?" Cotton asked.

The bald man moved quick to grab Cotton while Daddy Al pulled Allaina to her feet, a sign that the press conference was over. The remaining reporters nearly trampled Starr to shout out their own questions.

"Were you having an affair with the deceased?"

"Did you slaughter the victim?"

And again Starr: "Mrs. Knox, were you aware that this wasn't your husband's first dealings with the murder victim? Did you know he'd been seen with her on several previous occasions?"

Allaina hesitated in her flight from the room, and I saw Cotton glance at his wife with alarm. His worst fear, that she would believe the words, was all over his face. I knew from the few times I'd seen them together, and the stories repeated by Daddy Al and Gra'mère, that Cotton was devoted to his wife. His courtship of the tragic beauty had been followed closely in Black entertainment magazines and news shows.

The relentless media scrutiny eventually exposed the fact that Allaina's first child, a little girl, had died in a fire. Cotton knew the story, as did my family, and he was protective of his wife's pain. The one reporter who'd dared to mention it in their presence had been beaten that same evening after leaving a sports bar in Houston. It was reported in the press as a random mugging but Oakland knew better.

Starr looked down at his notes. "Several sources have reported seeing the woman in your company at least five times preceding the murder."

Despite the hushed warnings of his lawyers, Cotton stepped back to the podium, visibly angry. Allaina remained perched at the door. She looked like she was torn between fleeing the room and staying behind to support her husband. Daddy Al's eyes went back and forth between the two of them. Starr looked at Cotton and then at Allaina hovering in the doorway. She averted her eyes, and Cotton moved the podium to the right of his body. It gave him clear passage to the reporter pool. Starr was too intent on breaking Allaina's resolve to notice. He shouted his last question with his eyes locked on her.

"Who murdered your girlfriend, Cotton? Did you send someone to kill her to keep your wife from finding out?"

Allaina left the room on those last words, and Cotton was over the table in minutes. His hands were around Starr's neck before the man had a chance to blink. He choked the reporter to the ground while his lawyers tried to pull him back, but they were no match for his anger. The veins in Cotton's hands and his neck bulged as he planted his knee in the reporter's chest and dug in. It took three men to pull him off and while the press room went crazy, the barbershop was silent.

None of us knew how to process what we were seeing. We just watched, helpless, as a man's future burned before our eyes. Cotton's dose of sabotage was so potent he might as well have been hooked up to an electric chair.

He mainlined failure straight to the vein and it left us mute.

FOUR

"What I tell you? What I tell you? A coon show, hoodlums and thieves." Lester looked wildly around for support but I couldn't give it to him. Watching Cotton lose his cool, possibly his career, and seeing the fear and hurt in Daddy Al's eyes was too much to bear. I tried to shake the dread I felt, but I heard trouble howling in the distance like a train without brakes. A familiar feeling. I'd always found ways to invite danger into my life.

Once, when I was ten years old, Daddy Al took me, Holly, and Cotton fishing at Lake Chabot. On the way to the shore I fell behind the three of them, and when I veered onto another path none of them noticed. I panicked at the thought of getting lost so I circled back toward their voices. Later, when I retold the story of what happened next, I remembered hearing the soft buzz of warning but I kept going anyway. Moments later when I hit my head on a low-hanging branch, I was surprised—even as my face exploded in pain—that the branch was actually soft enough to crack open.

My walking into a beehive became a recurring joke at family gatherings. It always got laughs, and induced the same questions year after year.

Didn't you hear the bees, Maceo?

Didn't you see them?

Watching Cotton, fearing for Holly, gave me that same feeling, it just buzzed a little louder.

———

There was nothing left to see, so Andre turned off the television. Each of us retreated into our separate thoughts, and as soon as Cutty finished shaving my head I tossed two twenty-dollar bills onto his station. The haircut only cost fifteen. He used the broom handle to slide the money into an open drawer beneath the mirror. I motioned toward the black television screen.

"You saw the same thing I did. You still believe what you said earlier?"

"Even more so," he answered evenly. "Albert had a strong hand in that boy's upbringing. What he did up there was all him."

He was wrong, but my hands went up in defeat. What was the point? "Alright, Cutty, I'ma get up out of here."

"Well, take care of yourself."

"Yeah, you, too."

"You headed over to the Dover Street house to see the family?"

"Got a few things I need to take care of first," I answered.

"And these things are more important than seeing your people? That why you in here throwing money around?"

"I'll get over there when I get a chance."

"Guess you forgot how to answer a straight question."

"Just trying to save you some time."

"And the scar on your face? You got an answer for that?"

We held each other's gaze. I wasn't surprised by the question, just that it had come so late. The last-quarter moon carved into my cheek drew attention everywhere I went.

"What scar?" I asked.

I had a laundry list of scars, some visible, some not, and I didn't intend to explain a single one of them. I didn't drop my eyes and he didn't ask me again.

Few people ever did.

He looked me up and down. "Alright then, Maceo, but don't leave town without doing what you need to do. Get over there and see your granddaddy. You the only one blaming yourself for all the shit that happened."

It was a lie, but it was pretty enough to accept.

"Andre?" I called as I reached the door. "You remember the name of the cat who runs the Nightingales?"

"Still can't think of it, but he's related to that guy who died. You know, that dealer who used to live up near Knowland Park."

Before I turned around, before I faced him to hear the name, I heard the snake-laughter of my dead father.

"What guy?" I asked.

"Smokey Baines. That's it, and his cousin's name is Dutch. Dutch Baines."

Dutch Baines.

The name was a coffin nail, and I knew before I stepped outside that his appearance in Oakland was not an accident, that the death of the girl in Cotton's room wasn't one either, and neither was the fact that Holly was just *thatclose* to facing a murder charge.

It was the mark of an amateur to believe there wouldn't be retaliation for Smokey's death. I wasn't an amateur, and neither was Holly, but I'd left town before any markers had been called. Smokey's violent death was a by-product of the game he played, but so was revenge, and there was a long list of people for Dutch to take down.

It was so obvious I hadn't seen it coming.

I should have known better.

When I was old enough to understand the circumstances of my birth, I developed nightmares and a sixth sense for trouble. My father, the man who starred in most of those dreams, the man who killed my mother with a highball of cocaine and heroin, came from the depths of my subconscious to taunt me, and now he was back to feed off my fears. I'd invited his presence the moment I agreed to come home.

He danced in my peripheral vision with a grin and a tip of his hat. Without the Oakland soil to remind me, his ghost had grown weak and I'd allowed myself to forget all the ways in which his appearances spelled trouble, but now he was back and I felt his breath on my neck like a wolf hunting its prey.

And with him came death.

It was there like a promise.

FIVE

My first instinct after I left Crowning Glory was to smoke Holly out of hiding by feeding the grapevine, so I backtracked down San Pablo Avenue to Rook's Diner, my second destination of the morning. After the press conference I knew that the impending media scrutiny would eventually unearth all the secrets of Cotton's past. It was only a matter of time before the spotlight landed on Holly.

Holly, real name Jonathan Ford, came to live with us when I was seven years old. The product of an absent father and a drug-addict mother, he ran away from home and found his way to my family by finding me first. Billy and I, already inseparable, were playing baseball in Bushrod Park the day he appeared. He joined the game and in less than a week he was entrenched in the Dover Street house where my grandparents had raised their family. And in less than two weeks it no longer mattered that he was not a blood relation.

Daddy Al, the father of six girls, welcomed Holly, and later, Cotton, into his home with open arms. He raised his three stray boys with 100 percent of his soul despite the fact that my father had killed his daughter with drugs, that Cotton's father posed a physical threat to us all, and that Holly's family contributed nothing to his upbringing.

Didn't matter.

We were three fatherless boys who needed him and he was there.

It made us brothers.

————

Rook's Diner was a breakfast-and-lunch joint run by an ex-con of the same name. Holly used Rook's as a message center and a place to stash cash. He never kept a public phone line or permanent address for more than three months, so Rook's was the emergency go-to place for people he trusted. It was also his favorite place to eat breakfast, and the fisherman hours, four A.M. to noon, suited his vampire nature. Because of his mother's neglect he couldn't abide waking up hungry, so he ate at Rook's each morning around sunrise.

I honked my horn to get the attention of a homeless man sitting in a bus shelter at the intersection. He approached the car with his coin cup held out in front of him. Beside me in the car, Kiros sat at attention to watch the man approach.

"Hey, you know if Rook is still in business around the corner?" I asked him.

"Still there. Still expensive." He pointed across the street. "If you're trying to save money I could run into that corner store and get you an egg-salad sandwich for seventy-five cents."

I had to stop myself from frowning. I couldn't think of anything I wanted less than a liquor-store sandwich.

"I'ma pass on that."

"Fair enough, but since I helped you, you help me." He shook his cup again. "A little change or a couple dollars, so a brotha can get something to eat?"

I handed him two. "Grab yourself a sandwich, and bring me a cup of coffee."

The man hustled off, returning five minutes later with my coffee. True to his word, he also had a mashed-up egg-salad sandwich wrapped in cellophane. "For a couple more dollars I can watch your car and the dog while you eat."

"I think the dog got it covered."

He leaned in to get a good look at Kiros. "Yeah, that's a monster there. Well, then, I'll tell you what. I'll only charge you a small rental fee for the parking space."

I smiled at his hustle and gave him one more dollar and the coffee.

He pocketed it in a flash. "You need a receipt for your taxes?"

"I'm cool."

"Alright then, just cut through the alley, and you'll smell it before you see it."

He was right. I walked through the front door of Rook's and realized just how hungry I was when the smell of grease fat hit me dead in the face. I looked around and found not a single woman in the joint, not even a waitress, just tables full of men in Carhartt jackets, Pendletons, and steel-toe boots. My immediate impression was that of an industrial cartoon, rows and rows of shoulders and necks hunched over bowls of spicy-smelling chili. It smelled good, and Rook seemed to be doing steady business, but in my eyes you had to be a hell of a man to eat chili and onions at eight o'clock in the morning.

With that in mind I felt for the blackjack I'd slipped into my pocket and closed the door behind me.

SIX

I took an empty table near the back door and sat facing the entrance. The clink of coffee cups, the scraping of silverware, and the low murmur of voices locked the place into a cramped silence. A small handwritten sign wedged between open bags of cornmeal explained the lack of conversation: EAT FAST & KEEP THE BULLSHIT TO A MINIMUM.

Rook's wasn't a haven for strangers. Ex-cons made up a large part of the clientele, so suspicions ran too deep for nosy questions. Any information I gathered would come by way of osmosis so I tried to blend in by pouring myself a coffee and placing my pack of cigarettes on the table while I waited for a menu. My casualness didn't work; I could feel the eyes sizing me up. The only thing that saved me from overt suspicion was the fact that half of the men were watching the small black-and-white television, where footage from the press conference ran on a continuous loop.

Despite the volatile scenes on-screen, the silence imposed by the sign—and Rook's scowling presence—held until a man wearing a PG&E jacket reached over the counter to turn up the volume. The name tag on his pocket read JOE. Like Rook he appeared to be in his late forties or early fifties, hard to tell, but he wasn't chiseled from the same block of stone. Joe looked like he might have a few soft edges. Rook did not.

"Come on, man, let me turn it up."

Rook pointed at the sign as he moved potatoes, eggs, and bacon around the grill without talking. He stood at least six foot five and he wore a multicolored kufi and a T-shirt saturated with grease. His arms looked as if they broke rocks instead of bread, and I'd bet money he didn't have a playful bone in his body. I caught him watching me in an overhead mirror. He grabbed a greasy menu and tossed it my way. I caught it before it hit the floor.

"Let's just see what happened," Joe said again.

"You know what happened," Rook answered. "Cotton blew his cool—"

"And now, he's gonna fry." Another man, encased in overalls short enough to be culottes and tight enough to showcase his entire nut sack, offered his opinion to the room.

"Why you say that, Larry?" Joe asked.

"Yeah, *Larry,* why you say that?" The challenger was a younger man wearing a Raiders cap and a matching tattoo on his arm. "Sounds to me like you wishing the man bad luck."

Larry looked startled by the man's tone and the underlying violence in his voice but I was not. Despite the skyscrapers downtown and the ones flashing like beacons across the Bay, Oakland at times could feel like the piney woods of the most backward-ass state. Many residents still tended to settle disputes with their tempers cocked like guns.

Raider went on. "You seem happy about his trouble. You know something I don't?" The question was an equal mix of anger and sincerity. It would take more than newspaper facts to convince Cotton's younger fans of his guilt.

"I know he's guilty." Larry said the words like the jury had already come back.

"You know that, huh?"

"'Course I do."

Raider looked him up and down. "Then how come you didn't know not to wear those stupid-ass pants?"

There were a few snickers of tentative laughter. The remark was funny but the uncorked kid in the Raider's cap put everyone on alert. Just that quick, a quiet morning breakfast could turn to bloodshed.

"Why you actin' a fool?" Joe stepped in. "Cotton's guilty as sin." He pointed at the TV. "And that press conference proved it."

Raider stepped closer to Joe. "Old man, you don't know what you're talking about."

Joe snickered. He had at least twenty years on Raider, and just as much anger. "You can talk to your daddy like he's your youngest child," he said, "but you better step away from me. I'm a grown man and I say Cotton's guilty. Him and that fella he run with."

I braced myself for what came next.

"Who you talking 'bout, Joe?" Larry tried in his own way to ease some of the tension, but I could tell Raider didn't want Joe to finish his sentence. Neither did I. Rook, with his hand on a pot of boiling water, kept his eye on them both. "What fella?" Larry asked a second time.

"You know exactly who I'm talking about. That gangsta. Holly."

The Last King — 41

I was braced for the name, but it landed like a fist to the gut.

Joe continued. "Word on the street is that Cotton and Holly got in a fight with two thugs over that dead girl. She knew them. They knew her. One of 'em guilty."

"Joe," Rook interrupted, "read the paper to yourself." He looked at me long enough to make the others turn around. "And quit talking out of school."

It was quiet for a moment until Raider opened another route to the same destination. "What about the girl?" He faced the room. "These scandalous broads got to take some of the blame."

Around me I saw more than a few heads nod in agreement. Cotton's trouble was coming right on the heels of Mike Tyson's uncontested bout with Desiree Washington, and opinions on the matter fell hard along gender, age, and class lines. The grumbling around the room created a roundelay of disparate opinions.

Rook, with a voice made of gravel and quarry stones, cut right through the commentary.

"So you saying that one girl deserved to be raped and brutalized, and the other one deserved to have her throat slit?" I looked up at that. The paper had said "bludgeoned to death" and nothing else.

"Think about it, man!" Raider, planted solidly in the land of conspiracy, wouldn't concede to Rook's line of thinking. "Cotton and Tyson going down this close together! Something ain't right."

"Brothas acting like savages is what's not right."

"You just gonna let the girls off the hook?"

"Off what hook? One of 'em dead!"

"But still . . ." Raider said.

"Still, my ass. You hear what you saying? They're Black men, right, animals, so they ain't got enough sense to control themselves?"

Joe spoke up. "That's not what he's saying at all, Rook. Everybody just conversating about all the possibilities."

"Yeah," Raider continued, "'conversating.' That girl went up to his room on her own two feet. If you call the shot then you got to play it all the way through."

"Keep thinking like that, youngster. That's the same shit had me and most of my comrades locked down at Quentin."

He grabbed a pack of cigarettes from atop the grease filter and headed out the back door into the cold.

Joe watched Rook leave. "That man gonna kill somebody one day."

Larry nodded in agreement. "Maybe we need to put a cage around the grill and let his monkey-ass cook through the bars."

Everybody laughed, which broke the tension Rook had left behind.

SEVEN

The diner returned to quiet after Rook's quick departure, and on the grill, eggs, bacon, and potatoes sizzled by themselves as he enjoyed a cigarette in the alley. Minutes later the front door swung open, and before I looked up I felt the air shift. The silence in the room grew deep and cold and the tread of heavy boots echoed through the small space.

"Good morning, gentlemen." I recognized the thin, nasal whine of Detective Philip Noone and it made my heart sink. If Noone had found his way to Rook's it meant he had Holly in his crosshairs. It also meant he would be harder to find.

The detective hadn't changed much in the two years I'd been gone. He still reminded me of a cranked-up bullfrog, with wide-set eyes that lined up as far from each other as possible without being attached to his ears. It gave him the jumpy appearance of prey, of an animal with its eyes always trained to the side, forever on the lookout for predators. He sported a lopsided fade, an outdated Vandyke peppered with gray, and he still had the worst poker face I'd ever seen. Like the calving glaciers in old sixth-grade science films, expressions broke from his face like big clumps of ice. Once he spotted me in the corner, I watched him shift through all the emotions connected with my reappearance.

Disgust. Anger. Resentment.

Whatever it was, it wasn't a happy face he used to greet me with until he got an idea. "Maceo, I was afraid I might've missed you." Noone shouted his greeting, giving all the men in the room the impression that we were friends. He dropped into the seat opposite mine.

Raider turned and gave Joe a pointed look, then he slid out the front door. Larry and another man dropped money on the counter and followed right behind. Rook scowled at me as he came through the back.

Noone pointed at my scar. "Looks like you had a little trouble while you were gone. Did you get yourself a much needed ass-whipping?"

I didn't answer, but that didn't bother him too much. He was enjoying himself. He raised a hand to get Rook's attention. "Can I get some coffee and wheat toast," he motioned at me, "and whatever my friend Maceo wants for himself."

I shook my head but Noone insisted. "No, really, it's on me. The least your friends at OPD can do for you." His voice carried across the diner. He took pleasure in painting me as a snitch in a room peppered with cons. "How 'bout bacon, eggs, and an orange juice? You're a growing boy."

I stood to go but he dropped his voice and leaned in close. "Stay awhile, Maceo, don't spoil it for me. I was just coming in here to get a little work done, have a meal." He pulled a folder from his jacket and placed it on the table. "Then you just happen to drop out of the sky after two long years. I'm not a betting man, but today might be my lucky day."

He turned the folder around so that I could read the label: CORNELIUS KNOX.

"One guess," he said. "You're back here because Cotton's in trouble, and you suspect, or know like I do, that Holly's involved."

"I came back to see my family."

"That your story? Good idea to keep it clean." He switched gears. "You see the press conference?"

"Yep."

"What you think?"

"Nothing much."

"What's Holly think? You seen him since you've been back?"

"No."

"Know where I might find him?"

"No idea."

His eyes managed to center for a moment. "I never got your comments on the death of Smokey Baines. You know anything about that?"

"I know he's dead."

Noone's mouth pursed in irritation. The fake friendliness disappeared. "Holly's name has come up more than once in connection with a murder investigation. Several investigations, as a matter fact, and a slew of drug-related crimes."

"I wouldn't know nothin' 'bout that."

"Then I hope you stay out of the way. Don't interfere like last time."

"What last time?"

"Billy, Smokey, Reggie." He ticked off the names. "Should I continue?"

"Doesn't make a difference to me."

He sat back in his chair and shook his head. "No matter how old I get I'll never understand it."

"Understand what?"

"I'll never understand why your family insists on making me an enemy when I might be the one person who could help you in case, say, somebody wanted to find out who killed your grandmother's sister."

It was a cold card to play, and it let me know how hard his dick was for Holly. Celestine Bouchaund's unsolved murder was the equivalent of L.A.'s infamous Black Dahlia case. It had been unsolved for over forty years, and had been a thorn in my grandmother's side for just as long.

"You might be of help, huh?"

"To your family. And to Holly." He pulled a photo from his folder. In it, Holly sat in the stands of the All-Pro tournament with his hat pulled down low on his brow. A beautiful girl was at his side, one I'd never seen before. Her face was circled with red ink. Noone placed his finger on her chin.

"This is the murder victim. Holly was photographed with her the day before she was killed."

"So what? She was photographed in the stands of a basketball game with about twenty thousand other people. Are you looking for this guy, too?" I pointed to a man sitting a few rows up from Holly.

He ignored my question and closed his notebook. "That guy didn't leave his fingerprints in the room with a dead body." He had the grace to let the words sink in before he continued. Then he smiled. Big.

"While you think about that, Maceo, think about who inherited Oakland once Smokey and Billy died."

He saw Holly's name bloom in my face.

He nodded.

"The city belongs to your boy, but he ascended a poisonous throne. Got a gun aimed at him every day of his life."

"What you gonna do about it?"

"Do?" He laughed. "Not a gotdam thing but wait and see who pulls the trigger. This world, Maceo, is made up of heroes and fools, and since most of the time they're one and the same, it's only a matter of time before Holly gets caught."

He picked up his folder and my untouched coffee, and left me to contemplate all the ways in which the world could go wrong.

EIGHT

My first six months away from home, before I settled in Texas, I roamed the Western states and found myself killing time in Montana. I camped in the heavy thicket of woods on the edge of Glacier National Park, and after two days I was familiar enough with the disputes between the local ranchers and the naturalists who'd reintroduced wolves to the park to avoid bringing up the volatile topic with strangers. I overheard the conversations in bars, I saw the headlines in local papers, and I felt the collective glee whenever a stray wolf was shot after wandering too close to a herd.

One day I rode into town after a wolf was captured but not killed by local ranchers. They wanted to display their bounty, and he was chained into the back of a truck. I passed close enough to see his eyes, and the steady, haunted gaze of the wolf made me stop short. I'd been seeing it for my entire life.

I'd grown up on the Creole folktales of the *loupen acier,* the steel wolf that stole children and souls, but that's not what fueled the recognition. It was the look of my father, the look of expected failure that said, "There you are, I've been waiting on you."

If I could remember far enough back I'd bet money that the wolf had been there at my birth to kiss me before my mother had the chance. Or that he'd been the one to lean over my crib to lull me to sleep with stories of the pain in my future. Some kids had the luxury of remembering him as a spooky legend of youth but I knew him as the fifth wheel to me, Holly, Billy, and now Cotton. I'd always thought we were linked by the cruel fate of absent fathers but maybe it was a little more, maybe it was the fact that the wolf was the one who stepped in to take their place.

———

As I drove the streets of Oakland, Berkeley, and Richmond searching for Holly, I knew deep down I was really using the time to avoid Cissy. I had dues of my own to pay: one to my grandfather, and one to my aunt, though any debt I owed her would be impossible to settle. Cissy and I, only six months apart in age, were linked both by blood and by our connection to Holly.

The latter had been her downfall.

For years Holly had viewed women as a mere function of his body, nothing more, nothing less, not even believing in the intimacy of a kiss. Then his relationship with Cissy changed and so did he.

When I ignored all warnings in order to search for Felicia Bennett, the woman I loved, and the only witness to Billy's murder, he rode at my side despite his doubts because he understood my state of mind. But neither of us anticipated the cruel twist; that because he'd helped me with Felicia, he'd put Cissy in danger.

After Billy's death, Holly's climb to power bred him new enemies, and leading the charge against him was Orlando "Smokey" Baines, a man produced when a bully coupled with a coward. Holly was canny enough to elude Smokey at every turn but Cissy was not, and one October night Smokey beat her into a coma to send a message to Holly. Her recovery was long and painful, and I knew, because of my own involvement, that I could never live long enough to give her back what she'd lost. So when she asked me to come home to help him, all I could think was, *Who am I to say no?*

With those thoughts in my head, I crossed the Park Street Bridge into the island city of Alameda, where my aunt Rachel served as principal of a continuation high school. Cissy had lived with her since her release from the hospital. It was an act both of independence and defiance. She wanted to reclaim a portion of her old life and she wanted to continue to see Holly, who'd been banned from my grandparents' home. I knew this because Rachel and I had kept in touch during my absence.

I spotted my aunt at the edge of campus and ran to catch her in a bear hug before she could fully turn around. "You miss me, lady?"

Her smile was genuine. "Maceo, look at you, baby." She released me and ran her finger down my scar. "You never told me about this. When did that happen?"

"Awhile back."

"You see a doctor about it?"

"About being ugly? No cure."

She smiled again. "You want to talk about it?"

"Nope." I grabbed her hands. "But you got a minute to talk to me before I see Cissy?"

"Of course."

We retreated to Ole's restaurant on Park Street, my second diner of the day.

"You see Cotton's press conference? And Daddy Al?" I asked.

"Yes. Miss Antonia called me yesterday to tell me he was going." Rachel, the daughter of Daddy Al's first wife, called Gra'mère by her first name. It was a habit started during her father's courtship of Gra'mère when Rachel was still a little girl.

"How'd she take it?"

"She's upset. She's been upset ever since the story hit the papers. Daddy's still in L.A. with Cotton, trying to convince that reporter not to press charges, and of course, she's worried that Cissy will get dragged into all of this again."

"So, I'm not the only one who thinks this is about Holly."

"No, you're not."

"Noone told me they found Holly's prints in the room where the girl was murdered."

"Jesus."

"And from what I heard at Rook's, him and Cotton were with her the night she died. Apparently, they got in a fight with two men over her in the lobby of the hotel."

"Do you know who they are?"

"No, but they might be connected to a guy named Dutch." I paused. "Dutch Baines."

"I didn't know he was involved."

I was surprised. "You know about him?"

"Don't look so shocked, Maceo; I work with teenagers, impressionable girls, and him and those women of his have made quite a mark."

We paused when the waitress returned with our food. I'd ordered pancakes, bacon, eggs, sausage, and a side of grits. I was running on adrenaline and fear and needed to feed the beast. Rachel salt-and-peppered an egg-white omelet, then asked for an extra glass of ice and lemon for her water.

"You alright?"

She laughed and patted her stomach. "I'm fine. Getting older. Thursday night dinners take a little longer to get rid of."

"I missed that."

"Missed what?"

"Thursday nights. Seeing everybody."

She looked at me for a while before she went on. "You're different, Maceo. I can see it."

"It's the scar."

"No, not an outside different. You've changed." She paused. "So has Holly."

"You seen him lately?"

She shook her head. "We haven't heard a word from him since that girl got killed."

"You think he did it?"

"Two years ago I would've said no without hesitation, not because he wasn't capable but because he was too smart. He's always been an alley cat, nine lives and all that."

"But?"

"But sometimes when I see him now I get the feeling he wants to die."

Later, Rachel wheeled her BMW into a dead end on Chestnut Street at Clinton Avenue. I parked my car right behind hers and pulled Kiros from the car. Crown Memorial Beach was within walking distance and I could smell the Bay as we made our way up the front steps of the Victorian. In the distance I heard the noon bells from the nearby St. Joseph Basilica and the seagulls squalling overhead. Kiros took a seat on the enclosed porch when Rachel said he might be too much for Cissy to handle. She squeezed my hand, then slid a key into the lock.

"Cissy doesn't know you're back, Maceo. I know she called you, but she wasn't sure you'd come and I didn't want to get her hopes up."

She gave me a look of warning, then she swung open the heavy door. I crossed the threshold into the house and found Cissy sitting on a bench beneath the largest window in the room. She was framed by the weak sunlight breaking through the clouds, and she balanced a cane across her knees. Behind her the silty waters of the inner-island lagoon rippled with the wind.

"Cissy, baby," Rachel called in a soft voice, "somebody's here to see you."

While Rachel helped her stand, I took in the changes that had ravaged her appearance. The long hair that had once been her pride barely reached the top of her ears, and it was thin enough on the sides that I was able to see her scalp. Her shoulders were stooped, and the left side of her body sloped down lower than the right. Her hand curled in toward her body, clawlike, and the sure step she took with her right foot was followed by the slow drag of her left.

As I watched her struggle to her feet, I tried with all my might to keep my composure. Tears that felt like needles rapped at the back of my eyelids, but I knew that Cissy was proud of her progress and I didn't want to take that away from her.

"Hey, girl."

She looked up at the sound of my voice. The smile she flashed was broken in half by the one side of her face that wouldn't budge. Like the rest of her body, her left eye and the left side of her mouth sloped down, giving her a startled and slack expression. The beauty she'd been famous for as the youngest Redfield daughter was gone, just a faint shadow beneath a bruised and damaged façade. Our birthdays were only six months apart but in my absence she'd aged nearly ten years. The minimal progress I saw was cold comfort to me.

"Maceo." The word was slow and deliberate. "I missed you." She stumbled on *missed* three times before completing the sentence.

When I put my arms around her shoulders and kissed her forehead I felt the frailness of her body. "I missed you, too, Cissy."

I led her to the couch and she placed her cane on the floor before facing me.

"You home?" She inched her fingers across the couch until she reached my hand. I grabbed hers and brought it to my lips.

"I'm home."

"Good." She traced my scar, a mirror image of her collapsed face, with unsteady fingers. "Like me." She said. "You're like me." I saw from the mischievous glint in her eye that beneath all the destruction she still had a sense of humor.

I didn't know there were so many ways for a heart to break.

———

"Cissy has something she wants to show you, Maceo."

"Yeah, what's that?"

"She put this together in case you came back."

I looked at Cissy. "In case? You knew I was going to come back, didn't you?"

She nodded yes, then squeezed my hand. Rachel smiled at us and reached beneath the couch to pull out a scrapbook. She opened the first page and placed it on Cissy's lap.

"Remember this?" she asked.

On the first page of her scrapbook was a picture of me, Cissy, and Holly at my graduation from St. Mary's. I ran my hand across the surface. "Feels like this was taken about twenty years ago."

She turned the page and for the next five minutes I was treated to a photographic history of my friendship with Holly. The final pages of the scrapbook were filled with the clippings about Cotton. In more than one article the words *unidentified man,* which had jumped out at me earlier, were underlined in red ink.

Holly was the first person who popped into my mind after reading the newspaper, and apparently Cissy had the same idea.

"You worried about him?"

She nodded and pointed to two words scribbled at the bottom of the page.

Help Him.

"You want me to help him?"

She nodded again and closed her eyes to get the strength to utter her next words.

"You owe him." There was fire behind her eyes as she said it. "And you owe me."

———

Cissy went to bed after a couple hours, exhausted from our conversation about Holly, the family, her therapy, and her progress. I turned to Rachel once she'd gone.

"Daddy Al ever let up on Holly?"

"Daddy will never forgive Holly for what happened to Cissy. He loves him, but . . ."

"But he doesn't want him with his daughter."

"Would you? You have to look at this from both sides before you pass judgment."

"Holly wasn't the only one to blame."

"Maybe not, but they almost lost their daughter and they lost you."

"So they laid it all at his feet."

"Not all." She gave me a pointed look. "But most."

"Did Holly ever try to talk to Daddy Al?"

"Two years and neither one of them has said a word to each other. Both hardheaded. Neither one wants to budge."

"You know how to contact Holly?"

"Cissy had a pager number but it hasn't worked in over a week."

"How's she holding up?"

"How do you think? She's afraid, and she wants to know what happened."

So did I. Holly had the loyalty of ten soldiers, which meant there were only two things that would keep him away from Cissy. He was either trying to protect her from his enemies or he was out there trying to hunt them down.

NINE

There was a chance, after the random encounter with Noone, that he might have my license plate number. I'd parked on the street near Rook's, and as a former family friend, he knew about my love of muscle cars. The souped-up 1970 El Camino and the menacing dog would've been easy enough to spot, so I decided to make a quick switch before checking into my hotel. Holly was in hiding and I'd need a low-key car to track him down. Oakland was a blue-collar city to its core, a town built on the ingenuity of its citizens, and that craftiness was often used to ease the plight of poor people. I was counting on that as I squinted through the rain on my windshield in search of a storefront insurance agency. After traversing three blocks of Seventh Avenue I found it in the shadows of the West Oakland BART station, tucked beside a fish house and barbecue joint.

A neon sign in the shape of an automobile flashed in the window indicating that Black, a local loan shark and entrepreneur, was still in business. The insurance agent was an old man named Mr. Jenkins who hadn't sold a policy in about twenty years, so he made his rent by letting Black operate out of his office.

I doubled-parked, cracked a window for Kiros, and darted through the rain to get inside.

The place was empty, save for Mr. Jenkins dozing in front of a little black-and-white TV on his desk. He had his feet up on a chair, and his hat pulled down to shade his eyes. His clothes were neatly pressed and clean but he had an old man's way of matching colors, which meant they didn't. He sported gray slacks, a brown shirt, a red jacket, and a yellow tie like it wasn't a problem.

"Mr. Jenkins." I got a snore in return. "Mr. Jenkins!"

"What? What?" His legs came down from the chair as his hat rolled to the floor. I picked it up and handed it to him.

"Is Black here today?"

"'Course he's here." He cackled. "That boy love his money."

Jenkins was right. Black had attended UC Berkeley a couple years before I got there, but he'd been expelled when he'd sold his roommates' textbooks to a used-book store for cash. The man was in possession of a pirate's heart, and he never met a hustle he didn't like, but he didn't traffic in drugs, or anything to-the-letter illegal. He didn't have to. He made a decent enough living filling in the holes drilled by poverty and ignorance.

For residents with bad credit, no credit, or suspended licenses Black rented a fleet of used cars on a cash-only basis. It was the perfect solution for a high school boy wanting to take his girlfriend into the city for a date, or a mother with four kids and no wheels who needed to pay bills and make doctor's appointments. And if you didn't have cash, well then, he was also a loan shark who could lend you the money for the rental and gas until payday. Black had been in business for years in North and West Oakland, and I was hoping he had something for me to use while I was in town.

Mr. Jenkins straightened himself up. "Give him a minute. He went next door for some catfish. He'll be right back. Just have a seat."

I sat in a dusty chair and waited. Moments later Black entered with two paper-sack lunches and a bottle of blue Nehi.

"Hey, man." I stood up to greet him.

He nodded and handed one of the bags to Mr. Jenkins, who pulled hot sauce and pepper from his desk drawer. Jenkins opened his bag and rolled a napkin into the collar of his shirt.

"Maceo, right?" Black took a seat behind a tall counter in front of a glass case filled with keys.

"Yeah, Maceo."

"It's been awhile. What you looking for?"

"Need a car. Maybe a truck with a shell or something. I got a dog."

"Bartender!" Mr. Jenkins shouted from his corner, and Black rolled his eyes. "Bartender," he said again, "isn't there suppose to be potato salad with the number-two special?"

"It's right there, Mr. Jenkins, on the edge of your desk."

He picked it up. "Well, I'll be damned. It sure is."

"You alright now?" Black asked him.

He chuckled. "For now, but when you get a minute, I'd like a Courvoisier with a Coke back."

Black turned back to me as he cracked open his own lunch. "Mr. Jenkins is losing his grip, but he still comes to work every day. He's good company but sometimes he wears me out. So, you said you need a truck?"

"Truck would be good. Nothing fancy. Whatever you got."

"I got one I don't usually rent, but if that's what you want, you can have it."

"Yeah. How much for a week?"

He pulled out a calculator. "Twelve-fifty a day. Half now. Bring it back full. No dents. No tickets. Keep the registration in the glove box. Cash only."

Black ran his business on faith but he had enough rough-necks in his pocket to make sure his cars came back on time and in the condition he wanted.

I reached into my wallet. "Listen, I'm in my own car right now, so could you get somebody to drop it off?"

"That's another ten but I can do it. Where should we drop it?"

I gave him the location, paid the bill, and said my good-byes to Jenkins, who was lining up catfish bones in rows of three along the edge of his paper bag. When I closed the door I could hear him humming to himself.

———

"Can I speak to Winston Lamb?"

I was at a phone booth in downtown Oakland in front of the Lux Theater. The movie house had been closed for years but I still had fond memories of me, Holly, and Billy spending Saturday af-ternoons there watching kung fu flicks.

"Your name, please?"

"Maceo Redfield."

I held the line for Holly's lawyer. Winston Lamb had repre-sented Holly for years. He was famous throughout the Bay Area for his flamboyant presence in court and his high-end criminal clients. He had left a prestigious teaching post at Boalt Law School to defend Oakland criminals with deep pockets.

"Maceo, long time." Lamb was brisk. Time was money and I'd never paid him a red cent.

"I'm looking for Holly. Can you get a message to him?"

"If Mr. Ford gets in touch with me I might be able to pass on a communication, but, at this time, I am unaware of his location." Lamb spoke as if there was someone else in the room or listening in on the call. "I'd love to talk further but I'm due at the Criminal Courts building in five minutes. I'll pass along your message."

He hung up without taking a message, so I jumped into the car and drove to the courthouse building. I pulled up just as Lamb stepped out of a Lincoln Town Car. He looked the same, a compact man with a staccato speaking style and a predilection for bright colors. He was gay as a stereotype, open and loud about it, which didn't mean shit in San Francisco, but it was a brave stance to take in working-class Oakland. He didn't apologize to his unenlightened clientele, didn't hide his boyfriends, just did his job better than anybody on either side of the Bay.

"Lamb!" I kept the motor running and waved him over.

"Back in town?"

"For now."

"Good. Holly know you're here?"

"Naw, I'm trying to find him. I got a room over at the Seaport. I should be there for a minute."

He looked at me like he was trying to figure out my motives so I kept talking, hoping to gain his trust.

"Ran into Detective Noone this morning over at Rook's. He may have wrote down my license plate number, so I'm trading this car before I check into the hotel. Holly can find me there."

"Noone say anything important?"

"He told me that Holly's fingerprints were found in the hotel room where the girl was murdered. And word on the street is that Cotton and Holly argued with two men who work for Dutch Baines." I stressed the last name. "Something to do with the dead girl."

Lamb closed his eyes and exhaled loud but said nothing.

"I plan to check around as much as I can. Maybe in a couple days I'll stop in to tell you what I heard."

He nodded and looked up at the darkening sky. "I got a houseboat out in the Berkeley Marina, hardly ever use it. Nice place to lay low, though, since it's the last slip before you hit the open water. I'd go myself but the weather keeps me away."

"Sounds nice."

He avoided my eyes, driving the message home.

"Sounds perfect," I said, then watched him return to his car.

TEN

The Seaport Hotel, just a brick and a half away from being an out-and-out flophouse, sat squeezed between abandoned warehouses along the Oakland-Alameda estuary. I knew the place from my high school days when it was one of many low-end places that rented to minors.

On the outside it wasn't too bad. The two-story hotel was painted white with blue trim and somebody, at one point or another, thought it a good idea to slap pelicans and anchors on every open space. The rooms were spacious and looked out on the water, and the big windows, when they were clean, actually had a decent view of the Alameda Marina. Plus, it was cheap, private, and out of the way. Those details made it easy to abide the four-legged squatters and the thin walls that quaked when the working girls were on the premises.

It was familiar without being home. And the briny smell of the gray waters that flowed right behind the building was a comfort. I chose the hotel because I wasn't ready to camp out on Dover Street; wasn't ready for the constant barrage of family members with their opinions and problems. After my encounter with Cissy, the train, the water, and the bridges all represented a form of escape just in case my homecoming got too complicated.

Before I checked in, I drove past the building looking for police cars, or plainclothes cops, and when I found none I kept going until I reached the parking warehouse near the Coast Guard Island Bridge. Before I parked I did a visual check of the other cars, then backed my car into a space near the staircase. I left the motor running while I checked my surroundings. I'd picked up the habit after I'd made the mistake—only once—of thinking that my presence was welcome in a line of Texas day laborers who hadn't been hired in weeks. When I realized my mistake I was grateful for the El Camino's quick getaway power. The car's previous owner had painted the SS 454 a tuxedo black, but the cosmetics had been the least appealing feature when I purchased the car. All I wanted was an engine strong enough to keep me moving, and an open bed to use for hauling.

On occasion, when money was tight, I slept in the back with the tarp serving as my roof. The El Camino didn't come close to the 1967 Dan Gurney Cougar I owned before Smokey torched it but I appreciated the souped-up engine, clean body, and Ralley wheels.

Kiros followed me down the steps of the garage and across the street to the Executive Inn, where Black had been instructed to leave the truck. I found it, a mud-brown bucket, with the keys underneath the passenger seat. I drove back to the Seaport with Kiros at my side.

After I checked into the hotel, I retrieved Kiros from the car and wound his leash around my wrist before I lit up. He leaned his body against my leg, then plopped down at my feet. I loved the dog. His silent companionship had made the loneliness of the road bearable.

"You hungry, boy?"

He grumbled and I took that as a yes. There was a kitchenette in the room I rented so I made ground beef and rice, which I'd bought earlier, doused it in hot sauce, and mixed a couple of patties into Kiros's dry food.

I ate my meal at a rickety table near the bathroom and rehashed my morning. A big-ticket call girl, a high-profile basketball player, Dutch, and Holly. The buzz in my gut told me they were all pieces of an obvious puzzle. I just had to find a way to connect the dots with more information. While searching for Billy's killer, I found that I was a natural at getting information out of people. I came from a long line of secret-keepers, which made me trustworthy. And when necessary I used the local celebrity I garnered as a baseball star to get people talking. And when that didn't work I relied on the simple fact that people like to talk about themselves. A few well-placed questions, a sincere interest in their life and struggles, and the information flowed like water unless they had something to hide. I'd also done grunt work for a Texas process server, which helped me learn how to hunt down the people who didn't want to be found. So I decided to put my skills to the test one more time.

While the dishes dried on the counter, I went about giving the anonymous room a little permanence. I placed my hot-sauce collection on the windowsill, stacked the refrigerator with my last pack of Buena Noche, the seasonal Mexican beer sold in the Southwest, and threw a pile of dirty rugby shirts and jeans on the floor of the closet. On the rim of the bathtub, I lined up the paperback Westerns and *Sports Illustrated*s that had survived each of my moves.

Once that was done I headed to the manager's office and gathered old editions of the *Tribune* and *Chronicle*. Back in the room I ripped out everything related to All-Pro Weekend, the murder, and drug crimes in the East Bay, then I used a take-out menu from a Chinese restaurant to put together a list of the things worth looking into.

> Dutch
> Holly
> Cotton
> Nightingales
> Gideon Hotel

The San Francisco police had been unable to find anyone connected to the murdered woman, or even her name, but the *Chronicle* had the same photo Noone had shown me at Rook's. She sat five rows up from the Western Division bench looking intently at the action. There was nothing troubled in her face, nothing to indicate that her life was marked for extinction. Just a pretty girl who stood a better chance than most of attracting the attention of one of the ballplayers. I ripped the picture out and added it to my pile. After sticking it all in a drawer I gave Kiros the bed and stretched out on the scratchy sofa but sleep eluded me. I kept seeing the woman's manicured appearance every time I closed my eyes. If she was a Nightingale, then hair and nails were high on her maintenance list, which could only mean one thing. Whereas Cutty and his cohorts gave me one side of the truth, a salon run by ear-to-the-ground women would give me another.

I dialed Cutty.

"Crowning Glory." I recognized Andre's voice on the other end.

"Hey, man, it's Maceo."

"Wassup?"

"I got a girl here in town with me." I lied easily. "She wants to get her hair done, and I been gone so long I don't know where to send her."

"You can try Trim over by Lake Merritt."

"Is that new?"

"Yeah. You know Yolanda Landry, Emmet's wife? She opened the spot about a year ago."

That was good to know. I had a relationship with Yolanda because of Emmet. He was a good friend of Holly's, and he'd been present the night Smokey died. Emmet was a drug dealer whose capital was spent on keeping him and his wife in the finest clothes. They were ghetto stars to the nth degree, and often dressed in matching outfits and jewelry.

"That the best one?"

"One and only. Emmet poured a lot of money into the place."

Nothing new. Many of Oakland's successful drug dealers hid and washed their money through auto-detailing businesses, car lots, or hair salons for their girlfriends.

"Alright, I'll see if I can get her in."

"Good luck."

"Hey, listen. Did you recognize that man standing behind Cotton at the press conference? Next to my grandfather?"

"Who? Silas Lockwood?"

"Lockwood." I knew he looked familiar. He was a former player, at least twenty years Cotton's senior, who'd taken the coaching route once it became evident that the NBA wasn't in the cards. He enjoyed minor success as an offensive coach at UNLV, and even less at Sacramento State, before decamping to the Pro-Am circuit, and finally the European Leagues.

Last I'd heard he was a second-string coach in Spain, over-seeing a squad of former headliners who'd fallen victim to drugs and their own bad decisions. I'd met the man once when he'd accompanied Cotton to a family dinner on Dover Street. I hadn't liked him. He was rude and distracted, barely able to conceal the jealousy he felt over Cotton's success.

Any story Cotton told that night was followed by a larger, grander story starring Silas Lockwood as *that nigga*.

I found him to be cruel and cold but Cotton was devoted to the man.

"I thought Lockwood was coaching in Europe."

"He was in Europe but Cotton brought him home to handle his security. Apparently, Allaina got a couple death threats after they got married."

"Serious threats?"

"Serious enough to hire bodyguards."

"They catch anybody?"

"Not that I know of. It was in the news and then it wasn't. You know how it goes."

"Well, let me know if you hear anything else."

"No problem. My girl Lesley is the receptionist at Trim if you need help getting an appointment."

"Thanks, man."

I sat for a moment after I hung up the phone, then added Silas to my list.

ELEVEN

The rain dropped in sheets as I drove 580 toward Knowland Park. The public park and zoo were built into the hills and surrounded by redwoods and wildlife. The night Smokey died, the men who'd gathered to hunt him down joked that the hilltop home would be the pirate's bounty to divide among themselves. As I wound my way through the hills of East Oakland I wondered who lived there. I remembered that the house was in a cul-de-sac, and that Smokey had owned the two houses on either side.

The first and only time I'd been there, I'd come in through the back way, climbing through the woods with Felicia, Clarence, and Holly, so I made an educated guess, and counted from the tree line to figure out which one was his. Then I counted again. The space where his house had once stood was empty, a vacant lot, as was the space on the left. The one on the right, a nondescript ranch house, had a FOR SALE sign on the lawn.

The neighborhood was quiet and well kept, so I sat in my car and pulled out a cigarette. I turned my music up loud, just to bait the hook, then I waited. My presence on the street would gallop around the block like the Pony Express, and before long a nosy neighbor would either call the police on me or come out to talk. I hoped for the latter but was prepared for the first. If worse came to worst, I would tell the police that the real estate agent had stood me up.

I was midway through my cigarette when I saw a flutter of curtains from the house in front of me, and the front door swung open. The woman who emerged was in her mid-forties, blond, dressed in jeans, a black sweater, and a ski coat.

She motioned for me to roll down the window and I obliged.

"Can I help you?" She stood on the curb, just out of arm's reach.

I decided to roll with the excuse I'd prepared for the police.

"Yeah, I'm waiting on the real estate agent, but looks like she stood me up."

"Nice try." Her delivery was sharp and no-nonsense. "I'm the agent for that property and I don't have an appointment scheduled for this morning." She pulled out a cell phone. "Want to try again or should I call the police?"

"What's the deal with this property?"

"Are you a legitimate buyer?"

"Are you a legitimate seller?"

"Nancy Ollin." She pointed to her name on the FOR SALE sign.

"John Mason." I didn't bother to stick my hand out the window. "Are you selling the house and both lots?"

"Why are you here, Mr. Mason? I'm about two minutes from calling the police if one of my neighbors hasn't already."

"I had a friend who lived on this street once. Long time ago."

"Look, no offense, but we've had a lot of trouble on this street so people stick together and watch out for each other. You may be a perfectly nice man for all I know, but we have to be careful." Her gaze rested on my scar long enough for me to know she didn't believe her own words.

"How long has the house been on the market?"

"Two years."

"No buyers in all that time?"

"We had inquiries but not the right ones."

"What's that mean?"

"It means the last guy who lived here was murdered in his own home, then the property was burnt to the ground. There were abandoned cars parked at the bottom of the hill on the night of the murder, so fire trucks couldn't get in here. The whole neighborhood nearly went up in flames."

"The owner died in the fire?"

"No, he died from gunshot wounds. He was found inside with another man from L.A. So now everyone is a little sensitive about who buys here, especially with everything that's going on in the flatlands."

"Who owns the house now?"

"We all do. Everyone on this street."

"That's how you control who gets in?"

She didn't answer but I had her number. When Daddy Al and Gra'mère first moved to Oakland from northern Louisiana they'd tried to buy a home off Shoreline Drive in Alameda. Gra'mère had fallen in love with the idea of raising her girls so close to the beach, so the two of them grinned through the process of meeting the owners, placed their bid, then listened to the agent tell them later that the owners had accepted a better offer. Weeks later they learned that the neighbors had chipped in to buy the house to ensure the continued segregation of their street. I suspected the same thing was at play with Nancy Ollin and her cronies.

"Found a way to keep out the darkies, huh?"

She ignored my slur. "This is a nice street, and it's going to remain that way."

"Who'd you buy the house from?"

"The city. It was designated a drug property after the murders."

"And in all this time you haven't been able to find anybody worthy?"

"We've had some outside interference on that end."

"Meaning what?"

"Meaning there's a very determined party who doesn't want anyone else to have the house."

"You know the name of the person?"

"May I ask why you want to know?"

"Just curious."

"Were you connected to the man who lived in that house?" she asked.

"Nope, didn't know him."

"Well, I don't have any names either, but I'd like to find out. Their tactics haven't always been aboveboard, and whoever they are, they've shielded themselves well. We actually sold the second house once—it was still standing after the fire—but it burned down before the new owners could move in."

"Did the police ever catch anyone connected with the crime?"

"Which crime? The fire or the murders?"

"The murders."

"Never, and I don't expect they ever will. Fire destroyed all of the evidence. Anything else, or do you want to call my office for a real appointment?"

"No," I popped the engine, "you told me everything I need to know."

I made a U-turn as Nancy Ollin stood on the curb. Through my rearview mirror I saw her eyes scan my license plate. Didn't matter, I didn't have anything to hide. I took a last look at the scorched earth getting pounded by the rain as I headed back to the flatlands. Nancy and her neighbors might not know the identity of the mystery arsonist, but I had a pretty good idea.

TWELVE

Later that afternoon, the fog bank had moved out into the Bay, streaming backward through the Golden Gate Bridge, leaving the air dry and calm. I took advantage of that and pulled into the Seabreeze, an open-air market at the mouth of the Berkeley Marina. The picnic tables in front of the building were empty save for a lone biker outfitted in rain gear and the counter guy filling a cooler with ice. I parked alongside the tables, my truck facing the highway.

Inside the market I grabbed a cup of coffee and a pack of cigarettes to pass the time. The first cigarette warmed my lungs, and the coffee warmed my hands. I drank it as I listened to the seagulls spread rumors and complain overhead.

In the cars exiting Highway 80 I looked for the amphibious face of Detective Noone or signs I was being tailed, and found neither, so I figured my ruse with the truck was working and returned to my car. As traffic into San Francisco and Oakland bottlenecked behind me on the interstate, I followed an AC Transit bus down University Avenue and into the parking lot of the Marriott Hotel. Once a space opened up I pulled in and cracked the window for Kiros. He sniffed out a butcher's bone beneath the seat while I watched a group of suburban women exit cars carrying banners and signs for a cooking seminar.

I would look out of place in that group, and so would a cop, so I followed them inside from a distance. Twenty minutes later, after fending off three different women wielding black markers and name tags, I bought an umbrella from the lobby gift shop and headed into the cold air. The road was muddy as I trudged toward the boat slips but I kept going, looking into each car that passed me by. No one stood out so I finished a second cigarette, then dropped down onto the wooden walkway that served as a sidewalk to the yachts and houseboats along the harbor. Most were in top shape, well kept, giving the slip a uniform look of seaworthiness, but one, at the end of the row, had seen better days. It looked unkempt, lonely, and haggard, just the sort of place where Holly would feel at home.

The two-level houseboat was a patchwork of gray and brown cubes with a wooden railing around the perimeter. The railing was painted white and so were the tires tied to the bottom. It looked like a kindergarten project. I didn't understand the purpose of the oversize truck tires, but I didn't know anything about boats.

The boat on the left had a clothesline hanging along the side but even with that dog-patch decorating addition it didn't look nearly as bad as its neighbor. From inside a radio played the tinny sounds of bluegrass but I didn't see a human to go with the music so I kept going. Across the way a dog barked at my presence, then gave up when no one came to investigate. Doubling back, I used the tip of the umbrella to knock on the door of the one I figured to be Lamb's, and then I knocked harder on a side window. Nothing. I knocked again and stepped onto the plank. I walked the length of the boat, glancing in windows, knocking, trying to ascertain if anyone was home or if any of the neighbors would stop me from going inside.

I found a rusty iron chair around back with a wet newspaper crumpled beneath and an unobstructed view to San Quentin Prison, the Golden Gate Bridge, the San Francisco–Oakland Bay Bridge, and the Richmond–San Rafael, which had the goofy distinction of having been hit by ships and freighters on several occasions.

On the splintered railing there were telltale cans of pineapples and olives; a food combination that sustained Holly whenever he was left to fend for himself. He never grew out of his love for pineapples even when the thready fruit cut his mouth until it was raw.

I picked up the soggy newspaper and read the headline of the sports page: NBA STAR FACES CHARGES. With no visible neighbors to disrupt my pursuit, I shattered a window above the door and reached around the jagged glass to turn the knob. Inside I came across three pairs of the blinding white K-Swiss he preferred even to Cotton's Knockers, more newspaper articles about the case, and an old picture of Cissy. There was enough random evidence to convince me Holly had been there, but the boat was empty.

Before leaving I scribbled a note—"The Watch Dog's Back. M.R."—and left it on the counter beneath a can of pineapples.

———

The way back to the truck was marked by much of the same, dog owners on their way to the green, and commuters heading home from work. My truck, wedged between two oversize commuter vans, was barely visible, but I could hear Kiros barking as I approached. A few cars circled the lot looking for spaces, then sped by when I took too long.

A cloud spiraled overhead, releasing a cascade of pounding water, but out above the Richmond–San Rafael Bridge the sky was clear. That was typical of the schizophrenic Bay Area climate, where five different weather patterns could exist in a twenty-mile radius. It was possible to leave Berkeley in the middle of a thunderstorm and find clear blue skies and hot weather in Contra Costa County.

I picked up my pace as Kiros's barking increased and the rain battered its way through the thin umbrella I'd purchased at the hotel.

"What's up, boy?" I pulled the keys from my pocket as his paws slammed against the driver-side door. He was spooked. His fright registered just as I saw the reflection of a man standing behind me. I half-turned as the raised hand came down on the back of my head.

I felt rain on my face before the ground rushed up to meet me.

———

"I found him outside. Unconscious. There was a dog barking so I went over to see what was wrong, and he was lying on the ground."

"Sir. Can you hear me?"

There were two voices, one male, one female, and both battled their way through the thickness in my skull. I opened my eyes to find three concerned faces hovering above me. A woman, and two men wearing uniforms. The first wore the dark blue of the Berkeley Police Department, the second the red jacket of an EMS worker. I tried to sit up, but I felt a pain like a shovel slam me backward onto the ground. A light flickered in front of my eye. "Sir, I need you to open your eyes. Can you tell me your name?"

"Did you see anyone, ma'am?" The voice came from higher up, behind the paramedic. "Did you see anyone fleeing the scene?"

"No one," she answered, "and I wouldn't have seen him. It was raining so hard. I came outside because I left my recipe book; I'm here for the cooking seminar, and I heard the dog barking, like I said, then I found him. He was lying on his side, soaking wet, but there wasn't anyone else around."

"Did you pass anyone on your way out?"

"No one."

"What happened?" I asked. I forced myself to sit up, battling through the searing pain that gripped my intestines like a fist. I leaned over and threw up onto the gravel.

"Sir, can you tell me your name?"

"Maceo Redfield."

I saw the cop scribble my name into his notebook.

"Any idea what happened?"

"No, I remember getting in my truck but that's it."

The paramedic opened a bandage pack. "Alright, you have a nasty bump on the back of your head and a split lip. Are you hurt anyplace else?"

I tried to shake my head but the effort induced another wave of nausea. The air in front of my face filled with motes, and I threw up a second time. "Naw, just my head."

"Okay, we'd like to take you in, get a better look."

"That's alright. Just give me a minute and I'll be fine."

"Are you refusing medical service?" The paramedic gave a knowing look to the cop.

"Mr. Redfield, my name is Officer Glascott. I'm from the Berkeley Police Department. Can I ask you a couple questions?"

"Yeah, but I don't remember anything."

The fog in my head started to lift, and I noticed a small crowd gathered around the truck. Most of them were seminar ladies, a few employees of the hotel, and a Black man in green army fatigues and dreadlocks he'd tied back with a Jamaican ribbon. Underneath his coat he wore a white turtleneck and a sweater, but neither one hid the bleached-out bits of skin creeping up his neck and onto his chin and ear. He raised a hand to lift his collar and I saw the same patchwork on his wrist and fingers. Another man stood beside him with lightning bolts shaved into his box cut and baggy workout pants tucked into high-top Reeboks. He had the bulky upper body of a jailhouse weight lifter.

Both of them looked right at me, not saying a word, neither smiling nor frowning. I felt the back of my head and winced at the pain. That reaction got a smirk from the Jamaican.

"Mr. Redfield?" I turned my attention back to the cop and when I looked again both men were gone. "Mr. Redfield, do you have any idea who might have done this?"

"No. I just got to town."

"Are you on vacation?"

"Just got home." The stinging in my head dulled to a throb, though the skin of the cut felt like it had been split open with a hot poker. It sizzled every time I moved my head but my vision was clear. The presence of the two hulking men sobered me more than the raindrops and the irritated cop.

"From where?"

"Texas."

"You live in Berkeley?"

"Oakland. My family's in Oakland. I was just killing time, thought I'd come over here to check out the water."

"On a rainy day?"

"Wasn't raining when I got here."

"What about your wallet? Anything missing?"

I reached into my pocket, counted out all my cash, and located the credit cards I kept for emergencies. "Looks like everything's here."

"Have any idea who'd want to do something like this?"

"None."

"Did you leave town with any enemies?"

"Not that I know of. I just got back this morning and no one knows I'm here."

"What about the scar?"

"Ancient history." I turned to the paramedic. "Can I go? Everything alright?"

"Not alright, but you'll live. I suggest you see a doctor sooner rather than later. Take a pill for the pain and stay out of trouble."

The policeman handed me his business card. "Anywhere I can reach you while you're in town?"

"Like I said, just got here. Haven't picked out a hotel yet."

"And the one we're standing in front of, that wouldn't be where you're staying."

"Haven't decided."

"Well, when you decide, call and let me know where you can be reached. In case I have any more questions."

The two of them packed up, and I scanned the crowd for the men I'd seen but they were long gone. Maybe it was a fluke, but I doubted it; they'd been as out of place as I was, and if Kiros could talk I was sure he'd have picked them out of a lineup.

———

With the sky the color of silt, I made my way back to the hotel. My intent was to take a shower, feed the dog, and get a handle on the day's events, but once I saw the bed I knew I wasn't going anywhere. I hit it, and when I woke up once in the middle of the night, the rainbow-colored off-air bands flashed on the television. They didn't speak to me; they didn't blink encoded messages warning me to leave Holly to his fate. There were no whispered directions telling me to go back to Texas or to be careful. In short, I was on my own, and I'd stopped looking for messages in anything other than the lonesome howls of my father.

His words were enough. They were warnings I could count on.

THIRTEEN

Just after dawn the next morning a steamer rolled down the estuary waters, and the lonely foghorn snatched the last bits of my sleep away in its claws. I gave up the ghost of slumber, flung off the covers, and moved to the bathroom and the burnt coffeepot plugged into a socket near the mirror. It didn't take long to shower, feed Kiros, and clean the bandage on the back of my head. My headache had dulled in the night, faint enough to serve as more of a reminder than a distraction.

I went out and returned with copies of the *Chronicle, Tribune,* and *San Jose Mercury* to read about Cotton. Each article contained more innuendo than fact, which led me to believe the police hadn't come up with anything new. The name of the murder victim still hadn't been released but the *Oakland Tribune,* for the first time, alluded to her being a call girl.

There was no point in my going back to the houseboat, so I left Kiros at the hotel, then drove to Fifty-ninth and Shattuck in

North Oakland. The Nickel and Dime, a low-slung cinder-block building across the street from Bushrod Park, was the low-key restaurant-bar owned by Daddy Al since the 1940s when my grandmother closed Antonia's, her famous West Oakland supper club. The nightclub had been a popular "Harlem West" gathering spot for the Negro elite, and the site of the infamous unsolved murder of her sister, Celestine Bouchaund.

Gra'mère closed Antonia's the day after Celestine was found dead in an upstairs dressing room, and Daddy Al responded by opening the Nickel and Dime, a bar decorated with Naugahyde booths, a makeshift stage, and dim lights. He ran the bar and stage while my aunts, Josephine and Cornelia, managed the restaurant.

My grandfather believed in hard work, and each of his six daughters, and later Holly, Cotton, and I, began our working lives within those four walls. At the age of seven I earned a cool ten dollars a week filling the salt and pepper shakers and restocking the paper napkin holders. I moved up from that bit of grunt work to cashier, then to waiter, and after my twenty-first birthday I became a part-time bartender to help pay for college.

Daddy Al's trademark Cadillac was nowhere in sight but a delivery man from Kilpatrick's Bakery carried a box of bread into the restaurant, and I could hear the clash of pots and pans from the open door of the kitchen. Cornelia and Josephine served three meals a day, starting breakfast at seven o'clock in the morning, and they got a pretty decent pre-work crowd. A single cook stayed on once the main restaurant closed to provide the bar patrons with hamburgers and fries, fish and chips, and other greasy fare to help soak up the alcohol.

Inside the bar, chairs were on the tables, the booths empty, and the liquor lined up in neat rows in front of a smoky, gold-flecked mirror. The interior was permanently singed with the yeasty smell of stale beer and cigarettes but it felt, and smelled, like home.

Once my eyes adjusted to the dark, I watched the activity of the restaurant through the swinging doors that separated the two areas. Josephine, the eldest twin, was at the cash register smiling at a young man in a cable television uniform. Cornelia sat behind her, drinking a cup of coffee.

My aunts were known in Oakland as Redfield's Redbone Race-horses, and the twins, with their Creole coloring, were considered the thoroughbreds of the bunch. While Cissy and I were growing up, a mere six months apart, the twins called us Gra'mère's titty babies. They were beautiful and I loved them but they had sharp, viperous tongues that they wielded like weapons. I wanted to get them out of the way before going over to Dover. I took a deep breath and pushed through.

Cornelia looked up from her coffee as I came through the swinging doors. I'd caught her off guard and she stared, hard, trying to place me in the shadows of the room. Her intake of breath when she put it all together caught Josephine's attention. She looked at her sister, then followed Cornelia's eyes to where I stood. There was a concrete pause, a big gaping hole of silence that encompassed two years. They stood their ground, their eyes sweeping over me in waves, so I made the first move. I walked toward Cornelia, the tougher of the two, and tapped Josephine on the hand as I passed her.

Once I kissed my aunt on the cheek she forgot the distance and confusion long enough to reach up and touch my scar. "Boy," she said, "boy," and then she started to cry with relief.

The few customers scattered around the restaurant placed money on their tables and made their way out the door.

———

"You seen Daddy yet?" Josephine had gone into the bar and grabbed a couple beers despite the early hour.

"Just at the press conference." I took a long sip. "Only got back yesterday."

"And you came here first?" Cornelia asked. "To neutral ground?" Her initial happiness was fast giving way to the anger I knew would come. "Here at the bar with us rather than at Mama and Daddy's house?"

"Hush, Nelia." Josephine placed her hand on mine. "What're your plans, Maceo?"

I took a moment to answer. I didn't want to betray that Cissy had asked me to come back. That revelation would lead to the fact that my aunt Rachel had always known where and how to find me. That reveal would turn the twins against her.

"No plan, just time to come home." I dropped one of the newspapers that I had brought with me down between us. "Right on time, huh?"

"What does that mean?" Nelia flicked the paper. "That's why you home? That's why you came in here looking all beat-up? Didn't you learn a lesson the last time you got involved in other people's business?"

I held up my hand. "Nelia, I'm sorry about everything that happened before I left, but . . ."

"But what? What are we suppose to do with you being sorry? That don't help anybody."

"It got complicated. Not much more I can say about it."

She snickered. "So, you ran? That's something your father would've done." Something he *had* done after my mother OD'd in her hospital bed. "You're weak, Maceo, just like him." She rammed her pointed finger into my chest.

"Cornelia," my voice was sharp, "you think you got anything new to tell me? State your case, but unless its something new, something I haven't already told myself, I don't give a shit what you have to say."

She raised her hand to slap me, but I caught her wrist and forced it down to her side.

"I don't care what you want to hear," she screamed. "You can't come in here demanding anything, not after the way Cissy was hurt!"

I gently pushed Cornelia away, then I kissed Josephine on the cheek. "Listen, Auntie, I'ma get out of here. I'll see you later."

Cornelia's eyes blazed with anger. "Don't ignore me. Where you going? You have that raggedy-ass girl stashed somewhere?"

I was bewildered. "What girl?"

"The girl that started this whole mess."

"Felicia?"

"Who else? Wasn't she the one that had your nose open so wide you put the whole family in jeopardy?"

"I haven't seen Felicia since I left."

My answer left her speechless. She hadn't expected that. She'd assumed, probably like everyone else, that Felicia and I had been holed up together for two years.

"You weren't with her?"

I shook my head and pulled my gloves from my pocket. "No."

"Then you were just gone all this time, like none of us mattered?" She started to cry. "Maceo, you and Holly tore this family into pieces, and neither one of you were here to help put it back together. I don't know if I can ever forgive you for that."

In the quick moment before I answered her I recalled all the sleepless nights that solidified the fact that I would never forgive myself either. I answered as sincerely as I could.

"You're not the only one."

"Then do me a favor."

"What?"

She looked me dead in the eye. "Don't get involved with Cotton and Holly."

When I didn't answer, Cornelia left the room without another word to me.

I watched her go, then I faced Josephine. "I need a favor."

"What is it?"

"Don't tell Daddy Al and Gra'mère I'm here. I'd like to go over there on my own."

She nodded in agreement. Before she followed her sister I grabbed her in a tight hug. "You know I love you, right?"

"I know you do, baby, but you need to love yourself."

As I walked out into the gray afternoon I heard their voices raised in argument.

FOURTEEN

Bushrod Park, my main stomping ground as a child, was directly across the street from the Nickel and Dime and around the corner from my grandparents' Dover Street house. I drove up to Telegraph, then walked back down through Washington Elementary School to avoid seeing any more family members.

I was looking for Mike Crowley, a local boy who'd made good by starting a ragtag child-care program for neighborhood kids. The front doors of the rec center were propped open with phone books, and the smell of bacon wafted out into the yard. I stepped through the doors and saw that the gym had been converted into a dining hall. Long tables covered with paper tablecloths were lined with kids, their seating arranged by age, sipping orange juice and talking among themselves.

Crowley was at the front of the room wearing navy-blue shorts, tube socks, and a red Izod shirt. He looked like an NFL coach with his clipboard and the two whistles that hung around his neck. He walked from table to table, correcting the children on their silverware usage, quieting the ones who got too loud.

"Crowley."

I caught him mid-whistle and he almost swallowed it when he saw me. He wanted to curse, I could see it in the way he opened his mouth, shut it, then repeated the action.

"I know you're surprised." I gave him a pound while he tried to recover. "I know you want to cuss, but you have all these kids to think about."

"Man, I didn't think I'd ever see you again."

"You almost didn't."

"Did you go to Mecca? Have your hajj?"

I laughed.

"When'd you get back?"

"Yesterday."

"And you got conked in the head and popped in the mouth in less than twenty-four hours? You don't like the quiet life, do you?"

"Like it more than you think, but circumstances . . ."

"Cotton and Holly."

I nodded. "You got somewhere we can talk?"

Crowley blew the whistle. An assistant came running. "Taneisha, can I leave you in charge for about fifteen minutes?"

"Yes, Mr. Crowley."

"I'll be in the office. Holla if you need me."

The assistant took the direction, and one of the whistles, as Crowley and I stepped into his office, with a glass window that looked out over the gym.

"Nice setup you got here."

"Had to fight for it. The city didn't want me to serve breakfast in here, and the Parks Department was afraid we'd ruin the floors with the tables and chairs. Those floors being more important than the kids and all that."

"How long you been running breakfast?"

"And lunch, too. Almost a year once I realized half of my paycheck was going to snacks I bought for the kids who kept telling me they were hungry. I pressured the city, got Harry Livingston, your old professor, on my side, and the money kicked in, but I have to apply for renewal every six months."

"They keep you on your toes?"

"Them and the parents." He pointed through the window. "See those two boys? The twins at the end of the table?"

I nodded.

"Look at their feet. Six years old, both of 'em got on Baby Knockers."

"Didn't know they made them that small."

"They make 'em that small, and every little hoodrat mama in town makes sure her kid has a pair. The twins' mother hasn't paid her child-care bill in two months, and half the time I think whatever they eat here is the only food they get. No food, no consistency, no commitment to education, but 'my baby gonna have him some shoes.'" He rubbed his eyes. "Black people got it all wrong, Maceo. But damn, nigga," he let loose with a howl and slapped his hand on the desk, "where the fuck you been?"

"There's the Crowley I remember." I smiled.

"Well, shit, I couldn't say what I wanted to say in front of the kids. You walk in here looking like you been on a chain gang. Got a straight Creature Feature–ass scar on your face, a Band-Aid on the back of your neck, and it looks like you got popped in the mouth. What. The. Fuck."

"I went to Rook's to look for Holly, then I followed another lead and got knocked out in the Berkeley Marina."

"But you're still out roaming the streets?"

"That's why I'm here."

"Figured as much."

"You know where Holly is?"

"I'm not that connected. He went underground from what I understand though. He's been on the run for one thing or another since you left."

"What do you mean?"

"Smokey died, Billy died, and it was the Wild, Wild West in Oakland. The murder rate in 1990 was off the chain. That drug bust off the Mexican coast left the town high and dry."

"I remember that. The feds got a ton of cocaine."

"Twenty tons, and nobody could get drugs after that. Tempers got short and guns came out. It was a mess. Half the kids in that room got fathers or mothers in jail, smoked out, or dead behind all that. Then HUD instituted a policy last year where they started evicting people if they had family members involved with drugs." He made a face. "Who doesn't have an uncle or brother, somebody who got caught up in the game? How you gonna lose your house off some peripheral relatives? Don't make no sense. We had so many families put out last year that I turned my head a couple times and let them sleep in the gym. Almost lost my job, but what was I suppose to do?" He paused. "We all got our demons though, right, Maceo? I see you got one riding you like a jockey."

I didn't respond.

"Can I give you some advice? One friend to another?"

"Knock yourself out."

"Don't roll into town trying to be a hero. Don't let guilty knowledge take you down."

"What do you know about Dutch?"

"Not trying to hear me, huh?"

"Just trying to get some answers."

"Dutch is Smokey's cousin."

"Did he grow up in Oakland?" I asked.

"He was around for a while when we were kids, but he grew up out in Sacramento. When Smokey died, Dutch was down on a three-year nod for fraud. Airline tickets, credit cards, something like that."

"When'd he get out?"

"Right after you left, and it's been straight drama since he got here. He hit town and everything started to go wrong for your boy Holly. Nothing to take him all the way out, but he's been looking over his shoulder."

"How'd Dutch come back? Was he connected to somebody? One of Smokey's boys?"

"At first I thought it was just white-collar stuff, and the satellite crimes that go with it."

"But it was more than that?"

"Yep, and he lured everybody in like fish. He showed up New Year's Eve, in 1989, after the quake. He threw a party in the City, got Digital Underground, Too Short, and E-40 to perform. Turned it out. Everybody was talking about it for about six months."

"That wild?"

"First of all, nobody could believe those chicks."

"Hookers, right?"

"Yeah," he shook his head, "but not like the ones you see on the stroll. He calls 'em Hummingbirds or something."

"Nightingales."

"Right. He runs that with some white girl. Everybody think she bankrolled it but I think it's Dutch's enterprise and she's just his front."

"What do you mean?"

"He doesn't play the straight pimp role. He throws these exclusive parties, stocks the place with girls, and the men pay a membership fee."

"Slick."

"That's what I mean. He ain't like nothing we've ever seen before 'cause, you know, at the end of the day Oakland is country."

We laughed.

"You think he's out to get Holly?"

"That's my guess."

"Know anything else? Where he hangs out? Where he lives?"

"Nope. He keeps a low profile, lets a story leak out once in a while just to feed the mystery machine, but that's it."

"What about Black Jeff? Think he'd know anything?"

"He might know more about Holly than I do, but he's ho'ing the straight life now, so he probably can't give you too much info on Dutch."

"Straight life? What's he doing?"

"Oh, I ain't gonna spoil it for you. See for yourself, but be warned, he got chicks convinced his dick is made of kryptonite."

I laughed. "When I first got here and you were running all that 'back to Africa' drag, I thought you were gone, but I see the real Crowley is still in there deep down."

"I'm always real, baby. Too real. You can't do what I do and not be. Everything I told you before, even if I was just running my mouth, is all connected to Cotton or Holly, one way or another."

"I hear ya." I stood up to go. "I'ma get out your hair but I'll stop by in a couple days."

"You do that."

"Any words of wisdom?" Crowley usually greeted people with obscure rap lyrics, an amusing but annoying habit, but since I'd caught him off guard he'd skipped the intro so I decided to indulge him and request a couple lines. "Some musical advice I can take on the road?"

"Oh, I got something better. A little more potent than that."

"What's that?"

"Guilt, nigga, is a flesh-eating virus. Get some repellant before you get yourself killed."

I wanted to laugh, but it stung. I went in search of Jeff instead.

FIFTEEN

The hub of UC Berkeley's student life, the corner of Bancroft and Telegraph, was crowded with pedestrians and street vendors as I cruised the avenue looking for Black Jeff. The famous skateboarder, one of the few Blacks in the sport and the only Bay Area star, was always a font of information, and he made Telegraph his headquarters whenever he was in town. Black Jeff was known internationally for his skateboarding skills, and just as much for claiming the derogatory name that white skateboarders bestowed on him. Once he heard it being whispered behind his back, he used it to register for all his events. It forced his competitors, the organizers, and the announcers to say it to his face. It also helped to build his notoriety.

I made a second loop around the block before I spotted him standing on the cement wall in front of the Golden Bear with his skateboard at his side. In my absence his trademark dreads had been sheared and replaced with an Afroed Mohawk with cornrows along the sides for a little East Bay flavor. He wore a blue-and-white seersucker suit, huaraches, and a British flag wrapped around his neck like a scarf. There was just no pinning the man down.

I honked my horn and called to him through the passenger window. "Black Jeff."

"What the fuck?" He jumped off the wall when he spotted me.

I parked the car illegally and got out to greet him.

"Maceo, baby, I thought you were dead."

"I was." I gave him a pound that turned into a hug. He motioned to my scar when I released him. "How you living, man? You here on a charm offensive?"

"Something like that." I flicked his Mohawk. "What happened to the dreads?"

"World rotates on an axis. Got to stay ahead of the curve."

"I hear ya. You still skating?"

"When I'm not onstage."

He grinned at my surprise and looked at his watch. "Doing a show in two hours for some drunk frat boys. Park and meet me in the Lair. I'll give you a little taste of what you've been missing."

———

Ten minutes later I walked into the Bear's Lair, a campus pub. Black Jeff was in the middle of his warm-up onstage. The room was empty save for a couple of waitresses and busboys who'd stopped to watch the act. I didn't blame them. Jeff was kinetic on-stage, working a ska dance with a porkpie hat covering his Mohawk. Beside him a Japanese woman with blue hair beat a tambourine against the ball of her hand and chimed in on his vocals. His guitarist, a big, blond Viking, sported the dreadlock style Jeff had abandoned. A drummer played so hard he sweated onto his kit. Above them a banner announced the group as the Sunburned Poets, and I had to laugh. While the rest of us spun in circles, there was Black Jeff, shining, freer than all of us with his one-world approach to life.

Four songs later he joined me, drenched in sweat and out of breath.

"Gangsta business now, right?" He took a seat, then pulled out another chair for his tambourine player. She sat down and looped her legs across his knees.

"How you doing?" I nodded at her chin-up style, hoping she'd go away but she didn't budge and Jeff didn't ask her to leave. "When'd this all happen?" I asked him.

"About a year ago. I was fooling around onstage with some skaters in Amsterdam. After my tournament was over I stayed on to play a little and," he motioned toward the banner, "the Sunburned Poets were born."

"That's a cool-ass name."

"Dreamed about it. It was written in the sky above Mount Tamalpais and I took it. Before that I was calling the group Meredith Hunter."

Black Jeff raised an eyebrow to see if I got it. I gave him another pound to let him know I did. Meredith Hunter was a Black concertgoer, a rock and roller, stabbed to death by Hell's Angels while the Rolling Stones performed his death song at Altamont.

"No way to chart you, baby, you're off the Richter."

He laughed at the expression while his girl looked back and forth between us. He turned to her and spoke in Japanese. When she joined in his laugh I assumed he'd translated my words.

"This is Miyo Takumatsu," he said. I reached across to shake her hand. "We met in Japan. She jumped onstage while I was performing so I figured she wanted to be in the band."

"You perform around town?"

"Small gigs here and there. A little more in Europe, Canada, 'cause they'll tag me on to an exhibition. Check us out next week, if you're still here. We're opening for Fishbone at the Berkeley Square."

"Might do that."

"Are you gonna be here that long?"

Just that quick the conversation took a serious turn.

"How 'bout this? I know each day when it gets here."

"Which means what?"

"It means that's the best I can do."

"You get back this morning?"

"Yesterday."

"You seen Holly?" he asked.

"Nope." My hand went to my lip. "But I got this looking for him." I tapped the bandage on the back of my head. "And this, too."

"You know he went underground."

"Any idea where I can find him?"

He shook his head in the negative but I didn't believe him. Holly trusted Black Jeff. He'd even bankrolled his skateboarding when he first started out.

"Break it down for me then. What's been happening since I been gone?"

"More blood, more crack, more madness. N.W.A trying to make sure we all go to hell."

"All they fault, huh?"

"Basically, but I ain't trying to make you laugh." He paused. "Holly ain't checking for you, baby. The way you cut out on my boy, left him behind to follow after that girl—"

I cut him off. "I didn't leave with Felicia."

"You know that expression, 'possession is nine tenths of the law'? Well, perception is the same thing. You were gone. She was gone. Billy died. Holly lost his girl. His family. He ain't the same man. Matter of fact, he might beat the shit out of you when he sees you."

I pulled a cigarette from my pocket and lit up. Didn't have too much to say to that.

"Cotton's here, though. Touched down on a private plane after he melted at that press conference. Now he's out at his fortress in Timber Hills."

His gaze was steady. He was telling me something without saying the words.

"That place got White House–level security ever since Allaina got those death threats. They'll practically take imprints of your balls before you can get in there. He got off-duty cops, the grim reaper, and a couple Janissaries guarding the house.

"Hard for anybody to get in there without Cotton knowing first. Hear what I'm saying? It would be a safe place if you needed that kind of thing. There's a guard gate at the bottom of the hill, and another one right outside his house. Two separate checkpoints."

"He got all that security just because of Allaina?"

"Where you been? After Billy died everybody went buckwild in the town trying to get at the money. Jackers started kidnapping fools. You know the ones I'm talking about."

"The ones who can't call 911."

"Exactly."

"You think Holly's out in Timber Hills with Cotton?"

"I didn't say anything like that."

"But Cotton's there?"

"From what I heard. Couple of the fellas headed out there tonight. A little get-together."

"You going?"

He shook his head. "I keep it about the music and the skating." Behind us the guitar player tapped the mic to get Jeff and Miyo's attention. He stood up. "I got to roll, baby. Try to make the show." He pointed at my scar. "And quit sleeping with demons."

"You think Holly's caught up with Cotton?"

"Wouldn't know. But follow the money."

"What money?"

"You watched *Miami Vice* just like I did. It's either about money or a woman."

I stood up. "Jeff, you think you can get me in up there?"

"Like I said, I'm trying to stay out of all this."

"I hear you, but Holly could go down hard on this one."

I let him take his time coming up with an answer. "Alright, I'll call Cotton, tell him I wanna come through. Might be a little easier with all the fellas up there."

"Cool, you want to ride out with me?"

He shook his head. "You can use my name to get through the gates, but I'm not going anywhere near that. Once you're inside you're on your own."

"Fair enough. Hey, you remember Lemon Banks? Used to be Cotton's road dog."

Jeff nodded his head, slow, like he hadn't thought about

Lemon in years. I hadn't either until that morning. I'd woken up with a headache and the past on my mind. Lemon was part of the past, one of Cotton's oldest friends.

When Cotton first moved to Dover Street, Lemon would take a bus to see him every other weekend. The two of them were an odd pair: the gangly, awkward basketball player and the round, careless bright-skinned boy with a penchant for practical jokes and flashes of cruelty. Any trouble Cotton got into at our house always happened on the days Lemon came to visit.

During Cotton's rookie year with the Vanguards, the police were called to his Laguna Beach mansion on five separate occasions. Lemon made headlines the same year when he was pulled over in Cotton's custom-made Mercedes with vials of coke in the car. Later Cotton paid a quarter-million dollars in hush money to a female fan Lemon had assaulted after a game.

The connection between the two men didn't make sense in the abstract, but between the lines of the apparently one-sided relationship was the fact that Lemon's house had been Cotton's only sanctuary before my grandparents took him away. When Cotton ran from his father's abuse he ended up at Lemon's, where he would climb through a window looking for a safe place to sleep. And it was Lemon who became the only person to ever step between Cotton and his father's fist to take the blow himself. In turn, Cotton had him on payroll for years trying to protect him from himself. That lasted until his marriage. Allaina's first order of business had been to banish him from their home.

Lemon bad-mouthed the star and his wife to anyone who would listen. He would be a good source of any dirt concerning Cotton.

"I remember Lemon," Jeff said.

"Any idea what happened to him?"

"He went to jail after he beat up one of his girlfriends. From what I heard, he got raped inside. They were in there popping his ass like gum. Turned the man out. He went right back to the pipe once he hit the streets. Almost blew his heart up once, overdosed, did a stint in rehab, came out, and starting doping again."

"So, he's a bona fide crackhead?"

"Smoked out."

"You have a bead on him? Know where I can find him?"

"Heard he stays over in one of those welfare hotels on San Pablo. Smartest thing Allaina did was get that fool out of Cotton's life."

"Cotton and Lemon used to be pretty tight. Who replaced him in Cotton's life?"

"Holly. Two of them been thick as thieves since you left town. And with Holly comes Clarence, those Samoans, Emmet." He ticked the names off on his fingers. "You know the crew."

"Hard crew to penetrate."

"Exactly. Which means they know who killed that girl. Whether they'll ever say is anybody's guess, but I have to get out of here."

"Alright, Jeff, thanks for everything."

"No problem." He paused before he walked away, and gave me a lazy, knowing smile. "You thought you got away, didn't you? How long were you gone before you realized that Oakland had tentacles?"

I cringed at his accuracy.

"Give up before you drive yourself crazy, Maceo; this town will wear your ass like skin no matter where you go. Trust me."

"You talk like they got armed guards at the city limits."

"Don't have to." He tapped the side of his head. "Brothas locked themselves down without any help. I love Holly like family, but him and his boys are fighting for shit that don't even belong to them. The game don't love 'em, the city don't either."

"Heard Holly took over Billy's territory."

"Of course he did, and he went old-school on 'em when he took it. He let Billy's boys split it up between them, but they have to pay him a tariff to keep the peace."

Holly always had a Midas touch, but I bet he still lived like a pauper, and I bet he had at least seven men between him and any illegal transactions. In another life he might have run the CIA.

"So, you got six guys paying taxes to Holly. How come somebody hasn't tried to take him out before this?"

"They did." He paused. "Now you got five paying for six."

Holly had bodies on his gun, but I doubt it could ever be proven.

"Thanks, Jeff."

"No problem. But when you head up to that house . . ."

"What?"

"Watch yourself. Holly ain't the only one who's changed."

SIXTEEN

"Can I help you?" A man in a black slicker stepped out of a guard's booth in front of Cotton's house. The little hut was wedged into the trees a good distance from the main house, on the street side of the large iron gate. I'd waited until nightfall to approach the house, and I'd already passed through one checkpoint by using Jeff's name.

"Can I help you?" he asked again. The flashlight he leveled on my face felt aggressive. It also made it impossible for me to see him.

"I'm here to see Cotton."

"Is Mr. Knox expecting you this evening?" The formality coupled with the security telegraphed just how far Cotton had come.

"He should be."

"Can you step out of the car, please?" I did as I was asked despite the currents of rain blanketing the driveway. Cotton lived in

Timber Hills, an exclusive community in Contra Costa County built on Mt. Diablo. On either side of the winding roads that led up to the house there were drop-offs, like black holes, that fell deep into the canyons below.

As I stepped from the car to submit to the security wand I heard the piercing cry of coyotes calling to one another across the mountain range. Through the rain I caught the strong scent of canyon sage and eucalyptus while the darkness breathed around me like a predator. Out here the biggest perceived threat was animal, not human, and light-years away from East Oakland. But inside Cotton's house the reverse could still be true.

"Are you with the press?" The guard's voice had the resonance I associated with Black men, but because of the light trained into my eyes I couldn't see his face.

"No, I'm an old friend. He knows I'm coming."

"May I have your name, please?" From within the folds of his slicker I heard the squawk of a walkie-talkie.

"Black Jeff."

He waited like he wanted more but I didn't give him anything. "Just one moment. Please stay by your car."

He hadn't said "in the car" so I pulled an umbrella from beneath the passenger seat, and then because I learned too many lessons the hard way I grabbed the blackjack I kept in the glove compartment.

I slid it down into the back of my pants.

Through the gates and a small forest of oak trees I could see the massive structure that Cotton called home. In the circular driveway I counted a total of six luxury cars: a Mercedes, two BMWs, a Jaguar, a Lexus, and a 1970 Chevelle that appeared to be fresh off the showroom floor. They were red, and each license plate spelled out COTTON followed by a number from one to six. The cars were parked in numerical order.

At the bottom of the hill I saw another car weaving its way up to the house.

I stepped closer to get a better look at the guard, but he must have liked the uneasiness he'd created because he stepped back.

"Cotton always have this much security?" I asked.

Silence.

The car I'd seen in the distance, a black Corvette, streaked past us and drew the guard's attention away. I could hear his feet slapping through the puddles as he ran to the gatehouse. I waited for him to pull a gun on the driver, or at least drag him through the window for a beat-down, but he didn't. Instead he bowed and scraped like a slave.

"Good evening, Mr. Lockwood—"

"Open the fucking gate, man." The guard's Stepin Fetchit routine was cut short by the angry bark from inside the car. He hustled to swing the gate open. The wheels of the car kicked up gravel as he gunned it inside. As it pulled away I saw a woman in the passenger seat.

The humiliated guard turned his wrath on me. "Keep your distance until we get clearance."

His anger didn't matter; I'd just seen him behave as if he were the Black sidekick in a Shirley Temple movie. Plus, I'd heard the name of the driver. Lockwood. The handler at the press conference.

"Was that Silas Lockwood?" I asked when the guard remembered me.

"You ask a lot of questions." His walkie-talkie squawked again and I heard a female voice say, "Bring him up."

The guard led me inside and up to the house. The winged staircase that arched out like it wanted a hug was slick with rain and I almost fell twice.

When I reached the front door it swung open before I had a chance to ring the bell. I expected the guard to snap his heels and salute but he left me without another word.

A Black woman around sixty years old and dressed in a maid's uniform took my umbrella and handed me a towel to dry off. She rolled her eyes at the guard's retreating back.

"Was he out there acting like Sergeant Pepper again?"

I smiled. "Maybe he's mad about being stuck in the rain."

"He got a hat and a transistor. He's fine."

As I tried to soak up the water on my clothes I looked around the cavernous hallway. Cotton hadn't been looking for comfort when he'd bought the place; it seemed to be made only of sharp angles and granite. About as welcoming as a crypt.

"Cotton here by himself?" I'd already seen Silas, but I wanted to get her talking.

She rolled her eyes. "Cornelius is never here by himself. He got about ten friends upstairs in the game room, and some girl. You'll hear their voices."

She pointed me in the right direction and disappeared through a large door. I took a moment to survey the trophy case that held Cotton's bounty from his days at UNLV. In a center photograph Coach Tark stood with his boys, the '87 Runnin' Rebels, in front of the infamous Shark Tank where they'd trounced all comers until they met a heartbreaking end at the Final Four.

Their defeat left me sick for about a week, but the picture was probably taken months before any of them could even guess at their fate against Providence. It was the biggest heartbreaker of their history until 1991, when not even the showstopping trio of Larry Johnson, Stacy Augmon, and Greg Anthony could stop Chris Laettner and Duke's Blue Devils in the Final Four. Cotton was pro by then, but the loss still felt personal to me.

The maid returned to the hallway. "You lose your way?" She stood behind me with a glass of milk in her hand.

"No, I'm sorry, I was just looking at the picture."

"No need to be sorry. That's Cornelius's favorite one. I catch him out here looking at it all the time." She looked at me like she'd seen me before. "Tell me your name again, baby."

"Maceo."

"Maceo, hmmm. You can't be a ballplayer. You're too short."

She said it with the matter-of-factness of Southern Black women.

"I played baseball."

"Now that makes more sense." She remained in front of the trophy case. "Where your people from?"

"North Oakland."

"Before that."

"Louisiana."

"Antonia Bouchaund your grandmother?"

"That's her maiden name, yes."

"I thought I knew you. I'm Ethelene Ritchie. I used to work at the Celestine Home with your grandmother and Gloria Johnson."

"Nice to meet you."

"You didn't have that scar last time I saw you."

"No, I didn't."

We stood there in silence.

"It's been awhile since I've seen Antonia. I'm all the way out here, and it's easier to stay out this way on my days off."

"Well, it's a big house."

"It's something." She rolled her eyes again. "I was at Celestine the year Cornelius was with your family."

"Is that right?"

"Uh-huh, I spent a lot of time with him whenever he came to the center. He hired me when he bought this big monster."

"How long have you been here?"

"About two years."

"You must get lonely when they're in L.A." Cotton and Allaina actually lived in Laguna Beach, a wealthy community in Orange County, during the season, but like most Northern Californians, anything outside of San Diego or Disneyland was just L.A.

"I keep busy." She motioned to the staircase. "Well, tell your grandmother I said hello, and come see me next time you're here."

"I will." She disappeared for a second time through the door.

SEVENTEEN

I heard the faint sound of voices and music as I climbed the stairs, but I took the time to stop on the first landing in front of a portrait of Allaina. Stretching about six feet high, the painting encompassed the entire wall between the first and second floors. The pose was reminiscent of the *Madonna and Child,* but there was a little too much sauce and steel in the depiction to be entirely benevolent. Allaina had abandoned a modeling career in order to marry Cotton and follow him on the road, but I doubted that any fashion photographer had ever produced anything as ferocious as the portrait.

Dressed in a long, red dress with matching jewels on her neck, she cradled an infant Marquis in her arms. The little boy was naked, most of his small body covered by her arms and long hair. The smile she offered the baby was kind, but it was evident in her eyes that she would slit her own throat and use the blood to blind her attacker before she'd allow anyone to harm her son.

Cotton had found himself a worthy companion, and as far as I could tell the portrait was the only thing in the house that conveyed any sort of personality.

I moved on and passed three rooms, all dark, before I came upon the one where the men were gathered. Their boisterous laughter competed with the incendiary lyrics of N.W.A, and through the half-open door I saw a colony of shot glasses, liquor bottles, and overturned tables and chairs. Three large-screen televisions lined up against the wall played three different sporting events: boxing, soccer, and a horse race. There were two pool tables, a jukebox, a bank of arcade games, and stacks of videocassettes. The room itself was filled with the black leather furniture of new money and testosterone; the only thing missing was rottweiler and pit bull puppies.

In one sweep I saw everything a person might need to distract him from reality. It gave the gathering the feel of a bachelor party, or at the very least, the manic rainy-day recesses of elementary school. The drug game had made the men rich, but it was blood wealth, and they partied with the abandon of men who knew the hangman's noose was right above their heads. If I were a romantic I would have listened for the fiddles, but at the end of the game none of our ends would be that poetic. On some level they must have known it, because I could smell it. There was an unmistakable scent of sulfur in that room, a smell that made me think of hell. They had too much death between them to last. The veneer of protection they offered Cotton was riddled with holes.

Emmet Landry, an Oakland hustla, and Clarence Mann, a drug dealer from San Francisco's Hunters Point, sat at a table playing dominos with Clarence's silent and faithful Samoan henchmen, Declan and Luther. Bilau Arafi, a gangsta whose father was a prominent Black Muslim leader, reclined on the floor in dress pants, shiny liquor-store socks, and a silk shirt. He and Malcolm Rose, an old friend who went all the way back to elementary school, battled each other at Tecmo, an electronic football game.

All of them except Bilau had been present the night of Smokey and Reggie's murder, and all of them had held Felicia's life in their hands. I had trusted each of them in the most dire moments of my life, but as I looked around at the group I realized a sea change had occurred since my departure. It was obvious by the pairings that new alliances had formed, alliances that spawned new friends and enemies. In previous years, Bilau and Malcolm had barely been able to abide each other's company, but the number of the old guard was shrinking as fast as the number of people who could be trusted.

Holly, the man I'd come home to help, understood the shaky ground on which it was all built. I saw it in his face as I spotted him in front of the fireplace. He watched the others with the eyes of a cop, or at the very least, a con. He knew about the wolf's bounty firsthand. The knowledge had cemented our friendship because we'd learned about it as children.

When we were kids, a boy named John Claire—whom Holly bullied with a child's abandon—dropped dead on the school yard and Holly was the only witness. It was never known whether Holly pushed him and the fall caused his death, or if he fell on his own and hit his head, like Holly claimed. Either way, when Cissy and I were attacked in the alley off of College and Alcatraz, John Claire's ghost was there. The dead boy embodied the secrets we kept and the questions I never asked Holly for fear of the answers. But despite the phantom in the room, the mood among the men was festive, playful even, but Holly's demeanor was anything but, and for the first time since I'd known him I saw vulnerability in his face. I knew then that Cissy had been right to call me home, because I saw the fissures in that room as clear as day, and one of them ran right across the floor and ended at his feet.

EIGHTEEN

Through the window at the end of the hallway, a lightning flash shattered the darkness and illuminated an open door where I spotted Cotton talking with Silas. He was in a white nylon sweat suit with the gray stripes of the Vanguards down the sides. Diamonds flashed in his ears and on his wrist and ring finger. His white Kangol was pulled down low on his brow, and loose braids rested on his collar. He stood tall in the room—all angles and cuts, teak skin, and hooded eyes.

Behind me the music stopped abruptly to be replaced by the shit-talking and bone-slapping of the domino game.

Emmet's rough, pinched voice could be heard from the game room. "What you gonna do, huh, punk, what you gonna do? Take that."

Bilau shouted back. "Take what? Your money?"

The men laughed, then I heard Cotton's voice. I sunk farther back in the shadows, prepared to say I was looking for a bathroom if anyone caught me there.

"Why you bring her here, Silas? That's what you call looking out? If I ever expect to get Allaina home I can't have this kind of shit going down."

"She's scared, man."

"She's a hustla, Silas, and she hustled you. You supposed to be protecting my family. If I can't trust you then who can I trust?"

"Cotton, listen—"

"Listen to what? Listen to you tell me she's scared? Fuck that! I'm scared. I got the police on my ass, I'm suspended from the team, my shoe contract is up in the air, and Allaina . . ."

"I'm handling it."

"You think so? You were supposed to take care of the money for me, and you came back here with a drunk chick that might be connected to those fools."

I heard the sound of a door opening and I turned to find a woman leaving the bathroom. The light was on behind her, which gave me a clear view.

She was gorgeous.

She wore tight beige pants, or maybe just skin from the way they fit, and a white sweater that looked soft enough to pull through the eye of a needle. Her hair, just a shade darker than her skin, was rusty brown and curly. She finished all that off with mean, slanted cat eyes, a breeze of freckles across the bridge of her nose, and generous lips. Underneath that, though, she was a train wreck. She missed the light switch three times because of a shaky hand, and she gulped liquid from a tall glass like she'd just been rescued from the desert.

"You finished with the bathroom?" I asked her, stepping away from the open door to conceal my eavesdropping. She jumped at the sound of my voice.

"Oh, you scared me."

"Sorry about that. You alright?"

"Yeah, I'm fine. Have you seen Silas?"

"No, I just got here."

Cotton's voice rose in anger behind us. "Why should I care about that girl? Just get her the fuck out of my house!"

She sucked in her breath when she heard the words, and looked desperately up and down the hall.

"This is Allaina's house, Silas. You can't have a chick like that up in here. There's too much at stake. You know better than that."

I felt her arm on my wrist. "Can you get me out of here? Can you help me?"

I wanted to laugh.

This woman, not knowing a thing about me, was giving me the chance to play hero.

All I needed.

Her simple question gave me entrée back to a role I relished.

In my mind the Watch Dog was a rescuer, a safe harbor for women in trouble, despite compelling evidence that I was better suited for the role of Sisyphus.

Felicia hadn't been the first woman in my life to inspire blind devotion—only the most obvious—and this one, with her shady slew of problems, cruel eyes, and gorgeous body looked like she would be the next.

Two years on the road, a lifetime of lessons, and in that dark hallway it all came down to a simple question.

Did I have the answer?

I couldn't say, but I knew I was going to help her.

———————

The men from the game room spilled out into the hallway just as we made our way past. Bilau, laughing at something Malcolm said, shouted for his host.

"Cotton! Come out here!"

Cotton and Silas appeared then. He turned on a light, and they all stopped short when they saw me standing there with the girl. Cotton's brow wrinkled in confusion, Emmet smirked, but Holly, owner of a world-class poker face, gave me nothing.

"Gotdamn, motherfucker, what brings you to the valley of the kings?" Bilau, straightforward as ever, gave me a pound. I returned the greeting with a pound of my own.

Cotton ignored the conversation between the two of us and directed his gaze at the girl. "You gotta get up outta here."

"I was looking for the front door but I got lost." The challenge in her voice silenced everyone in the hallway. She twirled the glass in her hand and looked at each of the men.

Silas stood behind Cotton like he didn't know her, and I gathered from the way they all looked at me that everyone assumed I'd brought her to the party.

Bilau laughed again. "Maceo, baby, I got to give it to you. Your short ass be pulling down some hot chicks."

I didn't respond. Instead I put my hand on the girl's elbow to move her along. She decided then not to budge.

She was locked on Cotton.

"You have anything to say to me?" she asked him.

"Should I?" Cotton's voice was cold enough to drop the temperature another twenty degrees in that already freezing mausoleum.

The mood changed on a dime and I reached for my blackjack. She took the last swallow from the glass she was holding, then dropped it on the marble floor. The noise was like a gunshot. Everybody jumped.

She kicked the shattered glass away and I saw Cotton clench his jaw and fist in anger. She looked down at his hand and smirked. "Oops," she said, "sorry about that."

"Let's go," I said to her.

"I'm leaving. I'm leaving. I just wanted to make sure Cotton didn't have anything to say to me."

"Maceo, you gonna take her home?" Cotton asked.

"Trying to."

"Trying to?" Emmet, a shiny lunkhead—who didn't have the cognitive skills to decipher the intricacies of the situation—decided to get involved anyway. "You can't handle this girl?"

I didn't say a word and neither did she. I'd agreed to help her and I knew it was a mistake to take my eyes off her, Cotton, or the men ready to defend him against one drunken girl.

"Answer my question." There was a hiss in her words.

He was measured calm. "No, I don't have anything to say to you."

"You can't think of a single thing? Then how about I tell you something." Her voice grew stronger. Cotton actually stepped backward. "You want to hear it?" she asked in a whisper. "I'll tell you if you want to know."

"If I let you tell me, will you let my friend take you home?"

"Oh, you want to make sure I get home safely? Is that it? You're a gentleman now?"

"Will you go?"

"I'll go. I only have one word for you anyway. The word of the day." She slurred this and I heard the alcohol. "Want to hear it?"

"Should I?"

"Oh, you should. It might help you sleep at night."

"What is it then?"

"My word"—she paused—"is Dana."

"What's that supposed to mean?" I understood it before everyone else except maybe Holly. He caught my eye for a quarter of a second, then he looked away. "Her funeral's day after tomorrow. You and your wife are more than welcome to come."

"What are you talking about?" Cotton asked her.

"Dana!" She screamed it. "Dana, my friend; you killed her."

"What the fuck!" Silas tried to step around Cotton, so I moved in front of the girl. "I didn't bring you up here for this bullshit," he said to her.

"What did you bring me up here for then, Silas? You fucking pimp!"

She was nuts. She was surrounded by enough men to kill her and bury her in the canyons before sunup, like it was nothing, but she didn't back down.

Silas stepped up again and so did I. "Hold up, partna, I'ma take her home."

"Get out the way." He towered over me but he wasn't going to take me down easy.

"I can't do that. I'm not gonna let you put your hands on her."

Emmet broke the standoff with a snicker and his big, careless mouth.

"Maceo, you Save-a-Ho-ass nigga. You determined to be a trick. You left town with janky-ass Felicia, then you come back with this viper. Why don't you just pay somebody to suck your dick and save everybody the trouble?"

"Oh, shit." Behind him Bilau laughed openly. "You calling him out?"

Animosity had not existed between Emmet and I before I left town. We hadn't known each other well enough for that, but Felicia had changed the playing field all the way around.

"Fuck you, Emmet."

He put his drink down and stepped closer to me. "Fuck me? Fuck you, you coward motherfucker."

I grabbed the girl's arm. "Let's go."

Emmet stepped in front of us. "Go? You ain't got shit to say for yourself?"

Cotton tried to intervene. "Hold up, Emmet."

Emmet kept on going. "Where your girl at?" He laughed. I knew he meant Felicia when he looked at my scar. "What happen, she cut you? You betrayed all your boys to run after a chick who probably left you for dead somewhere?"

He bumped his chest against mine, so close I could smell the rancid scent of his own decay. Emmet was angry. But he was also hiding. I could see it. His pocky, dalmatian skin and the dark ring around his lips let me know he was not a stranger to crack pipes.

The wolf had already paid him a visit.

The knowledge made me fierce.

I snickered at him. "You want me to give up my secrets? What about yours?" Hardness flashed in my eyes. He saw it and wavered, then he bumped me again just to play the shot through.

He underestimated me when he did that.

By the time I put Oakland in my rearview mirror I had grown to hate the hesitancy in my own personality. I hated that in the time it took for me to make a single decision, everybody else had already made two.

And here were two more. I could see them.

I had the option of explaining that Felicia was a ghost to me, or I could have grabbed the girl and left.

I hit him instead. Then I smiled like a jackal.

It was uncharacteristic of the Maceo they knew, and I used that to my advantage.

I used the blackjack to split the skin across the bridge of his nose, and a good portion of his mouth. His lips popped like a grape.

Blood spurted before anyone could react, and I hit him again just to drive home my point.

Which was this.

The world had changed, and so had I.

———

I managed to get the girl out of the house and into the car before Emmet could get up off the floor. No one tried to stop us; they were too confused by the turn of events.

The truck kicked up rocks and twigs as I whipped the wheel and gunned it down the mountain. The canyon roads were harder to navigate on the way down, but I managed.

I looked at the girl I'd just risked a beat-down for and realized I didn't even know her name. She'd been brave in the house but in the car she was all tears.

I let her cry.

By the time she looked my way I was already back in Alameda County near Children's Hospital. She shivered against the cold and wrapped her arms around her chest. I turned on the heater and reached behind the seat to grab a sweatshirt.

She used it to blow her nose.

"You alright?" I asked her.

She looked at me, then she said her first words since we had got into the car.

"I thought I was the saddest person at the party."

Her voice was soft and defeated when she said it, then she released the contents of her stomach all over my car.

NINETEEN

My history with women had followed a pattern, from my first school-yard crush to Felicia. When I'd been faced with making a decision between a nice girl—the one who might pack an extra peanut-butter-and-jelly sandwich for me in her lunch box—or the one who'd be willing to lure me to the monkey bars to get beat up, I'd politely declined the sandwich every time and took the ass-whipping.

Cleaning up the vomit of a woman I didn't know was the equivalent of an adult-size beat-down. It was near midnight, it was raining, and as I sponged out the car in the parking lot of the hotel, I was sure I could read Kiros's mind. He seemed to say with perfect logic, Here we go again."

"I can pick 'em, can't I, boy?"

The dog stretched out on the pavement in front of the hotel to let me know he wasn't interested.

I didn't blame him. Oakland was riddled with the dust of

murders, unsolved crimes, and the tears of orphaned children, but it was just as lousy with the lessons I refused to learn.

Once I finished the inside of the car, I sat on the hood beneath the covered parking space and smoked a cigarette. The light from my room was visible from where I sat, and I could see the woman's silhouette against the curtains. I was on my third smoke before she came out.

She still wore the skin-graft pants, but she'd ditched the sweater for an old Raiders T-shirt of mine with Al Davis's infamous JUST WIN, BABY emblazoned across the front. Her feet were bare but she didn't seem to mind the rain and puddles in the driveway. She'd cleaned up well enough that it was soap and toothpaste I smelled instead of liquor and vomit.

"Hey." The word was just above a whisper. She nodded at my cigarette and leaned in to take a drag while I held it between my fingers. Kiros raised his head and looked at her.

"That yours?"

"Yep."

"What is it?"

"A dog," I answered.

She rolled her eyes. "What kind?"

Kiros stood to his full height and stretched. "A big one."

She didn't miss a beat. "Well, someone conned you if you believe that's a dog."

"Think so?"

"Uh-huh."

She held her hand out and Kiros came forward and licked it. Then he leaned against her knees and stretched his paws out across her feet.

I guess I wasn't the only sucker in the family.

"You want something to eat?" I asked.

"That would be nice." She squeezed my wrist when she grabbed my cigarette. "That would be perfect." Her voice was nice but her eyes were not. Though she tried to disguise it, the look she wore was hard and weathered, impatient and bruised.

She spoke my language without saying a word.

––––––––

"You always roll around town like a ninja?" She'd changed out of her pants and into a pair of sweats I'd dug out of a drawer once we returned to the room. Her knees were pulled up to her chest on the rickety chair that went with the rickety table.

I placed a plate of refried beans mixed with cheese and rice on a paper plate in front of her. Living on my own I'd grown adept at throwing together quick, jailhouse meals, and she seemed to appreciate it. My specialty was oysters heated in the can and topped with hot sauce and crackers, or ramen noodles with tuna, but I wanted to save those for a special occasion. With the amount of liquor she'd put down I figured she needed something a little more substantial. I handed her a glass of water and two slices of white bread to go with the beans.

"A ninja, huh?"

"Well, you came to my rescue like we were old friends. That's ninja, right? Or is it samurai?" I was glad to see she had a sense of humor, but leery of the fact that she'd switched emotions so abruptly. "You helped me," she continued, "and you don't even know my name."

"I thought it was Drunk-Woman-in-Danger."

"Funny," she shrugged, "but maybe a little bit true."

"What is your name?"

"Sonia. Sonny. Sonny Boston."

"You sure?"

"Yeah, I'm sure. Sonia is my real name but I go by Sonny."

"Boston. Is that real?"

"As real as anything else."

"Nice to meet you then, *Sonny Boston*." Sonny Boston was the name of an eight-cylinder chick with bodies in her past.

She shoveled a spoonful of beans into her mouth. "What's yours?"

"Maceo Redfield."

She rolled her eyes. "You're one to talk, *Maceo Redfield*." I watched her tear off a piece of bread and hand it to Kiros.

"And what's his name?"

"That's Kiros. No last name."

"Where'd you get that?"

"It's Greek; means a strategic time, a moment of destiny."

"A ninja with a dictionary." She winked at me to let me know she was kidding.

"That's what his first owner named him. He was a runt. Got him when he was about a year old."

"Him? A runt? That doesn't sound right."

I reached down and rubbed his ears. "He had a growth spurt once I got him." She tore off a corner of bread and ran it around the edges of her plate. "So, what was all that up at Cotton's house?" I asked her.

The playfulness fled. She continued to eat. I let it go. There was plenty of time for questions and answers, since she'd made no move to go home.

————

Later, I gave her and Kiros the bed and stretched out on the battered plaid couch against the far wall. The two of them were lights-out almost immediately. Once I heard her snore I got up to pull the articles from the drawer. Come morning I planned to hit the streets to get answers, the first of which was the name of the two men who'd fought with Cotton and Holly, but first I had to contend with my grandparents. I considered myself a man, but I knew deep down that until I looked Daddy Al in the eye I had not faced the final stage in my rite of passage.

Kiros yelped in his sleep, probably chasing down a squirrel, or a bear, and Sonny rolled over. She was a restless sleeper, whipping back and forth across the small expanse of the bed. I shoved the articles back in the drawer and returned to the couch. For the next few hours I listened to her mumble curse words in her sleep. Finally, she woke with a start and flashed her bloodshot eyes at me.

"I can't sleep," she said.

"I saw that."

"You been up all this time? What time is it?"

"Five."

She looked around the decrepit little room. "Why do you live here? You drying out or something?"

"Is it question-and-answer time? 'Cause that goes both ways."

"What do you want to know?"

"What do you think? Why would you bait a group of grown-ass men, then spend the night with somebody you don't even know?"

"I can't trust you?" She was adept at flipping my questions on their ear.

"You don't know me."

She shrugged. "You had kind eyes, so I went on instinct."

"I thought my eyes were sad."

"They are sad, so I took that to mean you knew how to be kind."

She was good. I had to give her that.

"You got all that while you were running for your life?"

"I think on my feet. Always have."

I stood up and stretched. My stomach growled, but it was too late to eat. "I need some water," I said. "Can I get you a glass?"

"Sure."

Kiros remained asleep, curled on the edge of the bed, as I moved around the little makeshift galley kitchen. When I handed her the water glass she trailed her fingers across my knuckles. I responded like I'd been hooked up to jumper cables.

"Why you so jumpy?"

"I'm scared of you."

She laughed and swung her legs over the edge of the bed until our knees were touching.

"Be still," she said. "Don't move."

I stayed put and watched her hands come toward my face. She ran her fingers down the length of my scar. I didn't flinch. Her touch was cool. Welcome.

"Looks like a tree branch."

"Rama del arbol."

She repeated the words, her fingers still resting on my face. "What's that mean?"

"Branches of a tree. A lady I knew in Texas used to say that to me."

"Well, can I say it to you now?" She moved closer. I let her touch my face until she got tired. Then I grabbed her wrist and returned it to her side.

"I know your game," I told her. "You're avoiding my questions."

"You want to talk about the scar?" she asked me.

I shook my head.

"So, there you go." She returned to her end of the bed to rest her head on the pillow. "But you will one day."

"That goes both ways, lady. What do you know about the night your friend was murdered?"

"I know she ended up dead." She fluffed the pillow until it suited her.

"I helped you. You don't want to help me?"

"I helped you, too."

"How's that?"

"You were about as welcome at that party as I was."

"That was one man giving me trouble."

"I didn't see anybody else jump to your defense." She chuckled. "I had it wrong before. You're a samurai, because ninjas usually travel in packs, right? Samurais are the lone wolves, but they wouldn't have you either. You're a Ronin."

"You're full of jokes," I paused, "or full of something."

"You mad, ninja? Don't be. I helped you and you helped me. When they write about it later they can call it misfit love."

Sleep came easy to me after that.

TWENTY

In the morning I woke up with morning sours so brutal that three caps of mouthwash couldn't kill it. I tried to wake Sonny but she brushed me off twice and pulled the covers over her head. I grabbed a phone book instead and searched the Yellow Pages for a boxing gym in the vicinity.

Fifteen minutes later I drove through the streets of the Fruitvale District, an area unofficially dubbed "Jingle Town" because of the fruit and vegetable carts adorned with bells that populated the largely Hispanic neighborhood.

At one point Fruitvale had been filled with Black families, and at a point before that—when Mexico still owned California—it had been filled with Mexicans. And at another point, before them all, the Ohlone tribe hunted and gathered along the shores of the Bay, and so it went.

Soup Can, one of the three old-timers who spent his days in the Nickel and Dime, had a theory about California and Mexico.

Any conversation with the old man included his take on the whole thing. Having been his only ride home on more than one occasion, I knew it by heart.

"You know, President Polk, when he started to carve shit up that didn't belong to him—this country in particular—he stole California from Mexico. It's only a matter of time before they take it back by hook or crook. They keep hollering about tighter border patrols but that don't mean nothing. That's just a little old Band-Aid on a big open sore. Blood will flow from that wound one of these days. Mark my words."

As I moved through the crowds on busy East Fourteenth, re-named International Boulevard, Soup Can's pronouncements rang true. The language filtering through the air and written on storefront windows was Spanish. The entire place had a south-of-the-border feel that reminded me of Texas.

I found Manny's Gym down a narrow alley strewn with garbage. The place was rundown, anonymous, and exactly what I sought. At the door I paid eight dollars for a day pass and a roll of tape. It had been over a week since I'd left my place in Texas and my body missed the regimen, my mind missed the diversion the exercise provided. While living in the border towns, killing time between odd construction jobs, I'd taken up boxing after wandering into a gym and recognizing the smell of burnt-up dreams.

Once I started to box, I found that inside the ring was one of the few places I didn't see my father in my peripheral vision. While I fought I could move fast enough to make him blur, mute his voice and his laugh. Landing a good punch sent him flying, because the moment I stepped over those ropes and onto the canvas, I knew I'd found a new way, a more accurate way to define myself. I took to the intimacy of the sport. I relished the way it forced me to be present in my own life. I'd been a spectator in it for so long that I grew to crave the simulated combat.

I took to the bag with gusto, doing my best to work my frustrations down to a dull roar. Boxing, and the time it took to train, filled the void left by Felicia, Alixe, and the Texas woman who'd come after that. It had been a good six months since I'd made any sort of connection that counted. My ferociousness on the bag let me know I needed something to exist in the prism between my family, Cotton, and Holly.

Sonny was the first thing that popped into my mind.

———

I was quiet as I opened the door, thinking Sonny might still be asleep, but she was on the phone with her back to me. The receiver was cradled between her shoulder and ear.

"Give me a little time. I'll take care of it. I just need a couple days."

Kiros barked, and she hung up the phone without finishing her sentence or turning around. I closed the door, expecting her to greet me, thank me, acknowledge my presence in some way, but instead she marched into the kitchen and yanked open the drawer where I'd stored the articles about Cotton.

When she looked at me her eyes sizzled with anger and distrust. "What's all this? You setting me up?"

"Setting you up for what? I just met you."

"Who sent you to follow me?" Her tone was shitty. In less than twenty-four hours we'd crossed through the choppy waters of fear, anger, seduction, and back to fury. Trying to navigate her moods was like trying to predict a quake. Guesswork at best.

"Nobody. Calm down and we might be able to help each other out."

"Why should I trust you? Why should I help you?"

At the kitchen sink I stuck my head all the way under the faucet to wash away the sweat from my workout. She fumed behind me, but I took my time. Finally, she reached out with her foot to push the back of my knees. They buckled, but I caught myself before I hit the floor.

I turned to face her. "You won't be happy until I put you out."

"Is that your plan?"

"What? You don't trust me?"

"My grandmother told me once not to even trust your teeth, because they'll bite you."

"Words to live by. But I got better ones."

"What?"

"Call the police."

She looked out the window, and I knew I had her.

Her response was weak. "Why don't you?"

"Cool. Now that we both know that's not an option, maybe we can help each other. You want to find out about your friend. I want to help a friend."

As she hesitated I sat and pulled my chair close to hers.

"Who else you gonna go to, Sonny?" I wiped the water from my face with a paper towel and kept talking through her silence. "The paper said that they hadn't identified the victim, but you said that you knew her."

"They know her now. I went in yesterday and identified her body, but they'd gotten fingerprints by the time I got there. They told me her name was Dana Hewitt."

"*Told you?* You didn't know that until yesterday?"

"I knew her as Ivy."

"So, you weren't that close?"

"She was my best friend. We came out here from Las Vegas together about two years ago."

"Then how come you didn't know her real name?"

"When I met her she introduced herself as Ivy Donovan. That's all I knew."

"How did the police come up with Dana Hewitt?"

"They got her prints. She had a record."

"For what?"

She averted her eyes. "Solicitation. In Atlantic City about five years ago. She moved to Vegas to get a new start."

"How did you meet her?"

"We both worked as cocktail waitresses at the MGM, then we got an apartment together."

"And Oakland was the most natural step after Atlantic City and Vegas?"

"We had a friend who lived out here, so we decided to give it a try."

"Who's the other friend?"

"Nobody. She got married. Her husband doesn't know about her life in Vegas, and she didn't like having us around so we lost touch."

"Did you talk to Dana the night she was killed?"

"Ivy. Call her Ivy. She was running out the door when I talked to her but she promised to call when she got back. I never heard from her after that."

"What do you think happened?"

She shrugged. "I don't know."

"But what do you think? Was she scared, different, anything out of the ordinary when you talked to her?"

"She was distracted the past couple weeks but she went through phases like everybody else."

"Where did she live?"

She paused before she answered me. "San Francisco. Russian Hill."

"You have a key?"

She nodded her head. "The police asked me the same thing."

"What did you tell them?"

"I told them she moved recently and I didn't have her new address. I didn't want them going through her apartment and finding things that would make them stop taking her death seriously."

"Like what?"

"Let's not play games, Maceo. You know like what."

"So, she was a Nightingale?"

She snickered at the name. "Whatever." She looked down at the newspaper article and pointed to the photograph of Holly.

"He was at Cotton's house last night. You know him?"

"I've seen him around."

"So, who's your friend? Who're you trying to help?"

"Cotton."

She looked skeptical. "Really? You guys are that close?"

"Close enough. He lived with my family for a while."

"And you're willing to risk your life for him?"

"My life? No. But I will help him out." I could tell she didn't believe me but she let it go.

She reached for my cigarettes and lit up. "So, what do we do now?"

"Find some answers. Help each other."

She tugged on the clothes I'd given her the night before. "You think I could get these back to you later?"

"Keep 'em."

"Okay. Can you drop me at Greyhound? I'll get a cab from there and think about what you said."

"I can take you all the way home. It doesn't matter."

Her eyes went into deep freeze. "*Nobody* gets to know where I live."

I raised an eyebrow at her attempt at eleventh-hour precaution. "Whatever you say."

"I'm serious. My business is dangerous."

"What kind of business is that? What do you do?"

"I work in bars." Her answer, straight-ahead, didn't stop me from giving in to the hilarity.

She rolled her eyes at me. "I'm not kidding. You don't know the shit I put up with."

"I know this. You're the queen of double-talk. Would you know a truth if you met it?"

"Does it matter?"

"So, we're back to where we started." She didn't bother to answer. "Let me change, then, and I'll get you out of here."

I closed myself into the bathroom to change into a hooded sweatshirt, brogans, and a pair of no-name rancher's jeans. After grabbing a black peacoat and knit cap from the closet, I shook my keys at her and opened the door. My impromptu outfit was perfect for the weather. The rain had let up during the night, but outside the air was crisp as a nun.

"Damn, it's cold." She pulled her soiled sweater over the sweatshirt. Kiros jumped into the back of the truck. "Will he be alright back there?"

"Kiros? He's a road dog. He'll be fine."

Five minutes later, after marinating in the scent of vomit, a line of blue-and-white cabs greeted us in front of the Greyhound bus terminal on Telegraph. The usual menagerie of bums and street people panhandled passengers who looked as broke as they did.

"Alright then, Miss Boston. You know where to find me if you need me."

She opened the door, then turned back. "Thanks for everything. I don't think I ever said that."

She hadn't, and apparently we'd sailed past anger and seduction and into the fresh waters of gratitude. "I'll be in touch," I said.

On the curb, she leaned into the back of the car to kiss Kiros on the top of his head.

He ate it up.

She hesitated for a second and came around to my door. She reached in to run her finger along my scar. "Thank you."

"You said that."

"But I mean it . . ."

"This time?" I felt my heart walk out onto quicksand but I was determined to play it hard.

"I'll be at Skates on the Bay tomorrow night. Stop by and I'll set you up with a drink."

"I'll see if I can get over there."

She smiled to let me know she saw right through my act. "Well, if you can make it, I'll be glad to see you."

"Will you give me some answers? Do you know the names of the two guys who hang with Dutch?"

"Do you?"

"Alright, Sonny, I'll see you later."

"Tomorrow."

She sauntered off before I could answer. I watched her walk away wearing my clothes. I watched her until her taxi sped off toward the freeway, then I checked on Kiros in the rearview mirror. He was staring right back at me.

We looked away from each other at the same time.

TWENTY-ONE

My grandfather is a murderer but he also has a quiet, steady sense of humor. He told me once that one of those things helped to cancel out the other but he never said which. In 1945, when he was nineteen years old, he married a girl named Elizabeth Cray who lived on a neighboring farm in Louisiana's Claiborne Parish. He married her to save her from her father's abuse, and he promised the young woman that she'd never come to harm on his watch. She believed him and he grew to love the plain-faced girl who was a stranger to him on the day of their wedding.

Her father, a man named Papa Cray who shared blood with the county sheriff, laughed at Daddy Al's attempts to alter the wheel of fate. He believed that Elizabeth was his and his alone, but he left the newlyweds to raise their young daughter, Rachel.

With him out of their sights, the couple prospered along with my great-grandparents by breaking horses, chopping timber, and growing corn and sweet potatoes on their land. Daddy Al named the farm Red Fields and grew happy and complacent. Two years later, while he was with his father at a horse auction and his mother midwifed in an adjoining parish, Papa Cray walked into Daddy Al's house like it was his own. He dragged Elizabeth through the woods while she clutched Rachel to her chest.

That evening when my grandfather returned, he found his wife and daughter abandoned beneath a tree. They were covered from head to toe in Elizabeth's blood. He got them home, called a doctor for his wife, then he walked through the forest of sweet gum, tupelo, and maple trees until he reached his wife's childhood home.

He found Papa Cray in the kitchen eating dinner like a man with a soul. Daddy Al strangled him with his own hands, then set the house on fire so Elizabeth could see the flames from her bedroom.

Maybe she smiled at the gesture, or maybe she believed that it was futile, that evil was evil and it traveled down through the blood. I can't say, but I know through family history that her body healed but her spirit never did. Because Papa Cray was the by-blow of the sheriff, Daddy Al fled across state lines to Arkansas until word reached him a year later that the sheriff was dead.

He returned to Red Fields to find his daughter talking in full sentences and eager for the safety of her father's arms. Elizabeth celebrated her husband's return, placed her daughter in his care, then took her own life while the family slept.

Daddy Al buried his wife in a family plot on the land, and when he left Louisiana for the last time three years later he vowed never to return. Besides being a murderer, my grandfather is a man of his word.

He didn't return when his own parents died, or even when

my grandmother insisted that my mother be buried there. He said good-bye to his daughter at her funeral in Oakland, then saw the body off at the train station.

When Billy died and I looked for meaning in every place but the most obvious, I went to my grandfather and asked him to drudge up the old memory. He obliged and he also told me that he'd lived too long not to believe in murder. His words were not meant to spur me on—they were words of caution—but I was blind at the time. I took a saying I'd heard my entire life—*Black justice, Southern-style*—and twisted it until it fit my own purposes, then I fled from the results.

Now I was back.

The legacy of blood and pain that went with the Redfield name was mine, but so was the history that bound us together. I was banking on that as I looked up at the three-story, brown-shingled house on Dover Street. It looked exactly the same as Kiros and I made our way up the front steps. I used my key to open the front door, then I took a deep breath.

Thursdays were a tradition in the Dover Street house, the one day of the week when friends and family knew they could find a good meal, and the entire clan gathered together. Gra'mère didn't scrimp on Thursdays, or the more informal Tuesdays—strictly for family; instead she started each meal right after breakfast, cooking and chopping with the help of her daughters and anyone else who dropped by with two free hands. I made my way through the front of the house with the sweet scent of homemade pralines and the spicy earth notes of red beans and rice in my nose.

"Josephine, that you?" Gra'mère called out from the kitchen, where I could hear the music of Canray Fontenot, one of her favorite zydeco artists.

"Josephine?" she asked again.

Her back was to me as I entered the kitchen. She was washing a pot of greens in the sink beneath the back window. Standing tall at five feet eleven, with brassy hair that had been prematurely gray since the age of twenty-seven, Gra'mère was a member of Louisiana's *gens de couleur libres* through a connection to the French and Spanish crowns. She was proud of her bloodline and still spoke the language of her youth.

"No, it's not Josephine. It's me." Fontenot droned on in indecipherable French, and water splashed loudly over the greens. "I used my key to come in." I kept talking, trying to fill in all the empty space in that room. "I brought my dog; he's in the front room."

When she turned to look at me I saw the gray in her hair, the age in her eyes and skin, but she was still the woman who loved me without restraint as she grieved for her own daughter. Ten years Daddy Al's junior at sixty-five, she still carried the ghost of the beauty she'd passed down to her daughters.

"*Cocodrie.*" Gra'mère had called me the word for crocodile since I was a little boy. When she opened her arms it was easy to walk into her hug.

"I missed you, lady," I said. "I missed you every day."

"I knew you'd come back."

———————

"What happened to your face? Who cut you like that?" Gra'mère took my hand in both of hers.

"Had a little trouble while I was gone."

"And it didn't heal any better than that? You seen a doctor? What happened? That why you came back?"

"I'm fine, I'm fine. I didn't come back because of this scar. The scar's nothing to talk about. I came back because I had things I wanted to say to you, and I could only say them in person."

We were seated at the kitchen table with a steaming pot of chicory between us. She pushed a plate of pralines across the table to me, possibly to avoid the impending conversation.

"Have a praline, baby." She pronounced the word with the bayou in her vowels. *Prah-leen*.

I shook my head. "I just wanted to say I'm sorry."

She pulled her hand away.

"I know it's not enough, but it's all I got. At the time it felt right for me to leave."

"You back to stay?" She neither accepted nor rejected my apology.

"I'm back."

"You have a lot of making up to do."

"I know that."

"Do you?"

"Gra'mère, I—"

She held up her hand. "You won't remember this, Maceo, but when you were a little boy you used to look over my shoulder whenever I came into a room. Like you were waiting for somebody else. Once you started to talk, and you explained your nightmares, I knew you were looking for your mama.

"That almost broke my heart. I felt like it was a curse or something, like you'd have megrims your whole life no matter what I did. I tried as best I could to make it up to you. We all did, even though we were grieving ourselves.

"Eleanor was your mother, but she was my baby for twenty-four years, and I still miss her. Albert misses her, and her sisters do, too. When she died we didn't run from you, or give you to Greg's family, and that would have been easy enough for us to do.

"I buried my baby and I kept asking myself what I could have done to save her. Desiree nearly died from grief because she introduced Eleanor to that life, but she didn't leave even though it was hard for her to face us. She left after she got herself together, not before, because she owed us that much.

"And even when she was stealing from us because of drugs, we didn't run from her either. And we wouldn't have run from Cissy for loving Holly. We never ran because that's not what family is all about. You get the good and you get the bad, but you stick. It's the only way to make it in this world.

"Me and Albert loved you like you were our child, but you never let either one of us all the way in. We knew that and we tried to love you harder, but you still left when the family needed you most.

"I love you, Maceo, and not because I have to, but you can't really heal things between us, or make up to this family, until you start to believe that. Y'hear me?"

I nodded.

"Now go see your granddaddy. He's out back." I rose, chastised and shamed, but one step closer than I'd been the day before.

"And give me a kiss before you go."

———

Daddy Al was in the garage, a freestanding space that had been turned into a wood shop. It was his domain, the place he could be found when he wasn't at the Nickel and Dime or managing the many properties he owned around the city of Oakland. The porch of my old cottage in back was lined with potted plants, and the lace curtains in the window let me know there was a new tenant.

Through the closed door I heard the low whine of a power saw and the blues music that Daddy Al played while he worked. In his wood shop he produced handmade furniture for friends and relatives.

He was facing the door when I walked in, so he saw me right away.

"Daddy Al." I nodded across the room to him and he put his tools down to come fast around the table.

"Come here, son. Come here." His tone was curt, but I recognized it as an attempt to control his emotions.

Son.

My knees nearly buckled at the sound of it. Daddy Al had never been stingy with love for his children, or for me, and he doled out affection whenever he could. I felt like a child, I was so grateful for the embrace he offered me. I took it.

———

"It's been over two years since anybody's seen or heard from you." Daddy Al closed the door of the garage to block out the cold wind whipping through the backyard. "You took the lost way back, didn't you?"

"It took me a little while."

"You let two years, an earthquake, and countless birthdays slip by before you came home, but home is where you came, isn't it?"

I nodded.

"Took you two years to understand that you can find your way back no matter what. Family is always an open door."

I wanted to believe him because I knew he believed it himself. He was invested in the benevolence of the Redfields but it wasn't true, not on the deep level that he wished it to be. He judged like the rest of the world, held grudges, and let himself boil with anger when he was disappointed, in me or my actions, but I held my tongue.

"You been inside to see your grandmother?"

"I saw her before I came in here to see you."

"What did she have to say?"

"Doesn't matter. What do you have to say?"

"You remember the last thing I told you?" He pointed out the window. "You were standing right outside near the barbecue pit."

I remembered. We'd had the coldest conversation of my life while Felicia's bloody clothes burned in the pit behind me. The two of us had stood there ignoring the acrid smell drifting into the early morning sky.

"You told me it was time for me to go."

"And what else?"

"That it didn't mean anything about how you felt about me."

"Did you believe me?"

"No."

"I know you didn't."

"You also called me your grandson instead of son, and you blamed me for what happened to Cissy."

"You and Holly were to blame."

"And Cissy."

"What?" He looked up, startled.

"You have to add Cissy to that list, too."

My voice was calm. There were apologies I had to make, but there were also new roles that had to be defined.

"You trying to blame Cissy for what happened? That's not what you're trying to do, is it? This isn't the conversation you came home to have, is it, Maceo?"

"No, I came back because it was time, and I missed my family."

"I must've misunderstood you then, because I didn't hear you say that the first time you spoke."

"Daddy Al, I'm sorry about what happened to Cissy. I'll be sorry about that the rest of my life. And I'm sorry that I left without telling anybody, or giving you a reason, but if we're really going to talk then we need to address the fact that Cissy knew, just like I did, the risks she was taking when she hooked up with Holly."

"That's easy for you to say, two years later, as you stand there in good health."

"It's not easy for me to say. It's the truth. Cissy was pulled in just like I was."

"You're not trying to justify yourself, are you?"

"No, I'm just stating a fact."

He frowned. "There are no facts here, Maceo, just mistakes."

"Then I made a mistake, and I'm sorry for that, but there's only so many ways, and so many times, I can say so. After that it's not up to me."

He returned to his table and picked up a hammer. "Everybody has to find their own way to be a man. I guess you took the road you thought was necessary."

"Can you live with that?"

"Can you?" His hammer came down hard on the leg of a table. The silence grew until I pulled on my gloves to leave.

I took my time formulating the next sentence. "Daddy Al, I think Holly is caught up in this mess with Cotton."

Ice crested over his eyes. He struggled to keep his anger in check. "How does that concern you?"

"You ask that after giving me a speech about family? Holly's family. He's my brother and he used to be your son. If he needs my help, even if he doesn't want it, I'm going to give it to him."

"So, what are you saying, boy?"

"I'm saying I'm going to help him."

"You asking my permission?"

"We're past that. I'm letting you know, out of respect and love, what my plans are."

"You're not going to be happy until you kill yourself, are you? Is that what you think it means to be a man?"

"Daddy Al, do you know that the only time my life felt real to me was when I was trying to figure out who killed Billy and find Felicia?"

I saw in his face that he understood what I'd said. The understanding didn't give him any relief. "If that's true, Maceo, it's the saddest thing I've heard in a long time."

There was nothing left to say after that. We were not going to meet in the middle. Not that day.

"I'll be back for dinner at seven. I'ma leave my dog, Kiros, here until I come back."

He didn't answer.

I left him to his work.

TWENTY-TWO

After leaving Dover Street, I drove to Lake Merritt, the natural saltwater lake in the middle of the city that had once bordered an area called Brooklyn. In the summertime, the trails around the water are filled with joggers and families, but on that mid-morning weekday the area was deserted because of the dismal weather.

I parked my car near Grand Lake Theater, grabbed a cup of coffee from Colonel Mustard's Wild Dogs, and walked down to Yolanda's salon. Through the windows I could see women in black painter's smocks, with their hair pulled back in severe pony-tails, working at their stations. Andre had been right when he said that Emmet poured a lot of money into Trim, but when I walked through the front door of the salon I saw that Yolanda's ambition went beyond her husband and the limited scope of his mind and drug dealing. It was evident in everything from the doorknobs to the sexy, mad-scientist flavor of the hairdressers and the borderline pornographic name. The place was the mark of a person on their way up, and Emmet appeared to be going fast in the opposite direction.

"Can I help you?"

A young woman in a stark black uniform sat behind a marble counter just inside the front door. Her name tag read LESLEY: RECEPTIONIST, and I assumed she was the girlfriend Andre had told me about.

"I was hoping to see the owner, Yolanda Landry."

"For an appointment? We don't service male clientele at this salon." She grabbed a card and began to write. "I can give you a referral."

"No, no, I'm an old friend." I hoped that was still true since I'd beaten the shit out of her husband the night before. "I just want to talk to her."

"Okay. Have a seat and I'll buzz her office."

I took a seat in one of the straight-back chairs near the window. A few of the women glanced my way but most were too entrenched in their beauty treatments, or gossip, to really care. A staircase led to an area marked SPA.

"May I have your name?"

"Maceo Redfield."

The girl said the name into the phone, then turned her back to me to finish the call.

"Everything okay?" I asked.

"Yeah, Rhonda will see you in a minute."

I hadn't asked for Rhonda, but I kept my mouth shut. Minutes later, another woman came down the staircase in a white lab coat, a sharp contrast to the black ones worn by the receptionist and stylists. The tag above her breast read simply RHONDA: SPA.

"Can I help you?" It was the second time I'd been asked that and I was still sitting in the same place.

"Yeah, I'm here to see Yolanda Landry."

"And this is regarding?"

"Something personal."

Rhonda rolled her eyes at the receptionist. "Can you say more than that?"

"No."

"Well, Ms. Landry isn't in today. Do you want to leave a message?"

"No."

"Okay, well"—she looked around—"I'll tell her you came by." She went back up the staircase and left me where I was standing.

I figured the receptionist to be my best bet after that. "Andre told me I might be able to get a friend of mine in for an appointment."

"Andre? My Andre?" Her face lightened. Their relationship must have been new because she still took pleasure in saying his name.

"Yeah, Andre Morehouse. Crowning Glory. Met him the other day. He was talking about you."

"He was? Really?" She smiled.

"Uh-huh. He said this place is booked but you had the inside track to get my friend an appointment."

She tried to hide a smile but I saw it. A leather appointment book materialized from beneath the counter. "What day you want to get her in?"

"How 'bout this week?"

She frowned and searched for an open spot. I leaned in close so my words would be lost in the chatter of the shop. "Is Yolanda upstairs?"

"No." She kept her head down. "She does the books and writes thank-you cards every morning at Colonial Donuts on Lakeshore."

"She there now?"

She nodded, then spoke up. "The first day I have open is next Friday the twenty-first. That okay?"

"That's fine."

"The name?"

"Chantal. Chantal Hunter." I had another palm to grease and I decided to go for vanity when dealing with Chantal.

"Great. Would that be for the salon or the spa?"

"Spa. Massage." I paused after I saw the price. "A little cheaper than that."

She giggled and wrote an appointment card after I paid. "She needs to bring this with her."

"Thanks. I'll tell Andre I saw you."

Her smile let me know she might be a bigger help to me in the future.

———

Colonial was a twenty-four-hour shop that trafficked in large doughnuts and big, cheap, steaming cups of coffee. Yolanda was at a table near the front window, flipping through an address book. White thank-you cards were stacked in boxes on a chair. Yolanda's ghetto-fabulous body was famous all over the Bay Area but she looked to be about a week shy of becoming a mother. Her belly pressed against the edge of the table, and her fingers were swollen as she wrote out her messages. The old Yolanda was still present in her jeweled fingernails and the colored beads sprinkled into her hair.

"Hey, girl." I tapped the table to get her attention.

"Maceo! Oh my god, what happened to your face?" She made like she was going to stand, but I waved her down.

"Don't get up." I hesitated, then leaned in to kiss her forehead. She didn't flinch, and I figured she didn't know about my fight with Emmet.

"What are you doing here?"

"Came to get some coffee."

"And you just happened to find me?" She raised an eyebrow.

"No, I heard you opened a salon so I went by to see for myself."

She beamed. "You saw the whole place?"

"Saw what I could. Rhonda wanted fingerprints and a blood sample."

"Miss Rhonda takes her job very seriously. She wouldn't let my mama in last week." Her smile was weak though she tried to keep the tone friendly.

"She one of your partners?"

"I don't believe in partners. She's an employee." Yolanda's baby-girl voice contradicted the steel in her eyes.

"How are you?"

"I'm fine. And you? What happened to your face?"

"Nothing."

She studied me for a minute and moved on. "So, why you come to see me? Felicia with you?"

"I haven't seen Felicia in two years."

"Really? Everybody just figured ya'll left together."

"Felicia's been a ghost since I left."

"That's too bad. I mean, you loved her so hard, I hoped you'd get her in the end."

"Worse things have happened. Speaking of which, you talk to your husband about me?"

"About you? Why?"

"We got into an altercation last night, out at Cotton's house."

"So that's where he was." Her smile dropped away and I knew I'd guessed correctly about her ambition. The couple that used to be joined at the hip didn't appear to be anymore.

"Emmet," her voice caught in her throat, "Emmet's changed. He . . ." I remembered the smoke signals around his mouth and stopped her.

"You don't have to tell me." I squeezed her hand. "I didn't come here to upset you. You want a muffin, some warm milk, or something?"

"No, I'm fine." She tried to recover. "And when I'm in a doughnut shop I eat doughnuts, the big pink ones with sprinkles."

"Can I treat you?"

"No, I'm fine. What do you need?"

"Gossip. Details. I figured since you own the hottest salon in town you'd know what was going on around the city. What people are saying."

"About Cotton?"

I nodded. "I think Holly might be caught up in this."

"Did you see his picture in the paper, next to the girl?"

"You know anything about her?"

"Just that she was a Nightingale, but everybody knows that."

"I heard they touched down pretty hard a couple years ago."

"They're my biggest account. We do a twenty-four-hour shift whenever there's a big party in town. My stylists fight to get those bookings."

"You ever work on Dana?"

"Who's Dana?"

"The girl in the picture."

"I worked on her, but I knew her as Ivy." That matched the information Sonny had given me.

"Do any of the girls ever show up with bodyguards, escorts, anything like that?"

Yolanda thought about it for a minute. "Ivy always did, and another girl named Fantasia. I just figured it meant they were Dutch's top girls."

"Anyone else?"

"Yeah, once in a while Ivy would come with this white girl named Tina. She looks like a million bucks, but she's worth about twelve."

"Same guys each time?"

"Yeah."

"How many?"

"Always the same two guys."

"What do they look like?"

"Hoods."

"Specifically."

"They never came inside, but one time Ivy wanted to give the shampoo girl a personal tip so she went outside to get money from one of them."

"You remember what he looked like?"

"Never forget. A real dark-skinned guy with light blue eyes. He had that condition, you know, vitiligo. It makes patches of your skin turn white. I saw it on his neck and hands when he handed her the money."

Patches on his skin? She was describing the man I'd seen at

the marina after my attack. "The guy with the patches. Does he have dreads?"

"Yeah, wears it pulled back with a Jamaican ribbon."

"What's the other one look like?"

"Popeye. Big chest and arms. You know them?"

I touched the back of my head. "Not before yesterday, but I got hit from behind and knocked out, and when I came to I saw the men you just described."

"Maceo." She reached for my hand.

I waved off her concern. "I'm fine. Makes things a little clearer though."

"How?"

"You know Dutch is Smokey's cousin?"

"I'd heard that. Nobody knew at first, not when he first got to town."

"Can I ask you a favor? Will you call me the next time one of those girls comes into the shop?"

"I'll think about it, but I'm not doing anything to jeopardize my baby or my salon."

"I wouldn't ask you to. You know what you're having?"

"No. We—I . . . I want to be surprised. I'm due in about three weeks."

"You ready?"

"I'm ready to stop being pregnant."

I laughed. "Anything else about the Nightingales?"

She winced and looked out at the traffic. "I hate that name. It makes them sound like they're more than they are. Those girls are hookers. Don't get me wrong, their money is just as good as anybody else's, actually it's better, but I don't like how they try and dress it up."

"You ever meet Dutch?"

"Once. I didn't find out until afterward that he was Smokey's cousin. Nobody knew when he first came back."

"What's he look like?"

"Nice-looking. Solid build. Tall. He was wearing a big wide-brimmed hat when I saw him, and club clothes in the middle of the day. Walks with a cane."

"Anything else?"

"I don't know how to put it, but there's something real deliberate about him, like he's controlling everything around him. He stays hidden but he makes sure that people keep his name in their mouths."

"What do you mean?"

"Well, he threw that party, and it was wild enough that people talked about it for about six months, but he stayed in the background, and no one knew he was Smokey's cousin for at least that long. Then everybody started to hear stories about the houses he had, or the people he knew, or the cars, and then the dogs."

"What dogs?"

"See, that's what I mean. Apparently he has a pack of bloodhounds that he keeps because—how did he put this—the sound of their barking sends chills down his spine."

"Why bloodhounds?"

"Because those are the dogs that hunters used to track down runaway slaves. Keeps him on his toes. Reminds him that he's being hunted."

I didn't know what to make of that, the calculated drama, the sickness, and the obvious bid to make his mark in town. From what I'd heard, he was too loud and showy, unlike Holly and Billy, who conducted their business in the shadows.

"Thinks he's Nino Brown or something?"

"Or something." She rolled her eyes. "You think he's after Holly to revenge Smokey?"

"Possibly."

"But why do it this way? Why go through all this trouble, all this planning?"

"I wondered the same thing myself." I shrugged. "But somebody who knows Dutch knows Cotton and Holly just as well."

She frowned. "Like Emmet."

"I didn't say that, but if Holly's caught up Emmet could be, too." I dropped my voice. "Dutch, his girls, and those stupid-ass dogs aren't an accident, and the shit at the All-Pro, that's not an accident either."

I could tell she wanted to change the subject. "Have you talked to Holly?"

"Haven't been able to reach him."

"Well, there's a big party next week. The salon's booked for two days. I'll let you know if I hear anything."

"Alright." I rose to leave. She reached for my hand.

"When you saw Emmet, could you tell he was smoking?"

I nodded.

"You think it's too late? You think he's lost?"

"How could he be, baby? He has you." She smiled at my lie. "And if Emmet doesn't get that . . ." I wanted to tread lightly but I also wanted to tell the truth. "Do you know how many men in this town would kill to have you?"

"That doesn't matter, though, when you only want one person."

TWENTY-THREE

Before I left town I'd been a Big Brother to Scottie Timmons, a good kid with a sassy-mouth mother named Chantal Hunter who'd proven to be a true friend when the crunch came down. Chantal, like so many other women in Oakland, was a single mother living off her wits and looking for a break. Daddy Al had given her one when he rented her a second-floor two-bedroom apartment in one of his buildings. He never regretted the decision, but Chantal tried his patience with her daily reports about the comings and goings of the other single mothers. She called herself the manager, snitching on anyone seen with shopping bags from Macy's and Capwell's even though their rent was late.

As I pulled up in front of the Bay View Manor, I hoped that my gift of a free massage would grease the wheels and get Chantal to talk. She was a well of information simply because she liked gossip; the juicier the better.

Next door to the Bay View, a necklace of burnt-out grass and dirt encircled a building that had once been a crack house. Chantal stood in front of it, dressed for the office and holding a stack of papers in her hand. The last time I'd seen her she was temping whenever she could get an assignment and supplementing her income with "Hot Body, Hot Clothes" parties where male strippers entertained women who bought bootleg designer outfits.

Her suit was nice, a little too tight, and more orange than pink but a step up from her usual attire. I honked my horn to get her attention. She shielded her eyes to get a good look, then broke into a generous smile when I exited the car.

"Why, Maceo, you little gargoyle. Aren't you supposed to be perched on top of a building somewhere? Give me a hug."

"Nice to see you, too, Chantal." I was grateful for her salty greeting; it was the closest I'd come to normalcy since I'd been back. "How's Scottie?"

"Scottie's fine. He'll be glad to see you. He liked the letters and postcards you sent. He wrote you back, but we didn't know where to send them."

"I was moving all the time, didn't really have a permanent place."

"I can't believe I missed your short butt. Man, my sister liked to cuss you out every time she thought about you." Alixe Hunter, my old girlfriend, was Chantal's half-sister.

"I bet."

"She wasn't the one for you anyway. 'Member I told you that from the beginning?"

"You did."

"Oh, give me another hug."

I did so gladly and came away drenched in her perfume. She looked good, slimmer, a little older, but settled and polished.

"I'm married," she blurted out.

"That right? Good for you."

"And I have a little girl. Eden."

"Scottie has a little sister, huh?"

"A daddy and a sister." She pointed to the apartment complex. "Me and my husband bought the building from your grandfather last year. He gave us a good deal."

I laughed. Chantal had been a hell of a de facto landlord; I couldn't imagine what she was like as the owner.

"I know why you're laughing, punk, but I'll tell you this: The rent be on time 'cause I don't play. I will come over here and kick on your door till I get my money."

"You ain't no joke."

"Never have been. I got this and another business." She opened the trunk of her silver BMW. "Here." She spread a T-shirt across the hood of the car.

NO ORANGE JUMPSUITS, INC.

Leave it to Chantal to get straight to the point. Orange was the preferred color of the Bay Area prison system. The less violent offenders could sometimes be seen on the sides of freeways wearing bright orange jumpsuits and picking up highway trash and roadkill.

Chantal joined me when my grin turned into a full-out belly laugh.

"Stop laughing! I got four after-school programs, and this year we have a team in the Midnight Basketball League."

"No Orange Jumpsuits, Chantal?"

"People love that name. It's catchy. If you had any sense you would know it's all about marketing."

I leaned over and gave her a kiss on the cheek. She pushed me off, hard, with both hands.

"Get back. I told you I was married."

"Who married you anyway?" I asked.

"Why you say it like that? He's a good man. I met him at church after his wife died. He's a deacon."

Just then a car matching Chantal's pulled up behind hers. She beamed at the man who ambled out of the car. I locked my face down just in case it wanted to betray what I was thinking. Chantal's husband was a good fifty, fifty-five, with a belly like one of those old-fashioned black stoves. He had hair only on the outer regions of his skull, but he smiled brightly when he spotted his wife.

Who was I to say anything?

"Maceo," she said as she pulled me forward, "this is my husband, Rosevelt Sykes. Rosevelt, this is my friend Maceo Redfield."

"Oh, yeah, Redfield. You're the grandson."

"Nice to meet you."

"You, too, son. Chantal invite you over to the house?"

"Yeah, Maceo, come have dinner with us. See Scottie?"

"I'll get by as soon as I can."

"I won't tell him you're here. You can surprise him, and see the baby."

"I'm sure she's as pretty as her mama."

Rosevelt beamed. "That she is. I can guarantee it."

"Where you staying?" Chantal slipped her hand into her husband's.

"At the Seaport."

"The Seaport? The roach house? We got an empty apartment in the building. You can stay there if you want."

"I'm fine where I'm at."

"You sure?"

"Uh-huh."

Rosevelt shook himself loose. "I'ma go and see after the repairs in the empty. Nice to meet you, Maceo."

"You, too."

"What you think?" Chantal barely let him get out of earshot.

"I think you did good, girl. Seems like a nice man." I pulled the appointment card from my pocket. "This is for you."

She raised an eyebrow. "What you want from me?"

"Just a little information."

"Well, I don't gossip like I used to. It ain't Christian." Last time I'd seen Chantal her Christianity had been limited to Donna Summer gospel albums.

"What you know about the Nightingales?"

"I know they ain't saved. None of them got the Lord in their lives."

"Besides that. You got inside scoop on any of the girls?"

"Not really. None of them grew up in Oakland, so they don't have ties to local folks. But I did hear a lot of them work the Gideon, the hotel where that girl got killed."

"What about Dutch? You know him?"

"I know of him. He tried to recruit a couple girls from my program."

"Where'd they meet him?"

"At a club in the city. Apparently, he sends other nice-looking girls out on weekends to invite them to his parties."

"What club?"

"Wherever the young people go. Townsend. Das Club. The Firehouse. DN8. Pick one."

"You sure you're not a cop, Chantal?"

"I work with teenagers. I have to stay connected. I tried to get my Bible group to do a prayer circle at that hotel but they didn't want to."

I laughed. "Anything else?"

"Yeah. I know you're worried about Holly, Maceo, but don't forget to look out for yourself. You're wearing that scar like a badge of honor but we both know you ain't really a tough guy."

TWENTY-FOUR

The next evening, with the sky the reddish purple of cheap wine and police helicopters buzzing above the Oakland Coliseum, the city's murder rate climbed from twenty-seven to thirty with a triple homicide at a MacArthur Boulevard motel. Once a popular destination for families traveling between Northern and Southern California, the strip had long since been given over to hustlers, prostitutes, and pimps. The owners looked the other way when people checked in with plenty of cash but no identification. As a result it took twenty-four hours to identify the three young men, but less than two for the six o'clock news to declare the murders a drug-related crime.

What else could it be in Oakland, on a broken-down stretch of land, where struggling business owners and homeless people mixed with teenagers in sixty-thousand-dollar cars?

The streets of the state capital were constantly filled with marchers protesting the wrongs done in foreign countries, but the outrage was absent when the tenants of the Sixty-ninth Street Village were barricaded into their own homes and forced to work as employees of the local drug crew.

In response to the crimes, the wealthy citizens in the hills tried, on several occasions, to secede from the city below. Their failed attempt was the death knell of the social programs of the sixties and seventies. They were no longer an option. The money from property taxes once used to feed the schools was recycled back into home security systems and state-of-the-art car alarms that shattered the streets like bullets. As the Breakfast Before School organizations closed their doors and the arts and music programs were safely returned to the children of the rich, the flat-lands burned.

The kids left behind by the absence of resources flowed into the streets and turned Oakland into a devil's playground. Entire cities overflowed with lost boys who bayed at the moon with their violence, and died just to be heard, while music and prime-time television told us we were happy. Who knew from *The Cosby Show* that we were in distress? The horror was reflected back to us in the murder rate alone, so it was no accident that when gangsta rap emerged it was met with open arms.

I understood the despair as I watched the helicopters through my window and looked at the three dead bodies covered with white coroner's cloth. As I listened to the newscasters turn the triple murder into a story and nothing but, I knew it was time to cross to the other side.

I just didn't want to go there alone.

———

I hit the boardwalk for a run with Kiros at my side. I had to clear my head, process the words of Chantal, Crowley, and Black Jeff.

Their warnings matched time with my footsteps as I weaved through the warehouses and bars of the Port District.

I ran past the Gingerbread House, a Creole restaurant housed in a pink Victorian beneath the freeway. I circled the county jail, nicknamed the Tombs by its residents, and talked myself into another trip to Timber Hills. Holly had seen me, he knew I was back, and I needed to make another attempt to connect with him.

On my way back through the marina, with Kiros keeping a steady pace beside me, I slowed down when I reached the yachts anchored in the waves near El Caballo. Memories flooded back.

Once upon a time, in the one October week that felt like a lifetime, I loved a woman who lived on one of those boats. The two of us met in the wake of Felicia Bennett, which meant, in the end, that we hadn't stood a chance, but I had tried.

I read the names along the side of each boat, *The Christina, The Encinal,* and *Lucy Dove,* until I found what I was looking for: *The Aeolian.* I searched the deck for signs of her but there were none. I wasn't surprised; it had been two years since we'd spoken, and she'd let me know that once I made the choice to go after Felicia, she'd cease to be an option for me. She was a woman of her word. The one time I tried to call, she'd hung up when she heard my voice.

Since then, whenever I took the time to second-guess my past her prophetic words as I rode out to look for Smokey echoed in my head: *Whatever happens tonight is going to poison you.* I'd listened when she said it, but I hadn't heard a word until it was too late and she was gone.

A tall redheaded man, bundled against the cold wind, stepped onto the deck from down below. He nodded when he saw me and Kiros standing at the rail, then he did a double take. "Jesus, what kind of dog is that?"

"A Cane Corso."

"That a mastiff?"

"Close, but not quite."

"What does he weigh?"

"Hundred and twenty."

"He friendly?" As the man came toward us the wind picked up his scent, the antiseptic odor of a hospital.

"You work at Highland?" I asked him.

"How'd you know that?"

"I used to know a woman who lived on this boat. She rented it from one of the doctors."

"That's right." He snapped his fingers. "A woman did live here before me. What was her name? Alicia or something."

"Alixe. Alixe Hunter," I offered.

"Right. She was a nurse. I met her when I took over. Was she a friend of yours?"

"In another life. How long you been here?"

"About a year and a half."

"So, she's gone then."

"Far as I know. I forwarded her mail for a while."

"Do you know where she went?"

"Medical school. Tulane."

I let that news wash over me. I wanted to be proud of her, glad that she kept moving forward while I spun in circles, but I realized that a part of me had hoped she'd be there to help me reconnect with Oakland, a warm body to smooth the transition. It had been awhile since I had that. Actually, it had been too long.

"Well, if I ever hear from her I'll let her know you stopped by. What did you say your name was?"

"It's Redfield, but you don't have to tell her that."

Somebody had the right to be free.

I walked away with the smell of rain in my nose and a promise to myself that I would start to believe in my right to the good things in life as well as the bad. For too long I'd let the oil slick of my mother's death leak forward to stain my future. It had to stop. It was time to be brave enough to believe that.

That was my plan.

That was what I was going to do.

Day after tomorrow.

TWENTY-FIVE

The guard from my first visit was camped at the bottom of the hill when I arrived at Cotton's house. Maybe he'd been demoted after letting me slip through, because station number one didn't include a swank little guardhouse.

He tapped the hood of my truck with his flashlight.

"What is it, man?" I asked.

"No way in hell you're getting inside, fella. I'm not losing my job over you, so you might as well back up."

I didn't budge.

"If you want to get out of the car"—his stance was aggressive—"we can talk about it in a little more detail."

"Listen, partna, unless you got a gun you gonna lose any fight we have."

"That right?"

I opened the door, leaving the blackjack and Kiros in the car. The two of us were toe-to-toe when the headlights of a black

Jaguar swept past and cut right through the tension. Allaina's face came into view in the driver's-side window. She sized up the situation, registered who I was, then called my name. She looked tired, and a little sad, but she was still one of the most beautiful women I'd ever seen. At the sight of her I felt foolish standing in the rain ready to fight a man for trying to do his job.

Allaina stepped out of the car. "Is there a problem, Curtis?"

"None at all, Mrs. Knox."

"Good. Think you can release my guest?"

"Yes, ma'am. The two of you have a nice evening."

"Maceo," she said, "why don't you follow me up."

Inside the house I directed Kiros to a rug in front of the trophy case.

"You here to see Cotton?" Allaina asked.

"Hoping to. He home?"

She looked at the diamond watch on her wrist. "Should be. He likes to read to Marquis before he goes to bed. We can go up to the nursery and take a look."

We passed the painting on our way to the top floor but Allaina didn't acknowledge it. I couldn't help myself, though. I had to point it out.

"Nice painting."

"I hate it."

"Really?" I paused in front of it, admiring for the second time the look in her eye.

"Cornelius had me sit for it after the baby was born. It was in the nursery, but I made him move it down here. I usually take the back staircase just so I don't have to see it."

"He just wants the world to see how much he loves you and his son. No shame in that, right?"

My tone was light, but her eyes flashed when she looked at me.

"Wants to show the world how much he loves me? Guess you didn't hear about the dead hooker in his room."

"Allaina . . ."

"Don't bother, Maceo, I know what you think. I'm just supposed to smile and be quiet, right? That's my job. That's what I signed up for when I married a star."

"That's not what I meant."

"Yes it is. I can see it in your face, and I see it in the faces of everyone around us. His lawyers, his friends, his teammates, the fans. They look at me and I can see them thinking, 'She got all that money, that big house, only thing she has to do is support her man and be quiet. Sit there like the nice little wife, look pretty, and don't say a word.' "

"That's not true."

"It's very true." Her voice bordered on shrill. "What do you think that press conference was about? How many acting coaches do you think I had behind the scenes telling me how to sit, how to hold my head, when to smile, when to touch my husband? His lawyers and the team flew in three different people to help me work on looking sympathetic in front of the camera.

"All these people in and out of our house, telling me what to do, protecting Cotton and all the money he makes for them, and not one of them asked me how was I doing or how I felt about hearing that my husband had another woman in his hotel room." She leaned against the cold stone wall. The tears that followed were sudden. "Not a single person has said they were sorry about what I'm going through."

"They're just trying to help you protect your family."

"I can protect my family on my own. There's nothing I wouldn't do for my son and his father."

"I didn't mean anything." I reached out to touch her arm but the gesture brought her up short. She stepped just out of reach and wiped her face with the back of her hand. Her body language indicated that the conversation was over; that the moment of weakness had been just that.

I took her cue and followed her up the stairs.

On the way to the nursery we passed a photography studio adjacent to the master bedroom. In her best hostess voice, without a trace of the previous tears, Allaina offered me a peak at the interior. She was all business and I followed her lead to allow her time to regain her dignity. She pointed out the skylights, the his-and-her's bathrooms, closets, and offices. I listened, smiled when it was called for, and acted impressed when I wasn't.

Finally, after I'd heard everything about the bedroom except when and where she'd bought the sheets, she opened the door into her studio. An overhead light illuminated a small room filled with black-and-white photographs. It was set up like a gallery, with Allaina's name on gold nameplates beneath each picture.

She tapped one of them and gave a smile I couldn't quite read. "Cornelius surprised me with these nameplates on Valentine's Day."

"Yeah? How long you been taking pictures?"

For years I'd seen her on the sidelines at Vanguard games with a camera around her neck, but I figured it was a bored housewife's hobby, a way for the former model to remain in the spotlight and separate herself from the other NBA wives.

"About five years. I got bored on modeling assignments so I started taking pictures. Once I became a professional wife I picked it up again just to add something to the games."

"You're not a basketball fan?"

"Of course I am, but you try and sit through twelve hundred and eighty-five games a season."

She'd exaggerated the number, but sometimes with the multitude of preseason and playoff games, the NBA season felt like twelve months instead of ten.

"My father used to take me to games when I was little. And one of my older brothers played in high school, so I know the sport."

"So you were a fan . . ."

"Before I was a groupie? Yes."

I didn't know Allaina well enough to know if she was kidding but I laughed anyway. She was obviously troubled, running hot and cold, as she and her husband faced ruin and suspicion.

TWENTY-SIX

I continued to look at the pictures while Allaina busied herself re-arranging camera equipment. Most of them were pictures of Marquis, typical shots of a child growing from infant to toddler, and only one showed evidence of the Down syndrome he'd been born with. When Marquis turned three, Allaina, against the shouts of many critics, elected for plastic surgery that erased the identifying features of a Down syndrome child. The move was controversial, and she took her blows in the press and with my family, but Cotton stood by his wife's decision. It was easy to say that a former model, someone's whose currency existed in her looks, wanted perfection in her child but I always thought it was something more. I thought she just wanted to give him a fighting chance.

Marquis's pictures gave way to the photos of Cotton, and where the little boy had been surrounded by people—his parents, other children, my grandparents—Cotton's photographs, all taken at games, were absent of bystanders, teammates, or fans. When others appeared in the background their faces were blurred or chopped in half by her lens.

The action shots fixed him in mid-flight, either coming down from or on his way up to the basket, but the best one of them all caught him in a moment of repose. The plaque below the photo read ALLAINA SERENA KNOX: MADISON SQUARE GARDEN, 1990.

He was on the sidelines, in profile, with a slight smile at the corner of his mouth and a light in his eye that looked like peace.

"I took that one the night he found out his father was dead." She came up behind me and ran her hand down the frame.

I remembered the death, remembered how the public nature of it had rehashed the details of Cotton's troubled childhood.

When he'd left Oakland at eighteen, Cotton went first to Iowa because his poor grades at Castlemont High School weren't good enough for entry into an NCAA school. Like many players before him he enrolled in an intensive summer session in the Iowa cornfields to train and study under the tutelage of a junior-college coach who helped to feed the Runnin' Rebel basketball machine by helping his players make grades.

Once on campus and miles away from the streets that had taught him to always keep his guard up, he gave an in-depth interview to the school paper. It was before his true fame, before he learned the destructive power of the sound bite, so he talked candidly about his past, lulled by the foreign aspect of the Ozzie and Harriet environment he had found in the Midwest.

He'd thought he was safe there, and he talked for hours to a budding female journalist whose open, trusting smile turned to a grimace as his story unfolded. He talked openly about his father, my grandparents, and the fact that he'd survived a childhood too brutal for most people to stomach. He stated that he considered his years between the ages of one and fourteen combat duty and he had the battle scars to prove it. He posed for pictures that accompanied the articles, revealing that the scars on his chest and arms had already turned into bumpy keloids.

Jermin Knox, Cotton's father, had left marks more permanent than DNA on the body of his son, and only later would Cotton think to cover them with tattoos. Until then his chest was a raised and ragged blueprint of his father's troubled psyche. The vivid grid of burns and welts captured in the picture indicated that his wary, tough-guy exterior was not manufactured. He wore the reasons for his rage right there on his body and it boiled beneath his skin until it seemed to fry the page. That photo and the gruesome facts of his abuse dogged him into the NBA.

After his phenomenal rookie year with the Vanguards, the article was reprinted as a sidebar in a *Sports Illustrated* cover story. It resurfaced a second time when his father, a former playground star who'd achieved local notoriety because of an audacious dunking style, took himself out of the game with a bloody "suicide by cop" on the streets of D.C.

As the story of Jermin Knox's death caught fire on the wire services and traveled around the world, Cotton's childhood was trotted out again for further viewing. The news of Jermin's death reached him at halftime during a game against the Knicks. As the story goes he was in the locker room, alone as usual, with his headphones blaring in his ears. The team owner, Harper Coolidge, had to tap him twice to get his attention.

Coolidge gave him the news after Cotton took off his headphones, but the star never bothered to turn down the volume. As the hip-hop he loved blasted from the headset, he learned the details of his father's demise. Coolidge gave him the opportunity to leave the game but he declined. Instead he returned to the floor at Madison Square Garden with brutal intent. It was the first time any of his fans saw him smile while he played. He was free. He broke his own record that night and scored thirty-nine points in the last half, taking him to a career high of sixty-seven in one game.

———————

"That was the game against the Knicks."

She nodded. "Cornelius didn't want me in the locker room so I didn't see him until after Coolidge told him. I took a picture when he walked onto the court, and this one after he scored his last point."

She turned to me.

"His father had started contacting him right before that."

"I didn't know."

"He didn't tell too many people, but he tracked us down while we were in D.C. for a Bullets game. He stood around the tunnel like a fan, then he just popped up."

"How'd Cotton take it?"

"How do you think?" She turned off the light and we left the room.

———————

Cotton was in the nursery with Marquis, sitting on the floor in front of a rocking chair while the little boy sucked his thumb. Marquis's eyes were locked intently on his father's face as Cotton made his way through a nursery rhyme. His rough, raised-on-rap voice mangled the kid's tune, but Marquis didn't seem to care. He listened, then tapped impatiently on his father's hands. Cotton kept going until Marquis tapped again.

Ethelene Ritchie sat across the room with knitting needles on her lap, watching them both.

"What is it, man? What you trying to say?"

Marquis answered with his hands, using sign language to tell his father what he wanted. Cotton laughed and started the rhyme from the top, his own hands telegraphing each word.

"When did Cotton learn to sign?" I asked Allaina.

She raised an eyebrow. "He's still learning. We all are. That nursery rhyme is the first thing they learned together, so they do it at bedtime. Marquis is only deaf in one ear but his hearing is weak."

Cotton finished the song, and Marquis laughed before jumping down and wiggling into his pajamas. Once he was dressed, Cotton swung the little boy into the air, rubbing the top of his braids against the child's stomach.

"You my boy, right? You my boy?"

When Cotton brought him back down, Marquis's arms automatically went around his father's neck. For an instant there was peace on his face, a mimic of the serenity I'd seen in Allaina's studio.

"Don't know what I'd do without you and your mama, little man. I'd give up everything I had to keep ya'll safe, you know that? You my boy. My son . . ."

"Give him to me." Allaina's icy words cut right through the calm in the room. "Don't get him all riled up before I have to put him to sleep."

Mrs. Ritchie looked up from her knitting, but I couldn't read the look in her eye as she watched the family.

"Give him to me, Cornelius." Allaina held her hands out for the little boy, but Cotton reached a hand out for her instead. Allaina stood there, inches from it, but she wouldn't budge. Cotton waited. They balanced like that until the tension dissipated under his gaze and she grasped her husband's fingers. It was a hungry gesture. Cotton pulled her to his side while he held on to Marquis. He kissed the top of Allaina's head, then murmured words I couldn't hear. There was obvious strain in the marriage, the specter of the dead hooker proving to be a powerful ghost.

"Maceo's here to see you." Cotton's head snapped up to find me in the doorway. There was no shock in his face as he realized I'd witnessed an intimate moment in his marriage. To him there was no shame in loving his wife and son the way he did.

"Can you give us a minute?" he asked.

I did just that, returning to the first floor where I sat with Kiros and waited.

TWENTY-SEVEN

"Hey, man, I saw the press conference. How you holding up?" Cotton had come downstairs to find me and Kiros sitting in the front hall.

"I'm holding. Only other option is to let go, and I can't do that." He gave me a pound. "Come take a walk with me. Give Allaina a minute to get herself together."

Kiros and I followed him outside and down a pathway cut into the canyons.

"You seen your grandparents?" he asked.

"Yesterday."

"Me, Allaina, and Marquis going over there Tuesday night for dinner. You gonna be around?"

"Should be."

We continued on in the dark, the light provided by tiny lanterns embedded into the stones. About ten feet down and around a bend of trees, we came upon an aviary wedged into the hill.

"Here we go." Before he opened the aviary's iron door, Cotton looked at Kiros standing stone still, his wet nose just a slick in the night air.

"Gotdamn, man, that's an insane-looking dog." He managed to smile despite the drama in his life. "He cool with birds?"

"Far as I know." I signaled with two fingers and Kiros stretched out on the walkway. "What's all this?"

"This is where I come to clear my head." He turned on another light. "Watch your step. It's wet from the rain."

He ducked into the man-size cage and pulled a string hanging from the ceiling. The light bloomed and the hair on the back of my neck stood up. All along the back wall were a row of open cages and eight silent, watchful birds. They had the taloned feet of the winged creatures seen in nightmares and small, black leather hoods pulled down over their heads.

Cotton grabbed a thick leather glove from a nail on the wall and clucked at a large gray bird that hopped onto his hand.

"This is Genghis." His arm swooped around until the bird was inches from my face. I stepped back as Cotton pulled the hood from its head. "He's a falcon." He kissed the top of the bird's head. "He was hurt when I found him, otherwise," he shrugged, "I wouldn'a been able to catch him. He nearly pecked my arm off."

"How long you had him?"

"Four years. Some people think haggards can never be tamed, but me and him got an understanding." He smiled at the bird with pride and affection. "He's still wild and I let him be."

It hurt me for a moment to think of Cotton in that big lonely house with his nightmarish birds. But a look around the cage at the spit-shined scales, the crystal-clear water bottles, and the clean floors let me know that he loved them like children.

"Sometimes I come off the road when we have a bye, or last year when I was out with my injury, and I come right up here to see him. I take him down into the canyons to hunt. He goes after ground prey—squirrels, rats, shit like that."

"How you get into this?"

"One of my coaches out in Iowa. He took me out a couple times with his sons, and I was hooked." I could tell that the memory was sweet for him.

"You come out here with Marquis?"

He shook his head. "The birds scare Allaina, but I sneak him out once in a while. He likes it." He ducked out of the aviary. "Watch this."

He lowered his arm and the bird took off into the air. Cotton turned on a floodlight and we watched as it swooped in and out of the beam. The bird's glide was beautiful, reminiscent of his owner's down-court charge.

Cotton turned to me. "What happened last night? How'd you end up with that girl?"

"Fluke. I came up here to see you, and she stepped out of the bathroom just as I came up the stairs."

"Where'd you take her when you left?"

"Home."

"Did she say anything about me? About the case?"

"Nothing I hadn't read in the papers. She told me that her and Ivy came out here from Las Vegas with another girl. Before that Ivy worked Atlantic City; got busted for hooking."

He was silent for a minute. "I hired a private detective. My lawyers got a man burning a hole in my wallet trying to find out about the girl. They trying to fry Holly on this."

"Heard his prints were in the room."

"Where'd you hear that?"

"Remember Philip Noone? He used to date Aunt Desiree?" Cotton nodded. "He's OPD. A detective."

"Thought this was a San Francisco case."

"It is, but Noone hates Holly so much I think he's probably working it on his own time. As a hobby."

"Shit. His prints, huh?"

I nodded, surprised that his battalion of lawyers hadn't already told him as much.

"They find any other fingerprints?"

"Not that I know of, but what about Starr?"

"What about him?" Genghis floated back, his wings creating a wind above my head. He landed on Cotton's outstretched arm, and I waited while he returned him to the cage.

"Is he pressing charges?"

"What you think? He shut the fuck up when I pulled out my checkbook."

"Yeah?"

"Everybody got a price, Maceo, I don't care how righteous they claim to be. Everybody got one thing, or one person, they'll sell their soul to have."

His voice was sad, resigned, but I couldn't read his face in the dark.

"How's Holly doing?"

"Holly's made of stone. The man's a soldier."

"What about the legal side?"

"Anything I have is his, he knows that. I got money, lawyers, a jet if he needs to get in the wind."

I was silent. I hadn't considered running to be one of Holly's options. It didn't seem to be part of his nature, but two years was a long time, and prison was its own death sentence.

"You don't believe me," he continued, "ask him yourself."

"Holly's inside?"

"He been here from the get. He was on one'a Lamb's house-boats but that spot got hot and he left. I got three lawyers that live down the hill, all on retainer, and nobody gets in unless I say so. This is one of the safest places he can be."

"He know I'm here?"

"You wouldn't be here if he did." I was taken aback by Cotton's bluntness but I knew it was the truth.

Inside the house we took the back staircase that Allaina had referred to earlier. It led to a sub floor, one probably built for servants. Kiros's nails clicked rhythmically on the stone tiles as we made our way down. Holly was in a kitchen that at some point in its life must have been for staff. It was in the basement area of the house with a TV mounted on the ceiling. The lights were low, the room lit by a single bulb above the stove and the shadowy flickers of the TV. A deck of playing cards was beside him on the long wooden table. He used a hunting knife to carve a bulky pineapple into smaller pieces.

He looked at me without interest when I entered the room, but his eyes landed on Kiros with a start. Holly looked at Cotton until the ballplayer held up his hands in defeat.

"What you want me to say, man? Allaina brought him in and Cissy's been on my ass all week. If you're brave enough you can deal with the two of them."

He left the room.

"Wassup, man?" I offered Holly a pound across the table but he ignored it and continued to hack away at the fruit. He wore the collar of his Carhartt up to his ears to ward off the cold, and his legs, stretched out in front of him, were encased in the requisite black Ben Davises. Like always, he wore his K-Swiss.

"It's good to see you."

He snickered and picked up the cards.

"I was out at Yolanda's this morning, heard a couple things about the Nightingales, found out the name of that girl that . . ."

He held up his hand. "Nigga, I ain't trying to fuck wit' you like that."

"Holly."

"Naw, partna, you made the choice when you rode out of town."

"I had some things I had to take care of."

"Me, too. Two dead bodies, and a year's worth of heat from the police. What about you? Was your shit that urgent?"

"Urgent for me at the time."

"Break it down for me, then. Three dead bodies and two years' worth of heat? Or was it white-boy shit? You had to find yourself?"

"Something like that."

"Maceo Albert Bouchaund Redfield." He shot me a contemptuous look. "You got four names. You coulda picked one and saved me the motherfucking trouble."

I ignored his comment. "You going to let me help you?"

"Help me?" He flung a card out on the table and ignored my question. "When was the last time you saw Felicia?"

"The last time you did."

"You ain't seen her in two years, then you show up with that nowhere broad from the other night?"

"I don't know that girl. She was standing in the hall when I got here."

"And you fired on Emmet for a girl you didn't know. That makes shit worse, 'cause it ain't gonna be you that dies behind a scandalous chick, *youhearwhatI'msaying*? It'll be anybody but you."

"So, you don't want to hear what I found out?"

"What? That Dutch is Smokey's cousin? Everybody in the town know that. He been here as long as you been gone."

"Why didn't you . . ."

"Why didn't I what, take him out? Smokey's cousin come up dead, where's the first place the police look?"

"So, you been a sitting duck?"

"It's the game, baby."

"Who were the two guys arguing with you and Cotton at the party?"

Silence.

"You can play it this way if you want, Holly, but know this: Dutch touched down to get *you*. Nobody else. And what kind of squad you got? Emmet's smoking crack, Bilau's an idiot, and Silas is about as shady as they come."

"That's your argument? I should add another untrustworthy nigga to my team?"

"Where your boys tonight? Any of them riding out trying to look for that Jamaican with the white patches on his skin?"

I got the first reaction since my return. It was there but it was fleeting. By the time I blinked, the surprise on his face was gone.

I kept going. "He runs tight with one other guy. They're in charge of guarding Dutch's top girls. Dana Hewitt, or Ivy Donovan, the girl that got killed, was usually guarded by them. So was another girl named Fantasia and a white girl named Tina.

"My guess is that those are the two men you and Cotton had a beef with at the party, and one of 'em knocked me out near Lamb's boat. Sonny, the girl from the other night, came up here

188 —   Nichelle D. Tramble

in a car driven by Silas. She's the dead girl's best friend." I paused. "You're more than a sitting duck, partna. You're a target."

I let the information hang in the air like an offering. Kiros followed me when I walked to the door. Before I crossed the threshold I left him with one more thing to whet his appetite.

"Ivy has a place in San Francisco the police don't know about."

I hit the switch for the overhead light as I left just so he would have a better chance of winning his game.

"If you need me, I'm staying at the Seaport. Room number's the same as my old jersey."

TWENTY-EIGHT

An hour later, after dropping Kiros at the hotel, I walked into Skates on the Bay in the Berkeley Marina. Outside, the white frost of wave caps crashed against the rocky shoreline and the wooden stilts that anchored the restaurant. I found a table near the window that was still covered with dirty ashtrays and salted margarita glasses.

"Sorry about this mess." A waitress appeared to clear off the table. "Can I get you something?"

"Cuervo Gold. And a water."

"The kitchen's still open. Would you like a menu?"

"No, I'm fine. Can you tell me what time Sonny's shift starts?"

She looked bewildered. "Is that a new guy?"

"It's a she. Sonny Boston. You might know her as Sonia."

"Sorry. Nobody here by that name."

"You sure?"

"Positive. I've worked here four years. We've never had a Sonia or a Sonny. You still want your drink?"

"Yeah, thanks."

The waitress moved off, and I was left wondering about Sonny's lie. I wasn't surprised; the truth seemed to be a liquid concept to her, but it made me wonder what pieces of information I could believe or if she was even going to show up.

I didn't have to wonder long. Moments later Sonny entered wearing a dress too thin for the weather and no coat. She slid onto the bar stool like it was made for her. At the end of the bar a man raised his glass in greeting but she ignored him. When my drink arrived I carried it across the room.

I rapped my knuckles on the bar to get her attention. "I thought you worked here."

She didn't miss a beat. "What made you think that?"

"Yesterday, when you said—"

"Yesterday I said I'd line you up with a drink if you stopped by. Order something and I'll take care of it."

"Just like that, you got an answer ready?"

She swiveled around in her chair and raised an eyebrow. "You back to acting like a cop?"

"How do you know Silas?"

She reached for the drink the bartender slid her way. "No chitchat, Maceo? No clever chatter to break the ice? Just a glove, a pointed finger, and a little Vaseline." She sipped her drink and beckoned for another.

"How do you know him?" I repeated. "Where'd he find you?"

"He found me here." She locked those mean, beautiful eyes on me and leaned over until her lips were on my ear. "I don't work at the bar, ninja, I work the bar."

"You a Nightingale?"

She snorted. "I'm a grifter. I run scams on whatever chump crawls into my web."

"That the truth?"

"Ah, the truth." She moved away. "That shitty little detail you're so obsessed with. I thought you came here because you missed me."

"Was that the first time you met Silas?"

"You don't believe in quiet, do you?"

"You're avoiding my questions. I thought we were past that."

She gave a sad little laugh. "You might want to be careful, Maceo. You talk like the two of us are friends."

"What's that supposed to mean?"

"It means you don't know anything about me. If you did you might slide off that bar stool and find yourself a nice girl."

"What good would that do me? A nice girl can't help me with what I need." We were talking about more than a crime.

She blew smoke rings into the air and poked her finger through each one. "I got edges, you know. Sharp ones."

"I'm not a bleeder."

"I'm just trying to give you a fighting chance here."

"Is that what I need to roll with Sonny Boston? A fighting chance?"

"You don't listen."

"What should I be listening for?"

"Warning bells." She leaned in close, using the heat of her body to close the gap between us. Her lips were inches away from mine as she talked. "You want me to say I've been waiting for you all my life? You want me to tell you that you're the man who can straighten me out, help me get my act together?"

I had to swallow twice before I could answer. "No, I just want you to tell me the truth. At least your version of what happened that night."

"Stop playing with me, Maceo." She hissed her words so loud a few people looked up from their drinks to check us out.

She was skittish as a colt, so I reached for her wrist and held on tight. She was also a little bit mean, and too beautiful to ever be permanent, but better men had been inspired by less.

I dropped my voice down to a whisper. "Don't run."

We were at a standoff, testing each other and trying to figure out a way to be brave because that's what it took. We were playing an old game and I was a die-hard participant despite my track record. Hard to imagine after my failures with Felicia and Alixe that I still believed in possibilities, but I did, and the second I sat at the bar it became obvious to me.

"Don't say later, Maceo, that I didn't warn you. No matter how this plays out, I gave you a chance to get away."

I smiled.

She didn't flinch at the gruesome sight of the scar that smiled at the same time. It was an eerie effect that gave new meaning to the expression "smiling out of the side of his face." She stood her ground and I recognized a kindred spirit, another person with a ruin of wounds just below the surface.

She leaned in to give me a kiss. "Let's get out of here, ninja. I have a story to tell you."

———

I trailed behind Sonny's sports car, a convertible Karmann Ghia, as we headed west toward Emeryville. She lived in a city 1.2 square miles long wedged between Oakland and Berkeley along the Eastshore Highway. Just as Interstates 80, 580, and 880 intersected, Emeryville disappeared. The small town was home to a couple of gambling dens, the most visible being the Oaks Card Club, a building tricked out like a casino but without the showgirls, slot machines, or other Vegas stylings. Yet it was still possible to lose Vegas-size money.

We pulled into the parking lot of a warehouse loft behind the Berkeley Farms milk factory. The security door of the grungy building was made of metal, and she had to push her way into her apartment, but once we got in I understood the effort. Inside she had a wide open space with no walls, just columns strung with heavy velvet curtains. It was at least two thousand square feet, with a bank of windows that reached to the ceiling and redbrick walls below. An octagonal chamber made of mottled glass sat in the middle of the room. It was open-air on the top and pipes came down from the ceiling. It was cool and odd all at once, which fit her, but I didn't want to imagine the scams she ran to afford the place.

I pointed toward it. "That a torture chamber?"

"Bathroom." She slid open one of the doors to reveal a room filled with candles, plants, and a freestanding bathtub big enough for three people. The toilet was enclosed behind a curtain but the shower was made of the same glass as the outer walls.

She noticed my curious look. "The glass is treated. Once you turn the water on and it gets steamy, you can't see inside." She winked. "There's a screen for people like you."

"I didn't say anything."

"Your eyes did. Want a beer? Glass of wine?"

"Beer's cool."

"Have a seat."

She filled a teapot with water, put it on the burner, then grabbed a beer from the refrigerator. I sank down into one of three couches that were low to the ground and overstuffed with pillows. She handed me the beer and disappeared behind a curtain at the end of the kitchen.

As the teapot started to hum on the stove I closed my eyes.

I was exhausted.

Behind me, Sonny's phone rang, and my eyes snapped open. I heard her voice, seductive and playful on the recording: "You've reached Sonny Boston. Catch me if you can."

A long beep followed, and then a male voice. "Sonny! You think you can play with me, girl? I know what you're trying to do . . ." She came up behind me and turned down the volume. She had changed into a black robe with an elaborate red dragon embroidered on the back.

"Sounds like you got trouble on all sides, lady."

"Nothing I can't handle." I saw her finger hit the erase button as the kettle wailed behind us.

"Sit down." I patted the seat next to me and shifted my body away to see if she would follow. She did, and just that quick the wind changed. We were at square one of a very familiar dance. I wasn't fool enough to think that Sonny worked without an agenda, but I knew that if I at least kept my wits about me—if I at least remembered at all times my first encounter with her—I could keep my head above water.

She picked up my beer. After a long swallow she handed it to me. Her robe fell open as she did so. I looked down. The skin beneath the open robe was flawless except for a single tattoo: a long string of dice that trailed down her hip bone and disappeared into the fold of her leg.

She moved in close and I stopped thinking right before I kissed her.

———————

We didn't bother to move to her room. Actually, she didn't invite me. She just slipped the bottle from my hand and threw her leg across mine. There was nothing beneath the robe, nothing at all, and even less between me and her when she reached down to unzip my pants.

I barely had to work, and bad timing or not, as Sonny labored above me I thought of one of Gra'mère's most tried and true sayings: *Now why would you want something if you didn't have to work to get it? When is something like that ever worthwhile?*

TWENTY-NINE

Sonny slipped off into the bathroom while I tried to catch my breath. I sat there motionless, breathing hard, sweating, and feeling like quicksand. Baseball. Boxing. It didn't matter. She'd still managed to wind me in more ways than one. I was fully clothed but exposed in the wide open space of her warehouse with my pants around my ankles, a condom wrapper discarded on the floor, and my conscience echoing in my head like the reverb at a handball court. I'd made a mistake; I knew it before it happened but I rolled with her program just to see where it led.

Through the glass of the bathroom walls I watched her take a shower. The performance was for my benefit, so I took it in as she rotated beneath the stream of water, slow, making sure I saw every angle. She was right, the steam hid most of the details but her silhouette got the point across. The soft, melancholy tune she hummed to herself made the hairs on the back of my neck stand on end. There was something so deliberate about the whole exercise that the song put me in mind of the warning music in horror films.

"What you doing out there?" she called to me.

"Watching you. Trying not to be a victim."

"Someone after you, Maceo?" She placed her hands on the sides of her face and leaned against the glass to peer out at me. I knew she couldn't see me but she faced my direction. "Is there someone out there who wants to do you harm?"

"You never know."

"No, we don't, do we. We never know." The intensity of her humming increased and I continued to watch. "What can we do about that? Is there anything we can do?"

"Not really."

"We could watch our backs." She wiggled her hips. "You watching mine?"

"I'm watching."

"Good. I'm watching yours, too. We can take care of each other, right, Maceo? That's why you helped me."

"I helped a woman in trouble."

"No, you helped *me*. You helped me because I was in trouble and now we're in this together."

"What is this?"

"This, ninja? This is life."

———

When she finally came out I was at the kitchen sink, still watching her and smoking a cigarette from a pack on the counter. She wore the dragon robe with a towel wrapped around her head.

"Take a shower," she said as she took the cigarette from my fingers, "and I'll finish this for you."

In the bathroom she'd left a towel for me on top of the sink, a brand-new toothbrush, and an unopened bar of soap.

I tried not to think of the reasons she'd have extra toothbrushes lying around.

My heart rate had just about returned to normal when I heard her footsteps clicking like a warning on the bathroom tile.

"Maceo," she called to me over the sound of running water, "you have any plans for the rest of the night?"

"Not that I know of."

"Then let's take a ride."

I turned off the water as a towel sailed over the shower wall. I wrapped it around my waist and stepped out into the steam of the small room. Sonny was fully dressed.

Her dress was black and small; it looked like a napkin, and she was holding a glass of wine in one hand and her purse in the other. She towered above me in her high heels.

The air was loaded.

We both knew she was asking me to go for more than a ride. She was asking me to go with her, wherever that led. The sex on the couch, quick as it was, hadn't been free. There was a price and it dangled before me like a sales tag, in shoes that looked like weapons.

THIRTY

The wind whipped Sonny's sports car across two lanes of the Bay Bridge before she regained control. I grabbed the door handle to keep my balance. "Slow down, Sonny."

"Sorry," she said, then accelerated across another lane.

"My truck would've handled this better."

"Maybe, but people on the block are used to seeing this car. We don't want to draw too much attention to ourselves."

The block she spoke of was in North Beach, a formerly Italian neighborhood that had been swallowed up by Chinatown. It was one of the hardest addresses to come by, but she wheeled through the streets like she was born to it.

"Here we go."

She pointed to a building made of redwood and glass at the end of a short, dead-end street. Wedged tight on the side of it was a steep public staircase that ran up to a small park.

"Can you get the garage door for me?"

I jumped out and pulled the door open with the key she handed over. She wheeled the car in and I pulled the door down behind us.

Inside the apartment the artwork was museum quality, the all-white furniture just off the showroom floor, and the view of the Golden Gate Bridge postcard-perfect. A spiral staircase connected the first and second floors.

"Impressive."

"Should be. Ivy earned every penny of this place."

"She live here by herself?"

"She didn't live here, she worked here."

"The police been here?"

"No. I gave them the address in Russian Hill."

"If she didn't live here, how do you know about this place? Why do you have a key?"

"Ask me a straight question, Maceo, or I won't answer you."

"I just did."

"No you didn't, and until you state it plain I'm not going to answer."

"Why we here then? How about that?"

"I just wanted to get some of her personal things out of here. There's a necklace I want to wear to her funeral, and some letters she kept from her mother. That alright with you?"

It was alright, but it still didn't explain the dress, the sex, or the secrecy.

"Sonny . . ."

"Don't worry about it. I thought I needed your help packing my friend's clothes, thought it might be too hard to do by myself, but I was wrong." She tossed me the TV remote from the arm of the couch. "Fix yourself a drink, watch a little TV. I'll be upstairs. By myself."

I called her name again but she kept going without a backward glance. I heard her heels clicking on the tile overhead, then the opening of doors. I flipped through the TV channels, trying to drown out the doubts pecking at the back of my head. On three different news channels, scowling pictures of Cotton gave way to the disastrous press conference. I watched with the sound off as the newscasters mimed their impartiality with elevated eyebrows and widened eyes. No mention of a lawsuit from Starr, which meant the money had already changed hands. Whatever the case, Starr's career would be forever stamped by the brawl. He could go on to win a Pulitzer or Nobel Prize, but any future story would always include the words "choked out by NBA star Cornelius Knox."

I cut away to an old movie to avoid the footage and was immediately met with one of Cotton's commercials. They hadn't stopped running because the executives at Flight Athletic Shoes understood the basketball player's core fan base, the hard-knocks kids who worshipped the holy trinity of Cotton, Tyson, and Tupac, and they knew that the Cotton Nation wouldn't abandon him in his time of need. The unbridled anger legitimized him, made him credible, which meant the ads would keep running, would keep earning money.

I turned up the volume.

It was the first time I'd ever seen the commercial, but I recognized the postcard images of Russia's Red Square behind Cotton. He stood alone in the center of the infamous square until a basketball dropped from the sky and into his hands. He squinted and zoomed in on a lone basket in the distance, then he twirled the ball to get his bearings. One bounce, and the impact shook all the surrounding buildings. As he revved up to make the sprint for the basket, the volume dropped out and the action went to slow motion. He ran and the famous landmarks of China, Australia, and Africa moved in and out of the frame. When his feet left the ground he hovered above the earth, and the dunk, when he came down, was so powerful that the sky shattered like a backboard and the entire planet went dark, as did the screen, before his trademark legend *Let Me Fly* appeared in white letters.

The imagery was effective; it sold him as the loner, as a man who could fly above the earth on his own steam just as long as there was no one else around, no one to get in his way or hold him back. Let him fly, let him live without shackles, and he was perfection in human flesh.

I flipped back to the news and ran right into the sight of a group of women picketing the Flight store in Union Square.

"Several women's groups have lobbied the NBA to permanently suspend Cornelius Knox from the National Basketball Association."

"Maceo?" Sonny saved me from the drone of the reporter's commentary by calling me from upstairs.

"Yeah?"

"Can you come up here for a second?"

I took the stairs two at a time and found her in the bedroom holding a dress and a pair of shoes. Her face was streaked with tears.

"I thought I could do this."

I took the clothes and threw them over a chair. Then I pulled her into my lap. "Don't make yourself crazy. We can call somebody else to take care of all this."

She wiped away her tears. "There is no one else. I'm the only one. It's been just the two of us for years. We talked about things, but I'm not prepared for this. The two of us lived fast but when you hustlin' and winning at it, you convince yourself that it's never going to end. We used to laugh sometimes about how easy it all was." She started to cry again. "I had to identify the body."

"You told me."

"The police want everybody to believe she was beaten to death but the sheet slipped while I was there, and I saw her neck. It was cut from ear to ear, like somebody meant to take her head off."

"They ask you not to tell anybody?"

"Yes."

"But you're telling me?"

She nodded. I appreciated that but I didn't tell her that I'd heard the same thing in a diner run by a man Holly trusted.

"They killed her like she wasn't nothing."

The tears came loud and hard after that and she buried her face in her hands. I grabbed her around the waist and pulled her backward until we were both reclined on the bed. She wrapped her arms around my neck, then brought her knees up until they connected with my chest. I held her as tight as I could while her tears burrowed beneath my skin.

"*Maceo, boy, you cursed. Anybody crosses your path is doomed.*" My father and I were on a rooftop looking out over the city of Oakland. Behind us birds chattered in cages.

"*What good you ever do anybody? Can you tell me that? What good are you?*" He did a quick shuffle as he taunted me, then broke into a two-step that ended in a dip. He had his back to me, unconcerned with the effect of his words.

"*Fly, robin, fly / up, up to the sky.*" He sang the lyric in a shrieking falsetto that resembled the call of a hawk. A flock of homing pigeons took off overhead, then dipped and rolled in time to his clapping hands.

My father pointed at the birds as they swirled above us. "*Look at 'em go, look at 'em. Every one of them smarter than you, with brains big as thumbtacks. You know that saying, 'niggers, rats, roaches'?*"

Laughter cracked from his blistered mouth like thunder. "*I used to say 'niggers, rats, roaches, and pigeons,' but that ain't fair.*"

A bird landed on his shoulder and pecked viciously at his ear, tunneling in and coming away with meat. My father ignored the bird as it drilled deeper and deeper into his skull.

"*How long you gonna stand there, Maceo? What you got to say for yourself? You're bad luck, baby boy, bad luck.*" He screamed the last of his speech as blood poured from his ear. "*When they kill your woman, you can join me here. We can rule together, father and son, kings of the underworld.*"

Without warning the birds begin to drop from the sky like rain. I woke with a start as his head tumbled from his shoulders and rolled to my feet.

THIRTY-ONE

I bolted upright, confused to find myself in the all-white bedroom, disoriented by the wall of mirrors that bounced my terror back at me.

"What's wrong?"

Sonny was at my side, still in her dress and shoes, pulling my damp shirt away from my chest. "What's wrong, Maceo?"

"Nothing."

I stood up and headed into the adjacent bathroom to splash water on my face and shake off the scent of ammonia and limes that always accompanied my father's appearances. Sonny followed at my heels.

"You're soaking wet. What happened? You have a bad dream?" I didn't want to tell her about it. I'd been lucky while I was in Texas, lucky while I roamed the back roads of the Southwest, to have left my nightmares behind. Now they were back, fresh on the heels of Cissy's deterioration, Cotton and Holly, and the beautiful woman at my side.

"You almost ready to go?" I asked instead.

"No," she looked at her watch, "we were asleep for over an hour." She grabbed my hands. "What's wrong with you?"

"Nothing. I just need a little fresh air. You want something to eat?"

"Not really, but you go ahead. Give me about forty-five minutes and I'll be finished here."

"You sure?"

"Yeah, I'm fine. Take my car. I'll be ready when you get back."

———

I left Sonny upstairs, eager to abandon the mirrored house that had induced the nightmare. I drove the hills of North Beach with no particular destination in mind until I saw a bus ad for Fisherman's Wharf and aimed the car at the water.

The Gideon Hotel, where the murder had taken place, was in Ghirardelli Square at the tail end of the wharf. I turned in to the circular driveway and gave the keys to a uniformed valet holding an umbrella. From the fancy green-and-gold façade I could tell the hotel had aspirations, like it wanted to grow up and be somebody famous, but the murder had tarnished its image.

Most of the tourists, though, were foreigners who appeared to be ignorant of the crime, or maybe they just didn't care. I didn't worry about it too long. Instead I trailed behind a group of Japanese men streaming out of a tour bus. The crowd in the lobby was filled with people in jeans and tennis shoes despite the oak-paneled bar that looked like it had been built for men in suits. It was the perfect place to get lost in a crowd if you were a working girl, or a man searching for a few empty answers in women or liquor.

I banked on that as I took a seat in a cushioned booth. Across the room a tuxedo-clad bartender realigned liquor bottles and smiled at customers without ever looking them in the eye.

"Would you like to order?" A waitress appeared before I got settled.

"A cup of coffee."

"Anything else, sir?"

"No, that's good for now."

She had the good grace to look embarrassed before she said her next line. "Sir, there's a two-drink minimum to sit at the booth unless you order a meal."

"Then bring me a coffee, cheeseburger, and french fries."

The meal took ten minutes, cost twenty-seven dollars, and tasted like paste but I ate it anyway, using the time to scan the crowd for a familiar face or at least a brown one. I saw my mark, a brother in the high-stepping band uniform of the hotel's bell-boys, and a little too much glide in his walk to be completely legit. He pulled cigarettes from his pocket and stepped into the alley through an exit door marked EMPLOYEES ONLY. Perfect.

I motioned for the waitress. "Can I ask you a question?"

"Yes."

"Is this the hotel where that girl was murdered?"

She stepped back and closed herself off. "If you would like any information about the tragedy I can refer you to the night manager. There's also a press agent on staff to deal specifically with journalists."

"I just wanted to know what you thought about it."

"Can I get you anything else?"

That was my answer, so I let her off the hook. "No, don't worry about it. I'm going to step out for a smoke. Can you bring me another coffee and leave my food here until I get back?"

208 — Nichelle D. Tramble

The alley was open on both ends with a pedestrian bridge over-head that linked the top floors of the hotel. I stepped into it while patting myself down for a lighter even though I had matches in my pocket.

"Say," I asked as I walked toward the bellboy enjoying a quiet smoke near the Dumpster, "you got a light?"

He reached into his pocket without answering. I took a long drag, then gave him a moment to get used to my presence. "Listen, brotha, I'm looking for a job. I just got into town—"

He held up his hand and threw the cigarette down near my feet.

"If you were looking for a job, *brotha*, you wouldn't be inside the hotel eating a fifteen-dollar hamburger. So, to answer your question before you ask, I ain't got shit to say about the murder."

I took the Broadway Tunnel back to Taylor thirty minutes later. The Gideon had been a bust. They were hell-bent on business as usual, which meant the murder didn't exist and by season's end neither would Ivy. She was already becoming a ghost, just as Sonny had predicted. Her tragic demise would become a sad story that would lose its shock value over time. There would al-ways be another scandal waiting in the wings, a story a little more tragic and salacious than the last.

Sonny had given me the keys to the car but not to the garage so I parked on Winter Place above the park. I tried Ivy's street but a couple of inconsiderate neighbors in wide-body Mercedeses blocked the street while they unloaded their trunks. I'd waited at the entrance to see if they'd move but they didn't even flash a blinker. I moved on, spending a good ten minutes searching the surrounding streets for a parking space that didn't require a permit. I found one on Winter Place and beat out another driver who'd flipped a U-turn to try to edge me out.

It got like that sometimes.

The park was empty, small, and dark, with broken glass littered along the path. It was too unkempt for the ritzy neighborhood, and that's what gave me pause. I looked around, saw no one, then remembered the double-parked cars. The pieces slammed together all at once and I took off in a run. My thoughts were on Sonny as I took the steps two at a time. The cars were still there when I reached the bottom. The first Mercedes idled at the corner with the trunk open, the second pumped white smoke from its tailpipe as its engine hummed. The windows were dark on both cars but I could make out the silhouette of a man seated in the first.

I remembered closing the door of Ivy's garage so when I saw it standing open, I crouched down and ran low against the buildings.

A man charged out just as I reached the front door, and I saw the unmistakable dreadlocks of that ridiculous Jamaican. My nuts shriveled up at the sight of him but I pushed through it like an athlete and swallowed my fear. I charged him, head down, body loose, and took him off his feet from the side.

We both hit the ground, but since I was prepared I had the advantage. I steadied myself enough to deliver two blows to his side, aiming for his kidneys. I heard an exhalation of air, and I kicked him in the side of the head, connecting with a satisfying thud, then I punched straight down, once, to his nose. I felt the concrete beneath him as the blow landed.

From inside the house I heard Sonny call my name, then I was lifted off my feet. Rasta Man tried to balance himself as another man gripped my body like a vice.

"Let's go! Let's go!" The man in the first Mercedes stood outside the car, barking orders at the two men.

The second man cut me loose just as Rasta released a punch. I blocked it, then feinted to the left to avoid another blow. The man at the Mercedes laid on the horn.

The two men ran, and I was tempted to pursue them until I heard Sonny call for me again. Lights went on in the surrounding houses, and I knew police sirens would not be far behind.

I went in through the garage, trying to recall everything I'd touched while I was in the apartment. Sonny was in the kitchen, holding herself up by leaning on the counter. Bruises were visible on her arms and legs. Her dress was torn and her underwear was discarded on the floor beside the refrigerator.

"We have to get out of here, Maceo." Her voice was frantic. She dropped to her knees and scrambled for the pieces of clothing. I reached down and handed them to her. "We have to go. We have to go now."

I helped her to her feet. "Sonny, let me wipe down our fingerprints upstairs, then we can—"

"I already did that," she said, cutting me off. "Right after you left. Before they got here."

I hesitated, but I had to believe her as a siren sounded in the distance. I made the decision, as I squeezed myself out from between the rock and hard place, to trust Sonny.

"Fuck." My UC Berkeley vocabulary fled. I didn't know what else to say.

"Trust me, Maceo. There's not enough time for you to go upstairs. We have to get out of here." She stood and grabbed a dish towel to wipe down the counter and the handle of the stove.

"Who were those guys?" I pulled her shoes off, just in case we had to run, and grabbed the remote control off the coffee table. I'd used it to surf the channels, looking for news about Cotton.

Outside, the neighbors gathered on the sidewalk talked amongst themselves and stared at the open door of the garage. All of them looked at us as we exited.

"Keep your head down. We're going out through the park."

Sonny nodded. She had her arm around my shoulder, but she gained strength with every step. Maybe the bruises looked worse than they were.

"Hey, you two! Hey, stop!"

One man, braver than the rest, yelled across the street, but he didn't cross to us. We were up the stairs and halfway into the park before Sonny spoke.

"Wait."

I thought she was hurt but she reached into a garbage can near the picnic tables and pulled out the shopping bag I'd seen in the apartment. There was a duffel inside. She pulled it out and left the paper bag in the trash.

"What's that?"

"Clothes. Let's go."

"What's it doing out here in the park?"

"I put it there."

"Sonny." I stopped dead in my tracks. The sirens grew closer.

"Alright, alright. Clothes, some letters, and personal stuff I don't want anyone to find. Ivy told me where to look for the papers in case anything happened to her."

"So, she was running scared? That's not what you said earlier."

"And it's not what I said now. They're personal. Things from her mother."

I grabbed the bag to lighten her load and was surprised by the weight of it. My arm dropped as I took hold.

Sonny looked away from me as we kept running.

THIRTY-TWO

"What happened back there?" We were on the bridge, with me behind the wheel. It was easier to handle the small car on the lower deck of the Bay Bridge as we raced toward the East Bay. I scanned the rearview mirror as we left the Treasure Island Tunnel but I saw nothing.

"Did that man rape you? I saw your underwear . . ."

"Naw, he didn't rape me." She paused. "He stuffed them in my mouth so I wouldn't scream."

"Jesus, Sonny. What happened while I was gone? Did you call somebody?"

"No."

"Then what?"

"Nothing."

"That's all you have to say? You lure me to a pump house in the city, get beat up, but before all that you manage to wipe your prints and stash a dress and some letters in the park. You got to do better than that."

I remembered the broken glass and the downed streetlights that lined the pathway. I wondered if she'd done that as well. When I met Sonny I'd nailed her as an eight-cylinder chick, and I wasn't wrong. She kept her engine running at all times.

She moaned, which caused me to look down at her bruises.

"Are you hurt?" I asked her.

"Sore. It looks worse than it is. I'll be fine once we get back."

"Back where?"

She reached across and laced her fingers through mine. "Your room at the Seaport?"

I pulled my hand away. "Why? Your spot too hot?"

"Don't be a fucking chump. Say what you have to say."

"What's to say, lady? You're writing this script, right?"

We rode in silence all the way back.

———

The Seaport never looked so good as we pulled into the driveway. Kiros greeted us at the door as I led Sonny inside.

She kicked the duffel beneath the bed, pulled it back out, then dropped it into the back of the closet on top of my dirty clothes.

"You should sleep with that duffel strapped to your back. That way it'll be safe."

To answer that she pulled her dress over her head to reveal the full extent of her beating. Her legs and arms were riddled with bruises—red, pulpy, and already turning black along the edges. It shamed me for a moment, to see what she'd withstood while I ate stale burgers at The Gideon, but I stilled my heart and remembered that Sonny had been orchestrating this drama long before I arrived.

"Maceo," she was naked as the truth, standing across the room with her hands down at her sides, "I don't want to fight with you."

"Then tell it."

"But . . ."

"You got to tell it or you have to go."

I threw her one of my T-shirts. She let it drop at her feet.

"You could've left me at Cotton's house."

"Sonny!"

Her shoulders dropped just a little before she grabbed a cigarette from the pack on the dresser.

"Listen," I held out the T-shirt until she took it, "I'm not trying to make things hard for you but I need to know the game I'm playing. Can you understand that? I told you I would help you, so you need to trust that or cut me loose. All I'm trying to do is help my friend . . ."

"Which friend? Cotton?" She raised an eyebrow to let me know she was calling me on my own truths. "This is Oakland, Maceo. It wasn't hard for me to find out about you. I know about Billy, I know about Felicia, and I know about Holly."

She dropped the name like a sword.

"I know Cotton lived with your family, that your grandfather saved him, and I know Holly runs this town and you've been gone for two years. I know you're a sucker for a pretty face, and even though you might mean what you say, you haven't been telling the truth either. Can we talk about that before I open a vein, spill my blood, then get caught with my ass out in the street?

"It's Holly you're helping, not Cotton, and at the end of the day, he'll protect you, but the only person who has ever protected Sonny is Sonny."

"You done?"

"Did you hear what I said?"

"I heard you. They heard you in Philly, too."

"Do you understand?"

"Who were those guys?"

She actually smiled, like I'd passed some test, then she pulled the T-shirt over her head and grabbed the sweats I'd discarded that morning. She winced only slightly as the fabric slid over the bruises.

"You sure you alright?" I asked her.

"I'm fine. After we finish talking I'll take a bath, a couple aspirin, and a shot of brandy."

"You tell the truth, for once you tell the truth, and I'll run the bath and then crush the aspirin into the brandy myself. Can you do that?"

"Will you run if I do?"

"I'm not going anywhere."

"You promise?"

"Promise."

"No matter what?"

"No matter what," I said, and I meant it. I meant it at that moment.

That's all that can be promised.

Ever.

THIRTY-THREE

"Me and Ivy came out here about two years ago. I told you we came from Las Vegas, but I'd been with her in Atlantic City before that. I met her at a private strip club in Manhattan where ballplayers hang out after games. It's gone now but it was the spot back then, and she was one of the top dancers there. Women weren't allowed inside the club unless they were dancers or guests, but I paid a bartender to let me hang out once in a while. He introduced me to Ivy.

"Everybody wanted to know her. Everybody wanted her *thing*." She looked away. "It's hard to describe if you didn't know her, but everybody loved Ivy. It wasn't about her just being pretty, there were always prettier girls, but she had this irresistible thing, this light, that people wanted. I used to watch the men at the club, and they would look at her like she was a crystal ball or something, like they could have or see everything they wanted in their lives just by looking at her."

"What you mean by that?"

"I don't know. I tried to describe it to her once, the effect she had on people, but she laughed at me. She didn't get it, she couldn't get it; if she did she wouldn't have been dancing and hooking."

"Where'd she meet Dutch?"

"In Vegas, but I always thought he'd seen her in New York, maybe in Atlantic City, and just took his time getting her."

"Why'd you guys leave New York?"

"Usual stuff. She had a married man taking care of her but his wife found out and we left Manhattan. We went to Atlantic City, but it was too small-time for us so we moved on to Vegas."

"How long ago was that?"

"Three years. When we got to Vegas Ivy got a dancing job our first night in town, and I went to work as a cocktail waitress at the MGM. The money was good, but it didn't come close to what Ivy made dancing, so I quit and went to work with her. I wasn't as popular, so I didn't get the best shifts. Mostly I danced in the middle of the afternoon or on Sundays. I lasted about six months before I got fired, and when Ivy suggested we move to Oakland I jumped at the chance."

"Why Oakland? Why not Los Angeles?"

"No offense, Maceo, but we heard Oakland was a little bit country, and it would be easier for us to set up a con in the Bay Area rather than in L.A."

I was offended, and maybe she was right, but Ivy hadn't gotten killed in New York or Vegas.

"So, she hooked up with Dutch before you guys left Nevada?"

"Yeah. He was a regular at her club, a big spender, and he set his sights on her the moment he walked in there. He was the one who suggested Oakland when Vegas got too hot. There were a couple other outfits that wanted Ivy for themselves and they came after him. He had to trade off three of his other girls to keep the peace over Ivy. All of us needed Oakland when he suggested it, so we left. Plus, he said marks grew on trees and we could pick 'em like apples."

"Marks, huh?"

"Yeah, we worked as a team when we first got here."

"Meaning what?"

"Meaning Dutch set up scams and we followed through."

"How?"

"Different ways. Everything."

"And Dutch set it up?"

"Most of the time. Him or his partner—well, she's not really a partner, she works as his front."

"The blonde? From Nob Hill?"

"You know about her?"

"Heard a few things. She fronts for him. Provides cover for his parties. Tina or something like that."

"Yeah, Tina Brunner, but I'm not sure if that's real."

"So the two of them would set up scams for you guys?"

"Mostly Dutch."

"How long did that go on?"

"For me, about six months. Ivy never stopped."

"And ya'll worked together?"

She hesitated but eventually nodded yes.

"Doing what?"

"What do you think, Maceo?"

"Sonny"—I reached for her hand but she pulled it away—"I need you to say it."

"You know what I am, Maceo."

"Maybe I do know, but"—I took her hand and held tight even when she tried to pull away—"is that the only thing you are?"

"It never was."

"Then tell me the truth and it won't matter."

"You believe that?"

"I know that."

She sighed and let go. "I used to trick for Dutch. Out here and in Vegas. I did singles in Vegas, doubles with another girl once I got to San Francisco. Once in a while I did them with Ivy, which was one of the reasons I got out. I wasn't any better than anybody else who made money off her, and I loved her. Not like you think. I loved her like a sister. The other stuff we did, that was just business."

"How'd you manage to get away from Dutch?"

"I just stopped. Dutch never really wanted me. Just Ivy. He would've let us all go just to have her, and I made it easy for him when I left."

"Ivy was a grown woman."

"She was a grown woman, Maceo, but she was a child at the same time."

"Was she the girl he depended on the most?"

"No, he had a couple more. One, specifically. He called the two of them First Ladies. He's big on theatrics, and Ivy and his other girl understood that. They played the game with him, worked all the angles."

I shook my head. *First Ladies?* That was in line with the stories I'd heard about the dogs, his New Year's Eve party, and the mystery surrounding his relationship to Smokey.

"So, they were a trio?"

"Yeah, the three of them were addicted to each other, like his blood flowed in their veins and theirs in his. You ever see an alcoholic or someone addicted to crack? That's the way it was with Dutch and Ginger."

"That the third girl?"

Sonny nodded. "Ginger just breathed Dutch. It was sick, but he owned her. Her mind. Her body. She had chances to break free but she never did. It was Dutch, then food, then water, then her own life. Dutch before everything."

"What happened to her?"

"I don't know. She disappeared. That scared the shit out of me, actually, and I didn't want to know the details. I thought Dutch might've killed her."

"Why'd you think that?"

She hesitated. "Because Ivy got jumpy if I mentioned her, and you couldn't even say her name around Dutch. I stopped asking because I didn't want him to turn on me."

"Was Ginger her real name?"

"Working name. Nobody trafficked in real names."

"So, you think he killed her."

"Maybe."

"Why? Was she trying to leave?"

"I don't know."

"Do you think Dutch killed Ivy?" I asked.

"That would be the easy answer, and it would make sense after Ginger, but no, I don't."

"What about the men in Vegas? The ones who wanted Ivy?"

"Probably not. It was over three years ago, and he paid them off with other girls and a lot of cash."

"What do you think, then, Sonny? You just gave me about three different recipes for murder."

"I don't know. I can't put it together. All I know is that the last time she was alive she was with your friends."

I let that slide. "Think about it. If Ivy was guarded all the time—"

"Not all the time."

"What do you mean?"

"She met somebody."

"Did Dutch know?"

"Not that I know of, but he would've excused it if he thought she was with a sugar daddy. He got bigger fees from exclusives, and if Ivy was in that situation she wouldn't have taken other dates; exclusives are too lucrative."

"Dates? Who arranged those?"

"Tina. She took referrals from clients who'd been a part of the program for at least two years. After a background check, the men would come to one of the parties, meet the girls, then pay a floor price."

"How much is that?"

"Ten thousand dollars."

"Which gets them what?"

"Anonymity. Beautiful women. No boundaries."

"Which means what?"

"It means that if a girl disappears on one of your dates, or things get out of hand, your name doesn't show up anywhere. Dutch has people who'll disappear the body."

"So that could've been the situation with Ivy, but the police found out before his clean-up crew could take care of it."

She shook her head.

"Why not?"

"Because Ivy was in the hotel room for two days before she was found."

"Dutch didn't know where she was?"

"No."

"Why haven't Dutch and Tina gotten busted?"

"For what? Party promoting? The men pay a fee to be part of a social club. They attend high-end parties with other business-men, network, enjoy some music, good food. What's illegal about that?"

"The girls."

"The girls are adults. Nobody underage. Party guests—"

"But—"

"But nothing. Dutch and Tina cover their bases on the legal side."

"So, where does the money come from?"

"Like I said, the men pay ten thousand dollars to join the club. Then there are monthly membership fees. The fees are pretty steep but no money ever changes hands between the girls and the men."

"Still don't get it."

"That's because you're making it complicated when it's sim-ple. Rich men go to parties filled with young, beautiful girls; beautiful girls go to parties filled with rich men."

"Ten thousand dollars for a few parties a year? Not enough to guarantee all the secrecy."

She smiled, and the sadness returned. "Think about it, Maceo: Ten thousand dollars and you don't have to care anything about the woman you're sleeping with. Ten thousand dollars and you don't have to care if she's been sick, if she's an orphan, or if she hates the sight of you. All you have to know is that she's flat on her back and you own her. Small price to pay if you ask me."

"How many men belong to the group?"

She shrugged. "Two hundred. Two-fifty. Ivy was never sure."

"All from San Francisco?"

"No, they come from all over the country."

"For the parties?"

"Yes. That's where they first see the girls. If there are a hundred men at the party, then there'll be two hundred girls in the room. Enough pretty, smiling, faceless women to keep everybody happy."

"Where do they come from?"

"All over. Some of them seek him out, others come on loan from other groups. Whatever it takes to stock the room. The men flirt and dance, and when they find someone they're interested in they get a business card with the girl's name and a phone number."

"Why a card?"

"Because nothing ever happens on the night of the party. Safety precaution in case cops get into the room. The phone number on the card belongs to Tina. When they call it they get the hard sell on membership into the 'gentlemen's club,' guaranteeing exclusive parties, networking opportunities—nothing about the fact that they're pedaling ass—but if they want to see the girl again they join. Three thousand dollars a month."

"Which means you own her," I said.

"Yes, and once the details are worked out, the girls meet their dates for dinner, somewhere public, and after that whatever happens between two grown people is their business."

"And these men are checked out by Tina?"

"Yes, and most of them are married, which Dutch likes. It narrows the possibility of them leaving their wives for the girls, which means Dutch doesn't have to replenish his crop that often. But somebody must've slipped through, because for the first time Ivy was beginning to imagine a life without him."

"She couldn't see that before? No one helped her?"

Her smile wasn't unkind. "You're looking at the world like love matters, Maceo."

"You don't think it does?"

"I've seen all the ways that it doesn't, and that reality has made Dutch a rich man."

"But sometimes—"

"There's never a *sometimes*."

"You believe that?"

"I know it for a fact." She paused. "I could go on a date with a guy ten or twenty times, but at the end of the day if I asked him straight to his face to help me get out of the life, he'd still fuck me after promising that he'd do anything and everything he could to help me; he'd still take what he came to get.

"Then"—she looked away and got lost in an old memory— "then maybe the worst thing that would happen is that he'd complain to Tina and ask for a new date, someone who wouldn't remind him that the girl in bed wasn't actually a talking doll. So, no, love never matters when money and sex are keeping company."

I let her wander around in her memories for a while before I asked my next question. "What happened tonight?"

"Dutch sent his boys to North Beach to clean out Ivy's place. They found me in there and"—she motioned to the bruises— "you saw what happened."

"Did you see Dutch?"

"He was outside."

"Who are the two guys? I think the one with the dreads knocked me out when I was looking for Holly."

"Just him?"

"Both. You know where to find them?"

"No, not even Ivy knew where Dutch lived."

"You know their names?"

"The Jamaican's name is Orieux, and the other one is a jail-bird named Derrin."

"Have you told me everything?"

"Everything I know. Anything else we'll probably find out to-morrow at Ivy's funeral." She walked into the bathroom, and when I heard the sound of running water I knew she'd told me everything she had to tell.

THIRTY-FOUR

One night after a fight in an El Paso bar, I woke up facedown in
a field of wild mustard. I rolled over to find a toddler, bottle hanging from his mouth, staring down at me. There was judgment in
his eyes. They said I was a fool. As I looked at my reflection in the
bathroom mirror, I searched for that same look of condemnation,
an indication that I'd just bought swampland in Florida from
Sonny, but there was none. I believed her, and I was too tainted
to judge anybody, not even myself.

Outside the rain continued to fall, and the sound of foghorns
bounced around in the night. In between the baritones I listened
for my father's laugh but I heard only silence.

I turned off the light.

It was three o'clock in the morning, and Sonny had fallen
asleep after the promised bath. She stirred when I closed the
bathroom door. I glanced over to find her eyes open and bright in
the dark.

"What's wrong, baby?" Her voice was sleepy. "You need me to take a thorn out of your paw?" I smiled but she couldn't see it. "You still awake?"

She sat up and turned on the light, then giggled when she caught a glimpse of my naked feet. I was short, but I'd been cursed with the long, pointed feet of a six-foot-tall man. It was an odd combination.

"What? Why you laughing?" I smiled, too.

"Your feet, Maceo." She giggled again. "It looks like you're doing a handstand."

"These are nice feet."

"No, they're not."

"Oh, we're joking now." I snatched the covers off her body, then I stopped. The playful gesture was made immediately sober by the spectacle of her bruises. She grabbed for my hand when she saw my face.

"Don't stop laughing, Maceo. We need the jokes. We need something."

Her direction to me was desperate; I could hear it in her voice. I could hear the fact that the self-assured girl who'd mastered the art of double-talk was about to come unhinged.

I leaned over to kiss her and she put her arms around my neck. "That'll work, too."

I turned off the light and climbed in beside her. We were due, after the last time, for a more honest coming together but I took my time. I lit a cigarette instead of moving forward and watched the ember burn into Halloween colors.

"You think Dutch will show up at the funeral tomorrow?" I asked her.

"He'll be there, and he'll have an audience."

"Can you handle that?"

"I'll have to, won't I?"

I reached for her hand, then wove my fingers through hers. She pulled them loose one by one. "You're not afraid of me are you, Maceo?"

"Nope."

The lights of a passing car shone through the window near the front door. I was shirtless and I saw her eyes drift to the tattoo on my chest, the hourglass with the butterfly trapped inside that symbolized '89 and the time I'd spent with Felicia.

"What's this?"

"This," I said, "is a cheat sheet, so I can always remember my time in hell. Anything else?"

"Yeah. One thing."

"What?"

"Who you trying to fool?"

Her lips were soft as she kissed me, and I grasped at the promise they offered.

"I know all about your love story, Maceo. Felicia was Cleopatra." She kissed me once. "Billy was Marc Antony, and you, ninja, were Caesar."

My laugh got trapped in her lips, and before long my clothes and hers were at the foot of the bed.

"Now you know everything, and you're still not going to run?"

"I'm not going anywhere."

I rolled on top of her, and she opened wide to let me in. Her hands traced the length of my back, trailing my spine as I hovered above her. She brought her hands around front to grab me, then she flashed a wicked smile and said two words.

"Bury it."

I did just that, and for a while we forgot.

The sound of foghorns cracked open the dawn, and I woke to the sound of Kiros's growl. A shadow passed in front of the window. I pulled myself away from sheets that smelled of sex and sweat and grabbed my pants.

"Sonny." I bumped the mattress with my knee to jostle her awake. "Sonny."

She opened her eyes and I put a finger up to my lips. I fished the blackjack from my pocket as she slipped into the bathroom with her clothes.

Kiros let loose with a rabid bark and I saw the shadow one more time.

"Maceo." The voice came from outside. I knew it enough to drop the blackjack. I opened the door to find Holly standing there—dressed in black, still scowling, a little cagey, but there.

"Let's ride."

How to explain the simple words that held eighteen years of history? When Holly first came to live with my family we shared one bike between the two of us. It had been mine before his arrival, and afterward it became ours. For years it was our only mode of transportation, and early on I established myself as the designated driver, pedaling through the leafy North Oakland streets with Holly balanced on the spokes of the back wheel.

When we became teenagers that one small bike turned into a car, a battered Buick we used to drive to A's games and high school parties. I was the driver then, too. I maintained the tradition even after the Buick turned into the classic 1967 Dan Gurney Special I used my tuition money to purchase. Holly had his own driver's license and enough money, once he entered the drug game, to purchase a fleet of cars for himself, but because of his chosen profession he liked to keep a low profile. And once his name became known to the police department he stopped driving all together in order to avoid being pulled over and searched.

So "Let's ride" is what he said when he needed to get someplace and he needed me to drive him there, and "Let's ride" was what he'd said when he agreed to help me look for Felicia. Those two words had turned his life upside down, and now we'd come back to square one.

He stepped over the threshold into my room and I stepped out of the way. There wouldn't be an after-school-special-type reconciliation, no sliced thumbs and blood pacts of fealty or confessions of loyalty and honor, just another chance—one last chance—to make it right.

One.

THIRTY-FIVE

Holly took a seat at the kitchen table and stretched his long legs out in front of him. His eyes were guarded as he scanned the room, taking in the two pillows, side by side on the bed, and Sonny's shoes abandoned in the corner. He summed it all up with a slight grimace but he kept his thoughts to himself. Kiros, standing at attention across the room, picked up Holly's uneasiness and locked him in his crosshairs with a roll call of menacing growls. Holly rotated his chair so he could watch Kiros with the same intensity.

"What brings you down from the mountaintop?" I asked him.

He continued to watch Kiros. He had yet to look me in the eye. "Do something about your dog, man."

The tone in his voice brought me up short. In the timbre of that simple sentence I understood that Holly saw me as the lesser of many evils and nothing more. My old friend was a survivor to the end, and my presence in Oakland offered him something he needed to stay alive. I realized then, as his low-grade contempt registered and my own anger flared, that on some level I'd expected my return, and the sacrifice of my own freedom and peace of mind, to be the gesture to clear all debts.

I was wrong.

"Nothing I can do about the dog," I answered. "He doesn't know you."

Holly turned to look me in the face. "School him then."

Holly had a habit from childhood that he called "rebuilding," a way to tunnel inside himself, regroup, and come up with the resources needed to survive any physical or mental assault. After he came to live with us, he told me that rebuilding was what he did when his mother's partying, whoring, and drug use got to be too much, and he had to find a way to hide in plain sight. I'd encountered him in the process of rebuilding after Cissy's attack, and Daddy Al's full-scale dismissal, and while he may have likened the process to shedding the unnecessary, I likened it to discarding the extraneous layers of emotion that made him human. When he was locked in the throes of it, he found a way to deaden his eyes and shallow his breathing to gather all his strength.

To come upon him that way felt a little like looking into the eyes of a corpse, and as he watched me from across the room with a thousand-yard stare, I remembered Rachel's words, *I get the feeling he wants to die,* and the cold chill that passed between us told me all I needed to know. That eventually he'd have to die, or become a machine in order to live the way he did.

The bathroom door opened before I could speak on my prophecy, and Holly shot out of his chair. The motion triggered Kiros. I had to grab his collar and plant my feet in the carpet to hold him down.

When the room settled, Holly stood with the front door open, his eyes going back and forth between Sonny and Kiros. "Gotdamn, man, I don't know which one's worse."

Sonny, a quick study, sized up Holly the same way he had her. One hustler reading the story of another. She reached for the cigarette abandoned between shot glasses and lit up. Then she blew the smoke in Holly's direction. It circled around him like a halo.

"Who might you be?" she asked him.

"Max."

Holly resorted to the alias he used with girls he didn't know.

"Well, Max." She said the name to let him know she didn't believe it, then she grabbed Kiros's leash. "I'll leave you to your business."

She slid out the front door after wrapping my jacket around her shoulders. The room felt small with her gone.

"Who beat her like that?" Holly asked.

"One of Dutch's boys. Same one I told you about."

"What about her face?"

"Didn't touch it."

He looked at me for a long time. "You know that's how a pimp beats his woman."

"I know all about it and before you say anything else, Sonny ain't Felicia."

"No doubt," he answered. "That chick ain't got the curves to be Felicia. This one's all angles, but at least she'll stab you in the chest so you can see it coming."

That was the closest I'd get to his approval but we both knew it didn't matter.

It hadn't mattered the first time.

THIRTY-SIX

Holly and I were seated at a banquet table in the back room of Kowloon Garden, a Chinese restaurant in an El Cerrito mini-mall where he did occasional business. The owners, immigrants from Shanghai, knew Holly as Jay and thought he was a music producer. Their daughter, a little more savvy, knew him by the same name and figured him as a drug dealer. That fact didn't stop her from sleeping with him and giving him a spare key to her parents' restaurant. He used it in the off-hours and always left something in the till to show his respect. He had similar situations all over the East Bay.

Finally, Holly broke the silence that had followed us from Oakland.

"What happened last night?" he asked. "After you left Cotton's house?"

"I went to Skates and picked up Sonny."

"That's her name? Sonny?"

"Yeah, Sonia. Sonny Boston."

He nodded so I went on.

"We went to her house for a minute, then we went to Ivy's apartment in the city. She used it for work, but she lived in Russian Hill."

"Then why'd you go to North Beach?"

"Sonny wanted to pick up some of Ivy's clothes and personal papers."

"She risked getting her ass beat for clothes and papers?"

"That's what she said."

"You wit' her the whole time?"

"Part of the time. I went to The Gideon to see what I could find out. When I got back, Dutch and his boys were already there."

"What did Sonny take from the apartment?"

"A duffel bag."

"Did you look inside of it?"

"No."

He didn't say anything and I remembered the weight of the bag when I'd taken it from Sonny in the park. Then I remembered the broken glass, the wiped fingerprints, and everything else Sonny had erased with sex. I talked through my embarrassment.

"When I got back to the apartment the garage door was open and there were two cars—Mercedeses—idling in the middle of the street. Tinted windows. I came up on the Jamaican just as he was running out. We got into it, then I heard Sonny calling me from inside.

"I found her in the kitchen and I hustled her out when I heard the sirens. We went out through the park, and she stopped to grab the duffel she'd stashed in a garbage can."

Holly raised an eyebrow and the absurdity of my trust was made clear.

"When'd she do that?"

"While I was gone. She said she'd stashed the bag in the park, then wiped the place for our fingerprints . . ."

I let my sentence drift off. We sat in silence.

"Why'd you come back here, Maceo? You ain't cut out for this shit. You were free and clear."

"I was never that."

"Naw, partna," he shook his head, "*I* was never that."

The anger between us crackled and whipped like an electric wire that had broken free from its base. There would be no way to contain it, or get it under control, without some damage being done.

"So, what you wanna do, man?" I asked in response to his anger. "You wanna stand up and fight? Tear this restaurant down?"

"Nope." The sneer on his lips reached his eyes. "I just want you to know this mission ain't about nothing but keeping me alive." His eyes blazed with unmistakable contempt. "I don't give a fuck why you came back." He dismissed my psychological discord with a wave of the hand. "You can handle that shit on your own time."

"If you don't trust me, why you here?"

"'Cause I know you ain't got the stones to let me down twice. You ain't got the courage to be a coward." He paused to let that sink in. "And I'ma use that to find out who's trying to take me out of the game. But if you leave this time, nigga, just keep running, *youhearwhati'msaying?*"

"That Holly's road to forgiveness?"

"What's to forgive? The world is yours, right? I didn't matter, Cissy didn't matter, Daddy Al and Gra'mère didn't matter"—he ticked them off—"Emmet, Yolanda, Clarence, the Samoans. It was Felicia and nobody else."

He paused.

"But if you sell me out for another chick—any chick—after I lost Cissy and the only family I ever had to ride out with you, I'll put you down like a dog."

"Fuck you, Holly. Cissy asked me to come back because you were in trouble, but you can kiss my ass if you think I'ma run after you like—"

"Like you ran after Felicia? Yeah, you gonna do it, 'cause I dare you to look Cissy in the face if you don't."

I stood up and pushed away from the table.

He sneered. "What up, man, you runnin' again?"

"I came back to help you, but I ain't beggin' you for nothing."

"What you beggin' for then?"

The question stopped me in my tracks. He stood up and came to where I stood at the front door.

"That's what I thought. Whatever you out here trying to do is for Maceo and nobody else. We all got a better chance of staying alive if you know that."

I held up my hands in surrender and gave him a mocking smile. "You're right," I said, "I put Felicia in front of everybody. But don't tell me you wouldn't have done the same thing for Cissy."

"I would've done the exact same thing, but I wouldn't have run when I was in the strike zone."

And there it was. My crime hadn't been my foolish desire to

have Felicia for myself, or the night blindness I had when it came to her. My crime had been that when the truth was revealed and the world had turned upside down, I didn't take the weight on my shoulders to turn it back around. I hadn't withstood the heat from the cops, my family, or the enemies Holly made while helping me. I had no answer for that.

"We straight?" he asked.

His voice was even, not kinder but even, as if he'd found a certain peace by shining the light into my eyes.

I nodded. Defeated. Tired.

"We straight," I answered.

"Cool then, baby." He offered me a pound. "'Cause if your balls actually dropped while you were roaming the earth we might be able to ride out and put these fools all the way down."

He issued a salty smile to take the sting out of his words. Then he pushed out into the watered-out sunshine of a Bay Area January.

THIRTY-SEVEN

"Did you kill that hooker?"

I tried, as I weaved through the cars on the Warren Freeway, to regain some of the ground I'd lost. Who likes to be read like a book? Holly could be right as rain about the reasons for my return, but I'd found a level of comfort in ignoring the realities about my life, and I didn't like having my coat pulled.

"Did I kill a hooker?" He snickered.

"Yeah. Noone said your prints were found in the room with the body."

"They were."

"You knew her, then?"

"Yeah, I knew her. Met her through Cotton."

"How's that?"

"How you think?"

"So you knew she was a pro?"

"Most of them are when Allaina's not around."

"So Cotton used Dutch's girls more than once?"

"He didn't use Dutch's girls, he had them around for his boys."

"Then who brought her to the inner sanctum?"

"Silas."

"What's that man's story? Why'd Cotton bring him back into the picture?"

Holly shrugged. "Can't figure it out."

"You know he was the one who brought Sonny up to the house that night. I saw him while I was standing at the gate waiting to get in. He went past me in a 'Vette."

"Sonny tell you anything else about him?"

"No, but she did tell me how Dutch and Tina run the Nightingales."

"Tina?"

"The white girl Dutch uses as a front. Tina Brunner. Yolanda knew about her."

"Blond?"

"From what I heard."

He nodded, slow, and cycled back to pull up a mental picture. "Yeah, I think I've seen her. Cool-looking, until she opens her mouth."

"That's what Yolanda said."

"When'd you see Yolie?"

"The other day. Went to her salon to find out what she knew about Dutch."

"Anything useful?"

"Just that they got a big party coming up next week, and most of the girls use her shop to get ready. She also told me that Dutch uses those two goons to guard his top girls. Same thing Sonny told me last night."

"What else she tell you?" Holly pointed and I crossed three

lanes to exit into the hills of Montclair Village. He pointed a second time and I headed to a park just off the freeway.

"She said that Dutch pissed off a couple different outfits when he stole Ivy out of a strip club in Vegas. He had to pay them off with money and girls."

"So, I'm hemmed up behind some pimp shit?"

"She didn't think so, said Dutch paid everybody off with money and other girls."

"You just swallowing everything she says."

"She told me the truth."

"She told you a story. We won't know the truth until everybody's lined up with something to lose."

I changed the subject. "You ever meet Dutch face-to-face?"

"I went to that New Year's Eve party he gave back in '89, but I didn't connect him to Smokey and neither did anybody in my camp." He frowned. It wasn't easy to admit that he'd slipped, that his game had holes. "I let those chicks and that white girl cloud my vision. He got an up on me because of that."

His answer was a partial truth. I could tell by the way he averted his eyes, but I wasn't going to call him on it. He still wasn't ready to play his whole hand, and I hadn't told him everything myself.

"You think he got you in his sights?"

"Yep. And I think somebody close to me is running their mouth. Dutch is right on my ass. I feel like I'm being hunted."

"You think Emmet's doing the talking?"

He nodded.

"He got a skid-row approach to life these days. It looked to me like he's been smoking. He started dipping into his product while they were investigating Smokey's murder. He couldn't take the pressure and it just got worse."

"Why you keep him around?"

"'Cause if I cut him loose he might feel like he ain't got nothing to lose. Might cause him to give up everything, and he knows too much as it is."

A car passed by as we talked, a nondescript four-door sedan driven by a woman. She pulled into the space in front of us. Holly noted it, then opened the passenger door. He pulled a piece of paper from his pocket and held it up.

"The top one is how you reach Clarence. The second one you can use to find me. Don't write it down." He held it up but he didn't hand it over.

"You out?" I asked.

"Yeah. You gonna be at the Seaport until you leave town?"

"I'm not leaving town." I remained silent until he nodded an acknowledgment. "Today I'm heading into the city with Sonny for Ivy's funeral, then I'm going to try and track down Lemon."

"Why you looking for him?"

"Covering all the bases."

"Does your girl know where Dutch lives?"

"If she does, she's not copping to it. According to her, not even Ivy knew where he lived and she was his top girl. Her and another Nightingale named Ginger."

Holly was halfway out of the car, but he stopped cold when he heard the name.

"Ginger?"

"Yeah. Sound familiar?"

"Naw. Anything else?"

"Yeah, the men who pay for the Nightingales also pay to keep their names away from anything dirty. Dutch'll disappear a body if things get out of hand."

"Like Ivy."

"Maybe. Maybe not. She was in that hotel room for two days before she was found." I paused. "What you know about that?"

He shut the door and stood on the curb. "More than I want to. Dutch might not have killed that girl, but he's the reason she's dead." He rubbed his forehead. "I don't know how to come at this."

"That's what I'm here for."

"What you got, a crystal ball?" He smiled without a trace of malice.

"Naw, baby, just a pack of gypsies that can see into the future."

"Whatever, nigga, just be ready to walk on that chick if it comes down to it."

"You got a place to stay?" I asked him.

He looked toward the sedan. "I got it covered. Thought it was better to get out of Cotton's house. Don't want to stay in one place too long."

"Hit me at the Seaport if you need me."

"Alright, man."

Our good-byes had been said, but he didn't move. I waited him out.

"Listen, partna, I didn't mean to strip you down like I did, but the number of people I can trust gets smaller and smaller every day. The game is getting grimy." He looked off as traffic whipped by on the Warren.

"Anything else?"

"One thing."

"What's that?"

"Cotton's lying about something."

He gave me a chin-up, then disappeared into the sedan idling at the curb. The escape hatch must have been in place from the moment he arrived at the motel because he hadn't made a call or sent up flares while he was with me. The man still operated with an ice-cold mind, but it didn't mean a thing, as we'd learned from Billy, if your inner circle was held together by spiderwebs.

THIRTY-EIGHT

On my way back to Jack London Square I detoured down San Pablo Avenue looking for the homeless man who'd fleeced me out of some cash on my first day back. I found him in the same spot, lining his shopping cart with plastic bags and stuffing his shoes with newspaper. I needed to find Lemon, but the legwork had to be done by someone who wouldn't stir up suspicion.

I honked the horn to get his attention. He ambled over to the car with a big grin on his face.

"Well, if it ain't old moneybags himself."

"Listen, man, what's your name?"

"Jasper DeCarlos Stanislaw"—he bowed deep—"attorney-at-law, jack-of-all-trades, president of these here United States; but since I don't like to be formal with my friends, you can call me Buttermilk."

"Alright, Buttermilk. How you strapped for time this morning?"

"I got a little bit."

"Cool. You ever heard of Burke House?"

He was slow to answer. "That hotel. The one downtown?"

"Yeah. Think you can get over there?" I glanced into the back of the truck. "I ain't got enough room for all your stuff in the car, but if you can get down there this morning I'll pay you to stay two or three nights."

He looked alarmed instead of grateful and stepped back onto the curb. "The first time I saw you I knew you wanted something nasty from me. I knew it, I knew it, I knew it."

"Hold up, partna, it ain't like that at all."

"I got pride. I may be broke, but I got pride. You just can't humiliate a man like this." His voice was high.

"Buttermilk—"

"Mr. Stanislaw," he corrected. "We are no longer on a first-name basis. You call me Mr. Stanislaw or you call me President."

I wanted to laugh, but I didn't have time. "Look, I'm trying to find somebody. I heard he got a place at one of the welfare hotels down on the stroll. If I went in there looking for him, people wouldn't talk to me. So, I thought if you stayed there, asked around, you could be my ears."

"And that's all? You don't want a key to my room or nothing?"

"Not even a little bit. All I want is information."

"Well, shit, who you looking for?"

"A guy named Lemon. 'Bout my age, bright-skinned, on the pipe."

"A crackhead! Crackheads'll cut ya if you give 'em the chance."

"That's why all I want you to do is listen. Find out where he staying, which hotel, what room, and I'll take it from there."

"Might be nice to get out of this rain."

"I bet it would."

"You got a deal then."

"Good. I'll go there now, pay for three days, and meet you at the Greyhound bus station about six o'clock."

"Bring me a sandwich?"

"I'll bring you a sandwich."

He reached in to shake my hand. "Then I'll bring you a crackhead named Lemon."

———

Burke House was on one block in downtown Oakland, not far from the Greyhound station, that was populated with welfare hotels, halfway houses, and shelters. In the lobby of the six-story brick building I found an attendant sleeping behind bank-teller bars with a newspaper open on his lap. There were a few chairs, a worn sofa, and a bank of pay phones down a long hallway all marinating in the pungent smell of people who'd given up. A few men and a woman lounged in chairs and watched a television bolted down on top of a vending machine.

The price for a warm bed with a hot plate was seven dollars a night so I splurged and covered Buttermilk for four. I'd hatched a story about him being an errant uncle but the attendant only cared about the twenty-eight dollars, the correct spelling of Buttermilk Stanislaw, and his own desire to get back to his nap.

THIRTY-NINE

Later that afternoon, a sharp wind whipped Sonny's dress around her legs and her hair into her face as we stood on the shores of Fort Pointe waiting for the chaplain of Funerals At Sea. Sonny had chosen to have Ivy's ashes scattered on the Bay, and she'd also changed the time of the service from four o'clock to noon in order to keep Dutch from attending.

Fort Pointe, in the shadow of the Golden Gate Bridge, was a defunct military encampment near the Presidio where tourists could pose for pictures in front of out-of-use cannons and listen to audiotapes about how soldiers had once roamed the shores. It had been over a hundred years since Fort Pointe had posed any real threat, and in its present state of decommission it served as a public park and a field trip destination for school-children, many of whom swarmed around us playing tag and tossing bread crumbs to the seagulls. Their loud, animated presence mocked the somber huddles of people who waited near the water's edge for one of five boats used by the funeral company.

Finally, the kids were ushered away after a gray-haired man in a three-piece suit pulled the teachers aside and gave them a profanity-laced lecture on being sensitive to the pain of other people. Gratitude rippled through the cluster of mourners as Sonny shivered against the cold.

I rubbed her arm. "Want me to get you a blanket?"

"Yeah, and I left my gloves on the seat."

I returned with her gloves and a tattered white blanket with SEAPORT INN printed in faded green letters. She wrapped it around her shoulders and turned to me.

"When you left with Holly this morning, I didn't think you were coming back."

"What made you feel like that?"

"Experience." Her answer was simple and nine tenths accurate. My conversation with Holly had cast a spotlight on my own gullibility. I fished a cigarette out of my pocket. She smoked it while I held it between my fingers. When she was done she stepped away and watched the overhead traffic crossing the bridge. In the silence, I listened to the steady mooing of the sea lions lounging on the rocks below. The noise was deafening, the smell even worse, but they looked more at ease among the bird shit and fish entrails than I did on land. In the distance two men on the deck of the boat adjusted flags and arranged folding chairs on the bow. Sonny watched them, too, but mostly she kept her eyes on me.

"The other day," I said, "when I came back from my run, you were on the phone. You hung up when I came in the door. Who were you talking to?"

"I don't remember."

"Want me to jog your memory? Tell you what you said?"

"Not really." She looked out toward the funeral boats. "There is something I need to do first."

"Like what?"

"Bury a friend."

She held my gaze until a ruddy-faced man in the navy blues of a sea captain had the good grace to make an appearance. He came toward us with his hand extended.

"Ms. Boston?" he asked.

"Yes."

"I'm Captain Stewart." He had a soothing voice, and though he'd probably performed over a thousand funeral services, his demeanor when he spoke with Sonny was sincere and kind. He took her hand in both of his. "I'm sorry about your loss."

"Thank you."

He looked at me. "Is it just the two of you this morning?"

"This is my friend Maceo Redfield, but I'm the only one going out on the boat." I was surprised by her words. "I want this to be private. Just Ivy and myself."

Stewart looked confused. "Ivy? I thought the service was for a Dana Hewitt."

"It is. Ivy was my nickname for her. She got poison ivy when we were little girls and the name stuck."

I looked at Sonny, amazed yet again at the smoothness of her lies.

"Of course. I understand. Would you like me to say a few words before we scatter the remains?"

"No, I'll do that myself."

"Are we ready then?"

"I'm ready." Sonny took his arm, then turned to kiss my cheek. "You don't mind, do you Maceo?"

"Naw, girl. Do what you need to do."

"You sure?"

"I'm sure. I'll be right here."

As the boat passed under the bridge and cleared the Marin Headlands, I heard car tires in the gravel behind me. I turned to see a blonde wearing sunglasses driving a gold Lexus. She circled the lot, looking out toward the water like I wasn't there before she headed for 101 North. While she was gone, I slid off the hood of the car and tabulated the number of people still in the vicinity. The schoolkids were far enough away that they were mere specks in the distance, and two elderly ladies sat on a bench sharing a sandwich. Another boat, carrying the largest group of mourners, took off while I watched.

The woman returned, just as I knew she would, and I did a quick scan of her backseat. It was empty but I stayed on my guard. She took her time getting out of the car, checking her watch and opening her umbrella before heading my way. Her entire outfit was white, which took a lot of nerve in the rainy weather, and her long, blond hair hung down her back like a statement. The smell of peppermint and the soft floral scent of her perfume reached me before she did.

"Tina," I said before she could open her mouth, "Tina Brunner." It caught her off guard, but only for a minute. She recovered and dropped the pretense.

"That was a stupid move your girlfriend pulled. Changing the time. Any idea why she would do that?"

I was taken aback, not by the threat but because of her voice. Tina looked Nob Hill in her thousand-dollar outfit and bone-straight hair but when she spoke she revealed the inflections of a woman who'd lived as the only white girl in the hood for most of her life. I bet when she relaxed she could pop vowels with the best of them. It stumped me. I couldn't understand why she'd spend so much money on the outside and not fix the sewer accent.

"I think she changed it to beat the rain," I answered.

"You must think this is a game."

"Can't be a game," I said. "I don't know all the players."

"Then let me introduce myself." The words came from behind me, and before I could answer or turn I felt a hand come down on my shoulder. It had the weight of inevitability. "Heard you been looking for me."

I turned around and looked right into the face of a gray-eyed Black man. He had the same wide-bodied menace as Smokey, coupled with a contempt and intelligence Smokey had never displayed. Up close he scared the shit out of me. So much so that for a moment I was tempted to holler, "Po-lice!" Then I remembered I was a tough guy.

Dutch was the only man in the park dressed for a Caribbean player's ball in a pale yellow linen suit and a Panama hat. His henchmen, Orieux and Derrin, took no leads from their boss when it came to style. They stood behind him looking like they toured with Full Force when they weren't killing people.

"Dis here the one that like the grimy girls." Orieux stepped to Dutch's side and I heard the clipped lilt of a patois that had been rinsed out in England.

Dutch stepped closer to me. "Any idea who he's talking about?"

"I couldn't even understand what he said."

Dutch's hand was around my throat before I could blink. I

heard the old ladies on the bench gasp and in the blur of my vision I saw them hurry off toward the chaplain's shack. Dutch backed me all the way into the trees that lined the parking lot. Tina followed at his heels.

"Not here," she said. She pulled Dutch's fingers off my neck one by one. "Don't lose the prize."

I coughed to help get wind back into my pipes. I doubled over and Dutch knelt down to look me in the eye. "You're getting involved in shit you don't understand. Your girlfriend is gonna get herself killed. You don't want to be a part of that."

"You looking out for me now?"

"Stand him up." Orieux and Derrin followed the order by grabbing me beneath my arms. The old ladies were gone and there was no sign of life from the chaplain's shack.

"You were one of the last people to see Smokey alive. Am I right? You, Emmet, Clarence, Holly, Felicia, somebody from L.A., and those no-talking Samoans." I was surprised by his knowledge but I didn't answer. "Tell me who pulled the trigger and we can end everything right now."

I remained silent. In response he delivered a quick shot to my gut. I doubled over for a second time and his knee came up to catch me in the face. Blood poured out of my mouth and covered his shoes. Yellow shoes that were dyed to match his suit. As I spit out blood I felt the rain that had been promising to fall come down all around us.

"Every time I look up you're getting in the way. You find something of mine in North Beach?"

"Dutch. Let's handle this the way we planned." Tina used the hushed tones of a parent talking to an errant child. She pushed him backward, gently, until she was able to wedge herself between the two of us. My captors loosened their grip and allowed me to stand on my own.

"Let him go," Dutch commanded. They did so, and once I was clear I spit blood onto the center of Dutch's suit. It made a nice pattern. He reared back to hit me but a voice yelled from the dock.

"What's going on over there?"

The five of us had been so locked in our drama we hadn't noticed the return of Sonny's boat. She walked toward us with Captain Stewart at her side. "Is there a problem here?" Captain Stewart looked at my bloody lip and the splatter on Dutch's shirt.

"No problem," I said. "I tripped and fell."

"And a little blood must've got on my shirt," Dutch continued.

"Son, are you sure you're okay? Do you want me to call the police?"

"No, I'm fine."

Stewart walked away. Dutch waited until he was out of earshot before he spoke to Sonny. "I want what you took from the apartment."

My mind went to the duffel bag we'd smuggled out through the park.

"I don't know what you're talking about," she said.

"That's the way you want to play it? You have a chance to fix this before it gets any worse."

"Fix it? Really? Are you a pimp who can perform resurrections? Bring Ivy back from the dead?"

"You got until tomorrow morning to make it right, Sonny." He turned to me. "Tell your boy, Holly, that with you back in town all the pieces are in place."

"That's what Smokey thought, too," I said.

Beside me Sonny smiled and slipped her hand in mine. It felt good, and it made sense on the wheel of crazy that I'd been using to chart my course of action.

"You picked the wrong team, baby girl," Dutch said.

"Yeah," she answered, "so did Ivy."

FORTY

"Let me get you a cold towel and some ice."

We were met by Kiros at the front door of Sonny's apartment. He sniffed at the blood that had splattered the hem of my pants, then walked away when he decided it wasn't fresh enough.

"Was Dutch talking about the duffel bag we took from Ivy's apartment?"

She returned from the bathroom with a wet towel. I wiped the blood from my lips and chin.

"That stuff belongs to Ivy."

"He didn't think so." I threw the towel into the sink as Sonny helped me peel off my shirt. Her hands rested on the tattoo on my chest. "Is it worth dying for? 'Cause he plans to kill you."

"I'm not going to die."

I ignored her answer and stretched out on the couch with the ice pack on my forehead. Sonny changed her dress and I stayed out of her way while she made a pot of tea, poured it out, then pulled meat out of the freezer for dinner. She separated a basket of laundry into three piles before dumping it all back into the same basket. She'd shown such bravado with Dutch, but the reality of her friend's death sank in as she tried to burn off her anxiety with useless tasks. Unlike Billy, there had been no pageantry associated with Ivy, just a bald sadness that let Sonny know she was on her own.

At the far end of the loft, the image of a clock was projected onto the wall. It was almost time for me to meet Buttermilk. "Listen, I need to meet up with somebody. Will you be alright here by yourself?"

She nodded and started a second pot of tea.

"I'll only be gone an hour or so."

"That's fine. Take these." She searched a drawer beneath the sink until she came up with a second set of keys. "Let yourself in when you get back."

"Don't go anywhere, Sonny."

"I'm not. I just want to lie down for a while."

"I'm serious. His boys came after you once. Don't antagonize the man any further."

"I'm not scared of Dutch, Maceo. He's a coward."

"Then you be one, too. That's how you'll stay alive."

"So Ivy wasn't the last person on this earth who cared about me?"

I shook my head.

"That's good to know." She smiled. "But maybe you'd better leave before you do something crazy like ask me to marry you."

I studied her for a minute, then I reached for a pen and paper. "If anything happens while I'm gone, call this number. Ask for Clarence, tell him what you know, then tell him to get in touch with Holly."

She let the paper sit on the counter between us. "You trust me that much, Maceo?"

"I have to, don't I? So don't bring any unnecessary heat. Dutch will slip. He'll take himself out of the game on his own. Alright?"

"Alright."

I hesitated. "You know I don't believe you."

"I'm glad you're here, Maceo. You don't have any reason to trust me, but I would miss you if you were gone."

I pulled her in for a hug, then a kiss. Before long we were behind the velvet curtains and reclined against the pillows of her bed. She ran hotter and colder than anyone I'd ever met and I told her so.

She leaned forward. "Is that what you think?"

"I just don't know how you switch from one channel to the next without skipping a beat."

In response, she swung her legs across my body and planted herself firmly on top of me.

"What's the matter, Maceo? You want to know if I'm working you?" Her voice was a whisper, her eyes locked on mine. She ground her hips, soft and slow, above me. Her eyes left my face and went to the horizon. They stayed there even when her head dropped down. She ran her tongue down the side of my neck, then along my scar. There was a smile on her face, even warmth, but she was far away when she looked at me again. She stopped mid-grind and pulled herself upright.

"When you see that look, Maceo, that's when it's time to go. That's when you'll know I'm working you." There was nothing to say to that. Afterward, the sex was fast and specific, like the punctuation at the end of a sentence.

When I stood to pull on my pants, Sonny remained stretched

out on top of the covers like the Cheshire cat. I half-expected her to disappear but she was all there, so comfortable with her body that she didn't even bother to cover herself with a blanket. From her window I could see the remains of an old baseball field etched in the dirt around the train tracks. The infield and home plate were sliced in half by the rails and I wondered which one had come first. I wondered if the yard workers gave up playing after the tracks were built or if they improvised and jumped the tracks while chasing down a ball. Before I turned away, I spotted faded white letters on the ground. VISITOR. HOME.

"Out on the boat today," I asked her, "what did you say that you didn't want me to hear?"

"I made a promise to Ivy."

"What was it?"

"Nothing much. I just told her I promised to bury Dutch with a stake in his heart."

On the street I used a pay phone to call Holly. It was a pager without voice mail so I typed in the return phone number and code eleven, the number of my old baseball jersey. I answered on the first ring when the call came back.

"Hello?"

"Is this Maceo?" It was a woman, and she butchered my name by placing a hard *k* right in the middle.

"Yeah?"

"He'll be at Millionaire's Row in fifteen minutes."

The location made sense and it was right up Holly's alley. Mountain View Cemetery, where Billy was buried, was also a park that serviced joggers and power walkers who weren't intimidated by the gravestones or the funeral processions. It had been designed by Frederick Law Olmsted, the same man who'd put together New York's Central Park, and it had a hill section dubbed Millionaire's Row because of its elaborate monuments. There were Kelloggs and Ghirardellis at Mountain View, the architect Julia Morgan, and, according to Daddy Al, even Elizabeth Short, the woman known the world over as the Black Dahlia.

I waited in front of a crypt built to resemble an Egyptian pyramid. I didn't recognize the name but I had a clear view of the narrow roads that led up to my perch on the hill. It was from there that I spotted the sedan carrying Holly. It was the same one that had picked him up from the park in Montclair.

"What happened to your lip?" he asked.

"Dutch. He was at the funeral. Had a message for you."

He waited.

"He said to tell you that with me back in town all the pieces are in place."

"What's that mean?"

"I don't know, but he named everybody who was at Smokey's house the night he died."

"Everybody?"

"Everybody. Including Felicia and Crim."

"So, Emmet's running his mouth?"

"That's my guess." I nodded toward the car. "Who's the girl?"

"Lisa. I been staying with her out on Eighty-first."

"She the one who called me?"

"Yeah, I planned to stay with her until tomorrow but her place is too hot."

"So what you want me to do?" I asked.

"Go by Rook's, pick up some money for me. I got about twenty thousand in cash over there, IDs, and keys to a car I keep out in San Jose." He paused. "Shit." He looked out at the southern end of the Bay. Oakland was spread out beneath us like a diorama, the water, hills, and bridges forming a chassis for the flatlands. From on high it looked too pretty to be so treacherous, but it was, and the nicknames for the various neighborhoods told the story: Dog Town, the Lower Bottom, Ghost Town.

"How long you gonna be gone?" I asked him.

"Long as it takes. You can hit me on my pager once you get the money."

"You could go to the house out in Louisiana." The house had been offered to me once as a refuge and I had turned it down.

Holly did the same. "I'm not gonna disrespect Daddy Al like that. Besides, I ain't letting these fools run me out of town for good. Just need to regroup, close ranks." He didn't look as sure as he sounded. "I'll tell Rook you'll be there about seven."

"Right after I see Lemon."

He gave me a pound, then hustled down the hill and back to the sedan. I watched him and Lisa drive off, his head barely visible in the passenger seat. After a while he disappeared.

At the Greyhound station Buttermilk was out front talking to another homeless man. He waved at me when he saw my car. Before I got out I pulled a bag of lemon drops from the glove box as an offering. Many people thought Lemon got his nickname from the shape of his head or the color of his skin, but it was because of his addiction to the sour candy he preferred as a kid. I didn't know if crack had cured that jones, but it was worth a try.

"Moneybags!" Buttermilk shouted. "I was just telling my friend Barry here about you. I told him that every time I see you, you got a new bruise. Look at that. Somebody popped you in the mouth. If you stop talking crazy to people, they might stop hitting on you."

"That's good advice."

"You ain't gonna take it though, is you? Don't matter none to me. Every time I see you with a new bruise I make a little more money."

"You hiring?" Buttermilk's friend opened a mouth absent of teeth.

"You should hire him, Moneybags. Barry's a good man. Us hobos got a union, and his dues is all paid up."

"Another time," I said.

Buttermilk tipped an imaginary hat at Barry and we moved off. He whispered with his hand on the side of his mouth.

"I found that crackhead you was looking for. He wasn't hard to find, 'cause crackheads tend to have big mouths, arguing, talking fast, itching and scratching. There ain't much dignity in that if you ask me. A drink'll put hair on your chest, but crack," he paused, "you know how many crackheads kill their mamas?"

I wasn't up to the social war between drug addicts and alcoholics so I cut off his tirade. "Where's he at? You seen him?"

"You been listening? He's at the Dunlap, right next door to the Burke House. I got your money back from Burke 'cept for the five dollars I paid the counterman to let me out of the contract."

"Tell you what. I'll help you move into the Dunlap; that way I can look around for Lemon."

"Don't have to look. Just told you. He ain't hard to find."

Buttermilk was right. Lemon wasn't hard to find. He was

parked in a third-floor bedroom two doors down from the shared bathroom. The smell was overwhelming, but his room was clean. I recognized him on sight, though crack had stripped his bones of the fat I remembered from childhood. A small transistor played talk radio on the windowsill above his single bed.

"Nice place." I stepped into the room and placed the lemon balls on the paint-chipped dresser. In response he gave me the slow, sleepy blink of a cow.

"I'm Maceo Redfield. You remember me?"

"Yeah, I remember you. Cotton used to live with you on Dover Street when we were kids. That why you here? I wondered how long it would be before ya'll found my hideout."

"You were expecting me?" I asked him.

"I was expecting somebody."

"Why's that?"

"'Cause I know where the bodies are buried." He stretched out his hand for the lemon balls. I grabbed them off the dresser and handed them over. I watched as he popped five or six into his mouth and made the requisite faces.

"What do you think about everything that's going on? Think Cotton killed that girl?"

"Nope. Don't have it in him. If he did he woulda killed his father. Cotton's a victim."

"Why you say that?"

"'Cause I know him."

"You seen him recently?"

He got up and opened the small closet near the window. The top shelf was filled with boxes of Knockers. Lemon pulled down a few and revealed the blinding white sneakers inside. None of them had been worn. I counted twenty-five boxes.

"That's my savings account." He popped more lemon balls into his mouth. "When my pockets get low, I trade a pair off for cash."

"So Cotton still comes around?"

"Whenever he's feeling guilty he shows up throwing money around, talking about the old days."

"What's he got to feel guilty about?"

"Guilty about the way he did his boy. There's no reason I should be living like this."

I let that go. There was no way to reason with a dope fiend, or a man intent on blaming others for the fate he'd created for himself.

"He never offered to help you out?"

He shook his head. "Allaina put a stop to that, but now that shit is coming back on him."

"I heard that you and Allaina didn't get along."

"We were cool at the beginning, before she had any power. She even tried to seduce me once." He reacted to my look of disbelief. "You don't have to believe me."

"I don't."

"Neither did Cotton, and look where that got him. Tell you this. If she didn't do it, how come I know she got a string of dice tattooed near her pussy?"

My mind flashed to Sonny sprawled naked on the bed, and the way the dice disappeared into the crease at the top of her leg. My blood ran cold, cold enough to freeze me in place. I couldn't talk.

Lemon looked me up and down. "What's wrong with you?"

"Nothing." I shook off the faint scent of ammonia and limes that seemed to seep up through the floorboards. My father was gathering his strength to make an appearance. I could feel it. "Maybe," I said, "you saw her tattoo at the swimming pool."

"That would be the easy answer, but it's not the right one."

"Why'd she try to seduce you?"

"Because I had her number. The moment she showed up I knew that was the end of my boy. He had it sick for her from the get, but I saw the real Allaina when she didn't think anybody was watching. That girl is broken."

"You talk to Cotton about it?"

He shook his head. "There's no talking to him when it comes to Allaina. Not then. Not now."

"What about Silas? Was he around when you lived with Cotton?"

"He came with Allaina."

"I thought Cotton brought him back from Europe."

"You thought a lot of shit that ain't true. Allaina knew Silas . . ."

"So she brought him in when she got those death threats?"

"Death threats?" He laughed. "Those weren't death threats. Allaina was being blackmailed."

"About what?"

"Couldn't ever figure it out, but she knew I was on her tail. That's when she had Cotton put me out."

"Any idea what it could be? Any guess?"

"Don't keep me up at night. That part of my life is done. Gone. My boy betrayed me and this is what my life is now. What does it matter anyway? Cotton ain't right and neither is she. Two broken halves don't make a whole."

FORTY-ONE

It was dark by the time I left the Dunlap. I found a pay phone on the street and paged Holly. I called three times and waited a half hour but I didn't get a return call. I tried to swallow my fears, but I'd known from the beginning that once the first layer was peeled away, the pieces would fall back to expose the wound and all its arteries.

The train I'd heard on my first day back wailed from the outer highway, but this time it wasn't a phantom sound. I tried not to let it spook me. I used the adjacent booth to try and reach Sonny, engaging both phones, but I got no answer. She'd told me she was going to sleep but I knew better. Minutes later the 880 Freeway disappeared beneath my wheels as I made my way back to Emeryville. The streets around her house were empty and I didn't see her car. I pushed open the front door and met darkness.

"Sonny?" I called out. "Sonny!"

Kiros was curled in a corner beneath the window. There were

two large bowls of water on the floor in the kitchen, as if she'd planned to be gone for a while. On the counter the piece of paper with Holly and Clarence's phone numbers sat where I'd left it. I tried Holly again from the house phone, then gave myself forty minutes to search Sonny's apartment while I waited on his call. A quick search didn't turn up the duffel but I hadn't thought for a second that it was in the house, and I knew it was no longer in my hotel room.

Kiros kept an eye on me as I walked around the apartment overturning pillows and cushions, opening drawers, and flipping through envelopes filled with bills, letters, discarded pieces of paper, and notes. I didn't know what I was looking for but I kept going. In her bedroom I pulled two boxes from beneath the bed. One was filled with clothes, the other with broken pieces of jewelry. Nothing useful. Sonny's apartment was like a hotel room. Despite the clutter it didn't feel as if there was anything she couldn't leave behind at a moment's notice. I thought about that as I headed out the door.

On Bancroft Avenue I turned down Eighty-first, searching the driveways of the one-story houses, looking for Lisa's sedan. While I overturned Sonny's apartment I remembered that Holly said he was staying with Lisa on Eighty-first, a street with a lot of drug activity and all the teenage villains that went with it. It would have been easy for one of them to spot Holly and turn him in for the underworld rewards. His reign had gone on longer than most, and there were meaner, greedier criminals born every day.

Three of the streetlights in the middle of the block were shot out, so I had a hard time identifying cars. I got all the way to East

Fourteenth without finding the sedan, so I made a U-turn at the hamburger stand and doubled back. At that moment I was glad I'd made the decision to rent a truck from Black. The El Camino would have attracted too much attention but I missed the security and power of the big car. The second pass revealed the sedan parked at the top of the driveway adjacent to the elementary school.

It was easy to miss. The streetlight in front was bent at the knee, where a car had rammed into it, and the lights along the side of the blue-and-white house were out. I heard gunshots in the distance, a sound that, since the onset of Oakland's drug wars, often marked nightfall, so I kept the truck running as I jogged up the driveway. A bumper sticker for Mills College with a corner ripped off was the same one I recognized from Montclair and the cemetery. It was the same car, but the last time I'd seen it the back windows hadn't been shattered and the back door was still on its hinges.

I left Eighty-first to stop at a pay phone outside the McDonald's at Eastmont Mall, where kids were already gathering for the Side Show, a makeshift car exhibition that was the bane of the local police force because of the souped-up cars paired with the equally reckless, sometimes underage drivers. While I waited for Holly's return call I watched a kid in a remade brown Camaro do spirals and doughnuts in the middle of the street, burning rubber into the pavement and barely missing the bystanders who cheered at his antics. Fifteen minutes later, when the same Camaro came up for a second turn in the spotlight, there was still no call from Holly. I tried another number.

"Oakland Police Department." A female voice came on the line followed by a steady beeping that let me know the call was being recorded.

"I'm looking for Detective Philip Noone."

"He's on a call, sir. Can I transfer you to another detective?"

"No, uh, just let me leave a message for him. This is Maceo Redfield." I squinted at the faded numbers on the pay phone and gave them to her. "I'll be at this number for about ten minutes."

The phone rang in five. "Noone here."

"Noone," I said, "this is Maceo."

"Well, well, well, your black ass must be in a world of trouble if you're calling me."

"Listen"—I cut him off—"let me ask you a question."

He was silent.

"You there?" I asked.

He grunted in response.

"Tell me this," I said. "If it all comes down and Holly's not involved, can you walk away? Can you walk away without pushing anything?"

"You questioning my integrity?"

"You stalling?"

"What you got, Maceo? Don't waste my time."

"Answer my question or I stop talking right now."

He blew out a long breath. "If he's not dirty on this, then he's not dirty on this. Simple as that."

"Is it that simple?" Oakland had recently been plagued by a crew of vigilante cops who called themselves The Fury and were more crooked and ruthless than the criminals and citizens they terrorized.

"It's that simple. Anything else?"

"That's all I needed to know."

"Now, what do you have?"

"Nothing, yet. . . ."

"But you're involving yourself in police business?"

"I can't help that things fall in my lap."

"After you knock them off the shelf." His laugh was dry. "Listen, son, your boy Holly may not be guilty but he ain't clean. Not by a long shot."

The line went dead, and I left East Oakland and the circus act of bored and restless teenagers trying to beat back another weekday night. On the drive back to the north side I tried not to think the worst about Holly's fate, but when I made the turn at San Pablo and Fifty-seventh, my father appeared in the rearview mirror. I closed my eyes, once, then twice, to shake him loose, but he stayed in the same place until I opened the window and let the cold night air scatter him into pieces. My nose burned with the acrid scent of his presence and I knew right then, though it wasn't confirmed until I spotted flames shooting into the sky above Rook's, that Holly was gone.

FORTY-TWO

Fire trucks blocked the alley as a group of people gathered at the corner of Stanford Avenue and watched the orange-and-yellow flames spiral and jump to the adjacent buildings. The roof of Benevolent Sect International, a Holy Roller outfit with Oakland tight in its grip, caught like a matchstick and caved in with a loud creak as the wood and beams gave way under the pressure.

"What happened?" I asked a man in a jean jacket.

"Rook's went up in smoke about thirty minutes ago. Don't know how it happened; the place been closed since this after- noon. Fire started quick, ate up the building on the left."

I watched the flames, then turned around to scan the crowd made up of neighborhood folks, some of them wearing house- coats and slippers as they watched the businesses burn. Across the street a second crowd gathered as people exited the 72 bus idling on the corner. When the bus pulled away I spotted the telltale signs of the Jamaican's silhouette, and when he stepped under the streetlight my hunch was confirmed. I hustled back to my truck, hoping that Rasta Man stayed put while I brought the car around, but by the time I returned he was gone. I circled the block two or three times, weaving in and out of traffic on San Pablo while I scanned the sidewalks, looking for him.

Before giving up and heading back to Sonny's, I went down Powell Street to Beaudry and hit a U-turn just as Rasta Man drove past in a decrepit-looking green Jeep painted in camouflage. Before I hit the gas pedal I looked in the rearview for my father but he was gone. I stayed at least three cars behind as Rasta Man drove west on San Pablo and picked up the Nimitz Freeway near Broadway. About ten miles down the highway he exited at Hegenberger Road and followed the loop until we were deep in the warehouse district that abutted San Leandro Creek. The streets were bare except for a meatpacking warehouse where a few men went about a shift change. Five blocks away, those same men were mere specks in the mirror as I cut the lights of my truck. Ahead I saw the red of Orieux's brakes before he turned into an alley. I jumped out of the car before I lost sight of him, then stayed low against the buildings as I made my way closer. I didn't know what I was getting into, or even if I was on the right track, and I didn't question the stroke of luck, or destiny, that had put me in the path of my attacker, but I didn't chance it either. I reached for a jagged rock lying loose on the ground. I tested its weight, then kept going.

I made it to the corner just as Orieux reached a low-slung, cinder-block building near the stagnant waters of the creek. He leaned against a large metal door as if he were eavesdropping. The sound of something from inside made him reach into his waistband and pull out a gun. I squeezed the rock I'd picked up and let go with a sizzler, the way I once had on the mound. The rock hit a window at the roofline of an adjacent building and the glass shattered, then crashed to the ground.

Orieux jumped, his gun at the ready, but he didn't have a target in the dark spaces between the buildings. I hid myself in the anemic shrubbery near my car as he backed away from the light. The extra precaution didn't help. While I contemplated my next move his head came off in a blaze of skin, bone, and muscle. I dropped to the ground and rolled beneath my car as Orieux's body hit the ground. His gun clattered on the pavement, and a stray bullet ricocheted against the gray buildings that were draped like sentinels along the shoreline.

The door to the warehouse snapped open and I saw Declan, or maybe it was Luther, come out and look down at the remains of the Jamaican. He grabbed the man's feet and pulled him backward into a dark alcove near the back of the building. I waited for him to go back inside before I ran toward the back of the warehouse. Through the filmy glass of a broken window, I saw an empty room streaked with blood.

I stepped away from the window, out of sight of the carnage, and right into the barrel of a gun. I recognized the feel of cold steel at the base of my neck, but not the wild-eyed look of Holly, who moved the gun in one swift motion from my neck to my temple. His face was swollen, caked with blood, and an open wound at his throat looked raw and angry. His eyes bore into mine, but I swear he couldn't see me, and I wasn't sure he'd care if he could.

"Holly," I said, hoping the sound of my voice would burrow down deep enough to lift him out. "Holly," I repeated, but it didn't register. He backed me into the warehouse, where overhead lights highlighted the gore. The floor was slippery with human waste.

With the gun pressed against my cheek I could smell the smoky discharge that let me know it had been fired. In the corner I saw Clarence standing with the Samoans. The three of them looked at Holly like he was a beloved dog but one they might have to put down no matter how much they'd hate it. Before my options evaporated I tried, again, to bring him back.

I said his name. He responded by jamming the barrel into my ear. My head was forced into an awkward angle so I turned my body to compensate. My eyes landed on a second body, and only then was I able to grasp the pornographic violence of that warehouse. The place stunk of piss and shit, blood and burnt skin.

The second body was draped over a chair, the leg bent at an odd angle, the fingers of the right hand torn off. The rubbery pose of the body confirmed for me that the man was dead. Flies had already started to gather and feast.

"Holly, man, what the fuck?" I'd stepped into a war zone and I didn't know, despite the gun in my face, who'd been the instigator of the mayhem. Clarence's boys were killers, maybe even Clarence himself, but Holly was the one with the gun, unable to register my presence or shake the haunted, traumatized look in his eyes.

"What happened, man?" I kept my voice steady. "I went by Rook's. Somebody set it on fire. I followed the Jamaican from there."

The pressure eased on the gun, so I kept talking. "I saw Lemon, too, caught up with him over at Dunlap. He said that Cotton had been there. You know about that? You hear about that?"

Holly dropped the gun to his side, which allowed me to face him. There were burns on his arm, cuts on his scalp, and bruises across his bloodied knuckles. But beneath all that chaos, I saw enough resolve to let me know he was still in there somewhere, holding on with a tenuous grip.

Since I'd known Holly I'd defined my role in our friendship as secret-keeper. I was the crown prince of unasked questions but this time, now, there were just too many to be enveloped by coded silence. There was a body count, and my best friend held a gun in his hand, the way I always knew he could. Like he was born to it.

"Who's in the chair?" I asked.

That question more than anything else seemed to bring him back. He blew a long stream of air through his cracked nose.

"I fucked up, Maceo." His words were so soft I wasn't sure he'd even spoken. "He wasn't snitching. It wasn't him."

His words left me to process what my eyes refused to see. I thought immediately of Yolanda and the day I'd seen her planning her future even as it disappeared. It was Emmet in the chair, shoeless, undignified, the clothes he wore with so much style shredded and stiff from the dried blood of his wounds. I wasn't a fan of Emmet, but once upon a time before it all went wrong he'd ridden to my aid. My mind filled with images of Yolanda, pregnant and hoping that it would turn out alright.

Clarence dropped a hand on Holly's shoulder. "We're all that's left, baby," he said as he turned away from Emmet's mangled body, "me and you, and we're gonna handle it. We're gonna handle it all."

The two men exchanged a pound while I looked on. "No doubt," I heard Holly whisper, "that bitch ain't gonna win."

FORTY-THREE

Fifteen minutes later Holly and I were on Highway 80, moving north toward Oakland. My hands shook as images of Orieux's head exploding off his shoulders replayed in my mind alongside stills of Emmet's battered body. Beside me Holly used discarded newspaper to clean himself up.

"What happened at that warehouse?" I asked.

He remained silent, which was his right. But I had a right, too. I wasn't going blind into a mission where I couldn't distinguish between friends and enemies. I was too shocked by what I'd witnessed, too floored by my own naiveté, and I needed answers. I'd come back to Oakland to seek redemption, and on some level to be a savior, but not to be a fool. I wasn't going to hide, not one more day, not even for my boy.

I gave him one more chance.

"What happened at the warehouse?"

When he didn't answer I pulled the car off the freeway near

the Oakland Coliseum and cut the engine. The Raiders were still being held hostage in Los Angeles, so the big gray open-air structure was used for car shows, local events, and A's games. It was an eyesore, seventies architecture gone wild, but it still stood, hoping like the rest of us that the silver and black would come home. At that moment, though, football was the last thing on my mind. I got out of the car and motioned for Holly to do the same.

He took his time unfolding himself from the passenger seat. He sighed as if I were an overcurious child who needed to have the ways of the world explained one more time. His voice was hoarse when he spoke. "You think I killed Emmet?"

I didn't answer, didn't fill in the blanks with my own assumptions. I wanted him to answer, explain his world, this life, and the way it was lived. When he faced me the look in his eye was primal. He had a reservoir of anger, and I could tell by the fierce clenching and unclenching of his fists that he was straining to keep the tide at bay. We stood in silence as cars passed. The rain continued to fall steady and hard.

When he finally spoke I heard his words in my heart before they registered anywhere else. They brought me up short. I'd never heard Holly speak with regret. Not once.

"I chose this life," he said, "I chose this life when it looked beautiful."

We returned to the car, to the mission that would either be a beginning or an ending.

———

Ten minutes later, when the Tombs, downtown Oakland's county jail, came into view off the freeway, Holly pointed to the exit. "Go by Lemon's place." We exited near the police station, a

stone's throw from the welfare hotels on San Pablo. Outside the
Dunlap, a coroner's van was double-parked while a few of
the residents milled around out front. I didn't see Buttermilk
in the crowd as we got out of the car. I gave Holly my coat, despite the cold, just to hide some of the damage that had been
done to him. It did no good because even without visible signs of
his torture he had the look of combat that made at least two people cross to the other side of the street as he passed.

We circled the block, twice on foot, without finding Buttermilk, so I drove to the Greyhound station in search of his
partner, Barry. I found him inside eating sunflower seeds and
watching a black-and-white TV attached to the arm of the plastic chair.

"'Member me?" I slid into the seat beside him. "Buttermilk's
friend."

"I remember," he said, but he kept his eyes glued to the fuzzy
reception on the twelve-inch television. "You didn't give me no
money."

"Can you use some now?"

He perked up. "I can always use some money. What you need
me to do?"

"I need you to go over to the Dunlap. Get Buttermilk for
me."

"This about the crackhead that got killed?"

"You know about that?" I asked him.

"Everybody know." He rubbed his fingers together, then
stuck out an open palm.

"You'll get paid, man. Take a walk with me first."

He followed me outside, where Holly sat in the truck I'd
parked at the curb. He rolled down the window when he saw me

approach with Barry. Without drawing attention to the car I stood close enough for Holly to hear our conversation.

"So, you said it was a crackhead who died over there."

"Where's my money?" I gave him a dollar. He frowned. "Is that all?"

"Earn the rest."

"It was that crackhead. The one you was looking for. Somebody stabbed him." He took his time folding the dollar I'd given him. Once he'd slipped it into his pocket he held out his hand.

"How do you know it was the man I was looking for?"

"I just know."

"Did Buttermilk tell you that?"

"He didn't have to tell me. I saw it for myself." Holly shifted and I knew he was listening. "We were keeping an eye on him. Somebody came after him once you left. Butter heard them arguing, tearing up furniture, then the other man ran out."

"What man?"

"A tall man. A real, real tall man. Smelled like he bathes on a regular basis." He cleared his throat. Loud. I gave him a five-dollar bill. He nodded in appreciation before he continued. "He had a nice car, one of them fast, red things. Parked it away from the hotel but I saw him get in. He went up on the curb when he drove off."

"How'd you know Lemon was stabbed?"

"Lemon? That was his name?"

I nodded.

"Me and Butter went in there. We saw. He was stuck like a pig. In the gut and in the throat."

"Why were you in the room?"

"Why you think?" He held up a foot encased in brand-new sneakers. Knockers. Blazing white. "For these, man. Shit, don't you know it's cold outside this time of year?"

I did know. I gave him another bill, then I drove back to Emeryville.

FORTY-FOUR

Inside the apartment Kiros had moved to the couch but the place was just as I'd left it. Overturned and empty. Kiros looked up, issued a long growl at Holly, but kept his distance.

"Who stays here?" Holly asked. "The girl from Cotton's house? Sonny?"

I nodded.

"Where's she at now?"

"Don't know." I pointed at the bathroom. "You can go in there. Clean up. Do what you have to do."

When he came out I handed him a beer, then got back to the conversation we'd started on the side of the freeway. I'd given him a reprieve, not an exit. "What happened?"

Though Holly rarely drank, he downed the liquid in one long swallow. He'd placed a makeshift bandage across his throat. His voice was hoarse when he spoke.

"I got snatched up on Eighty-first. Clarence's boys were in the neighborhood. They saw it go down, but they lost us in San

Leandro. By the time they found me, you saw what happened. Emmet was already dead."

He reached for another beer.

"What happened the night of the All-Pro? Was Cotton being blackmailed?"

He nodded. "By the time he called me in they'd already got him for about three million dollars. He wanted it to stop. He called me in to straighten it out."

"How'd Ivy come in?"

"She was the money drop, but she was also a weak link. I worked her for information, tried to get her to turn. She was close, but then Dutch's boys saw her with me and Cotton."

"Who found her in that hotel room?"

"Cotton found her the night she was killed. The police found her two days later."

"How's that?"

"Do Not Disturb sign, air conditioner on high."

"Were you with Cotton when he found the body?"

"No, Allaina was. He called me afterward."

"Allaina?"

He nodded.

"Lemon said Allaina was the one that brought Silas to town."

He looked surprised, then his face turned to stone. "What else he tell you?"

"That Allaina has a tattoo at the top of her leg. A string of dice." I paused. "Same one Sonny's got, and Sonny used to work for Dutch."

He rubbed his fingers across his eyes, pained, and I saw the open, pink meat of his knuckles. "What the fuck did this nigga do? Is Cotton setting me up?"

I couldn't answer that, but I knew who could. And she did it without being present. It took an hour, but once everything was overturned it came down to a photograph. A single picture with Las Vegas as a backdrop and Sonny, Ivy, and Allaina smiling into the camera. On the back were three names: Fantasia, Ivy, Ginger.

I held it in my hand and remembered Sonny speaking of a third girl named Ginger, a woman who'd gotten married and shaken her friends, two friends linked to her past—Ivy and Ginger—which meant Sonny was Fantasia, a name I'd heard more than once.

Holly was quiet as he held the picture in his hand.

"Where's the money from Ivy's drop?" I wondered out loud. *And where's Sonny?* I asked myself.

————

We sat there until nearly midnight when the lock finally turned in the front door. Sonny took the state of her apartment and Holly's presence in stride before dropping the duffel at my feet.

"Looking for this?"

————

The money was spread out before us on the table as Sonny dressed Holly's wounds. She redid the work he'd attempted, cleaned the splinters out of his throat, and poured peroxide on his cuts until they bubbled clean. Finally, I pulled the towel from her hands and sat her down between us.

"Did you help Ivy blackmail Cotton?" I asked. I already knew about Allaina's involvement but I wanted Sonny to pass a test for me.

"It was always Allaina."

"Why was she blackmailing her own husband? She has as much access to Cotton's money as anybody."

"She didn't want Cotton, Maceo. You look at the world like it's simple. Cotton was a mark."

"What do you mean, a mark?"

"Allaina worked for Dutch just like me and Ivy. She was on con and Cotton was her mark. Silas planted her there. He knew Cotton and he knew Dutch and Allaina from Sacramento. When Silas coached at State, Dutch supplied him with whatever he needed; money, cocaine, little girls. By the time he came up for air, Dutch owned him. It didn't take much to get him to flip on Cotton."

"How'd they pick him?"

"Bad luck and stupidity. Cotton trusted Silas, which he never should have done. He wanted him to be his father or something, but Silas was jealous of him. When Cotton met Allaina in New York it was a setup.

"Silas spent months feeding Allaina information about Cotton. By the time she met him she knew everything about him, which made the scam easy. She knew what he liked, what he didn't like, what he was afraid of, all the drama with his father," she nodded at me, "his relationship to your family. He was a john every minute of the day but he never knew it. Only person who did was Silas. He got a kickback so he kept his mouth shut. Dutch had his hand in every one of Cotton's pockets . . ."

"Until Holly showed up," I finished.

Sonny nodded. "Allaina had gotten rid of Lemon. She discredited him enough that Cotton wouldn't listen to a word he said about her." She nodded at Holly. "You were nothing but a lucky break. It wasn't ever about you. Silas heard Cotton talking about Smokey. It took him awhile to put it together, but when he did, Dutch saw all the money he lost when Smokey died come back into his life.

"Dutch had already worked it to make it look like Allaina was getting death threats. Cotton had Silas hire security. Dutch's boys. Without knowing it, Cotton bankrolled Dutch's whole enterprise. He could've stopped there because Cotton was easy, the perfect victim, but he wanted to destroy you and he got greedy."

"Lemon saw through all that?" Holly asked.

Sonny nodded. "So Allaina got rid of him as fast as she could. If Cotton had had other people in his life the scam wouldn't have worked, but he didn't. He was insulated, didn't have a safety net. How many times have you heard Cotton say that if he didn't know you before he got famous he didn't trust you? And the one exception he made to that rule—Allaina—turned out to be the most poisonous viper in the nest."

Holly shook his head as Sonny went on. "Cotton kept his agent, manager, coach, and teammates at arm's length. They knew about his business, but not a thing about his home life. He didn't socialize with them and Allaina didn't socialize with the wives. It was perfect," she paused again, "until Holly came along."

"What about Ivy?" I asked.

"Ivy was a pawn. Ginger—I mean Allaina—used her. Ivy *thought* she was in on everything, and she might have been at the beginning, but she found out recently that they planned to cut her out and skip town."

"You said Ivy was close to getting out. Did Dutch know that?"

Sonny nodded at me but she kept her eyes on Holly. "I told Maceo, the other day, that Ivy met somebody who made her see the holes in her life." A look passed between the two of them. Sonny's eyes watered. "Are you Jay?" she asked him.

He glanced at me before he nodded.

"She loved you," Sonny said.

Holly didn't say anything, neither did I, and we gave Sonny the time she needed to get herself together. She crossed to the windows that looked down on the railroad tracks. In the distance, San Francisco sparkled in the night sky. She resumed her speech with her back to me and Holly.

"I never walked a track, not once, in all my years with Dutch. Neither did Ivy. We did arranged dates. Never the streets, and as long as we had that . . ." She didn't finish and she didn't have to; her tone said everything. Somehow, in her mind, the distinction lifted her above the rest, and maybe that's what allowed her to sleep at night. I didn't press it, but there was a story there, a reason why Sonny sold her body. But I would never ask the hows and whys. She'd have to tell me on her own because I didn't have the arrogance or ignorance to ask a desperate or poor person what they'd stoop to in order to survive. I wouldn't ask because I knew too much about life. Besides that, the answer was in the question.

Survival.

I gave her a minute, then I pulled her back to the couch. She sat as close to me as possible, the money spread out in front of us, her hand wrapped in mine.

"How'd you know about the money?" I asked.

"Ivy told me the night she died. She'd planned to tell Cotton everything. That's why she went to meet him at The Gideon. Allaina must've found out about it." She motioned to the money. "And I bet you a million dollars she killed Ivy. Ivy was going to blow the scam and reveal Allaina's connection to Dutch. And Ivy knew, just like I do, that Allaina would die before she'd let anything happen to Dutch."

We sat in silence as it came together. The three of us could only guess at the words exchanged between husband and wife when Cotton walked into the room and found Ivy's dead body, but the final result was that Allaina was gifted, a world-class con artist, because somehow her words, pleas, and explanations had convinced her husband to take the heat for her crime, and set up his oldest friend in the process.

FORTY-FIVE

When Sonny finished talking, Holly went to a phone booth to call Clarence, and when Sonny went into her room I made a call myself. The receiver was back on the cradle by the time they'd both returned. This time I knew Holly's hand before he revealed it. It was easy. All roads led back to Timber Hills.

Thirty minutes later the three of us were at the first guard gate of Cotton's house. It was empty, and so was the second. We turned the cars around, parked them at the bottom, and walked back up the hill. When we got to the top the house was dark. I had the duffel bag slung over my shoulder.

"Let me stash this," I said. "Me and Sonny will meet ya'll around back."

Holly nodded but Clarence didn't acknowledge me or her. He still viewed me as a parade of mistakes. I left him to his silence and followed the trees down into the canyons around the hawk cage. Sonny stored the duffel bag behind a rock near the top. We made it halfway to the house before we were met by the two guards I'd encountered before. They both had guns and I remembered that Sonny had said that all of Cotton's security was on Dutch's payroll. One of them, the one I'd argued with, pulled the blackjack from my pocket as I held my hands in the air. I didn't fight him but as we walked toward the garage I scanned the grounds for something, anything, to defend myself with. We walked past all eight of Cotton's cars—parked outside—and I couldn't find a single thing to use as a weapon.

Inside the garage we came upon Holly on his knees in front of Dutch, nearly unrecognizable because of the fresh wounds on his face. His sweatshirt was stained the color of plums, and his arms were pulled so tight behind his back I thought his shoulder blades might pop out, but he didn't falter, not even in his battered state.

In the center of a floor covered in plastic Dutch sat in a chair holding a cane between his knees. The cane was caked with blood, the bottom cracked off and jagged. Behind him Derrin, Orieux's former partner in crime, affected an elaborate stance of boredom, like a bloodied prisoner and a crazy man holding a cracked cane were everyday business.

Dutch leaned forward so he was close to Holly's face. He didn't raise his voice but it carried in the empty space. I heard every word. "You know what's wrong with you low-rent niggers?" He used the word like a white man. "You don't have the soldier's soul to keep you strong."

In response, Holly spat blood on Dutch's white shirt.

Dutch looked down at the stain, and without a change of expression he brought his cane down on Holly's shoulder. Derrin pushed me forward. I landed at Holly's side. In the corner

Clarence was dazed but conscious, a trickle of blood trailing down his forehead.

Dutch followed my gaze. "He's next. After you."

"Then quit talking, nigga." Holly spoke between labored breaths. "Do something."

Dutch snickered. "Look at you, the last king, on his knees like one of my girls. This is just where I knew you would be. If it took me three years, ten, didn't matter: I was coming for you." He motioned at Clarence. "That's one." He pointed at us. "Two and three. Who I got left? Three or four more people, Felicia and her brother and anybody else who stood by and watched my cousin die, then made a profit off of it. No matter, I kept you on the street so you could make my money."

He laughed and poked the jagged edge of his cane into Holly's windpipe until he grunted in pain, and the open wound ran fresh with blood. Dutch ground the loose splinters into the skin by twisting the handle of the cane, then he reared back and struck Holly with it. The blow toppled him over. I took the weight of his body and we fell together. That's when Dutch's shoulder was splintered by a bullet.

The blast sent Dutch backward in his chair, the guards opened fire, and in the confusion I scrambled away. Through the back window of the garage above an abandoned office I saw the muzzle flash of a gun. Dutch tried to scramble for Derrin's dropped weapon, but the bullets hitting the ground kept him back. The guards ran toward a side door, guns drawn, and I saw them drop, one then the other, from blows to the back of the head. The Samoans.

Holly got to his feet and tried to shake the blood out of his eye. His left eye was swollen shut. He nudged Clarence with his foot while I untied his hands. Clarence moaned, which was all Holly needed. He picked up the chair that Dutch had inhabited so casually while he tortured him, raised it up, and crossed the room in three strides. He slammed the metal legs of the chair into Dutch's side. The wheels hit him in the back of the head and sent him to the ground. Holly was on him immediately, driving his fist again and again into Dutch's head. When the man was unconscious Holly stood up, breathing hard, and kicked him in the ribs. I pulled him back.

"Save him" was all I had to say.

One of the Samoans helped Clarence to his feet.

"Where's your girl?" Holly asked.

I looked around. In the chaos I didn't notice Sonny slip away. I thought of the money as did probably everyone else in the room. But I was wrong; she came back with Tina and Allaina. I don't know what she said to get them there but they came in like friends, not like women under siege. Holly and I exchanged looks. Allaina sized up the room, not noticing Dutch near the back tire of the lone car, and put her money on Holly. She played her last card. Concern.

"What happened?" She walked toward him with her hands outstretched. "You alright?"

Holly stepped back as she got closer, and to her credit, knowing when a con was up, Allaina dropped all pretense.

"Where's the money?" she asked.

Holly shook his head. "That all you worried about?"

"What else is there? My husband?" Tina remained silent as Allaina worked the lead.

Cotton chose that moment to make an appearance, coming through the side door from which the guards had tried to escape.

He held Marquis in his hands, and had a shellshocked look on his face. Allaina, for just a moment, looked panicked, but Tina had the good sense to try and run. Declan, or maybe Luther, stopped her in her tracks.

Allaina recovered quickly. Her eyes teared up at the sight of Cotton. "Help me." Her voice cracked at the end and then the tears spilled.

Cotton stared and I could tell that even after all that, all he'd probably heard, he still wanted to believe that she loved him. He'd been undone by the most simple of desires: the desire for a father's love and the need for a woman's heart.

"Motherfucker, what's it gonna take?" Holly's disgust was apparent. He'd read Cotton just as I had, and he'd seen the potential for more destruction if Allaina got away. He nodded, and the boys dragged Dutch into the center of the room by his feet. At the sight of him Allaina screamed like an animal and ran to his side.

She dropped down next to him, incoherent with grief, oblivious to everyone else. Marquis was half-deaf, but he understood the tenor of her pain, and his screams soon joined hers. Cotton looked lost. Holly's voice rose above it all.

"Look what you sold your boys out for, a chick with all them miles and she never gave a fuck about you."

"What could I do?" Cotton's voice was weak. "She's the mother of my boy." He held Marquis tight. "This is my boy, man, my only boy."

The word seemed to rouse Dutch. He looked up long enough to lock on Marquis, and play his trump. "Bring him to me," he said, plain enough for us all to hear. "Bring me my son."

Allaina looked up, triumphant. Even losing, she was still

going to win. She was still going to take the only thing that mattered: his son. Before it all dissolved I registered a shadow coming up behind Clarence. The final player. Silas. Before I had time to think, or second-guess, I acted on the same instinct that had probably driven Holly when he wanted to save my pitching arm. Blind faith. I jumped in front of Holly and right into the line of fire.

Epilogue

Outside, the flickering lights of five patrol cars, a fire truck, and two paramedic vehicles lit up the house like a carnival. In the midst of it all stood Daddy Al. Calm. Strong. Focused. He wore his signature black Stetson as red emergency lights swept back and forth across his tall frame. The wide-brimmed hat cast his face in shadow but I was glad to see him there.

I'd called him from Sonny's house when Holly left to phone Clarence, and my grandfather—steady as a rock—listened to everything I had to say, then listened harder to the telling silences that spoke of a night slipping out of control. He'd obviously made the decision to call the police when he didn't hear from me at the designated time, a precaution I'd tried to brush off, but as I reclined on the gurney feeling the searing heat of a wild bullet, I was grateful.

Silas had taken a shot at Holly, a shot that might've killed him, but I'd stepped up, like he'd done for me so many times before, and took the brunt of it. We'd both hit the ground as police burst through the door, and from there we watched Allaina, Dutch, Silas, and Tina turn on each other with lightning speed. They shouted accusations at each other as they were handcuffed and led away.

Detective Noone came in afterward with Daddy Al and Mrs. Ritchie, who told what she knew in an unbroken stream of venom aimed directly at Cotton's wife. Marquis witnessed it all, until Daddy Al gently took him from his father's arms and led him away. Cotton was so impotent with grief and betrayal that he ignored Marquis's screams for his mother. Allaina ignored them as well but for different reasons. She was focused on Dutch, shouting at the paramedics to take care of him, keep him safe, and not let him die. Cotton watched it all, mouth open, tears in his eyes as the farce of his marriage played out for all of us to see.

He reached out for Allaina as she passed in front of him but she lurched away, then spat at his feet. Before he had time to react to the slight, his lawyers raced onto the property to protect their franchise. Behind them television crews set up to project conjecture around the globe. They would never know the whole truth, which was good because the lack of facts would leave just enough room for good copy.

While Cotton's lawyers flanked him on four sides, the EMTs worked to stem the flow of blood from my shoulder, and a handcuffed Holly slumped against the hood of Noone's Crown Vic. He was spent from yet another betrayal with the same theme song as mine. Holly believed in the expression *his boys,* the loyalty that came with it, and yet he'd been done in by it twice. The words *his boys, my boys, my boy* had a terrain all their own, a whole universe of meaning, and it was that covenant that caused Holly to look everywhere but at his friends for the most obvious signs of danger.

I watched him until Sonny came up beside me and reached for my hand. While she stood there Daddy Al left the staircase after handing Marquis off to Mrs. Ritchie. He walked past the crowd of lawyers, cops, and Cotton as he tried to reach Holly. When Holly spotted him I saw him tense against the blow that had been coming for over two years. Holly knew he had to pay for Cissy. He knew he had to pay for it all, because he'd told me once that from the moment my family took him in he knew he had an expiration date, that the honorary Redfield title was just that. To prepare himself for that inevitability he'd made himself hard, forgot how to cry, and learned to trust nothing but his own survival instinct, yet when Daddy Al's hand came down on his shoulder in a gesture of support, I saw him break. He shattered into so many pieces I had to look away. I had focused for so long on all the ways Holly and I were linked by failure that I forgot our strength. Daddy Al. As long as he was there we could never be completely lost.

———

Later, after being released with a flesh wound that had ripped open the skin and muscle of my shoulder, I spent the night on Dover Street with Sonny, recounting the events of the night to Cissy, Gra'mère, and the twins. Emmet had been labeled a snitch, but it had been Cotton who fed information to Dutch in order to save his duplicitous wife from what he thought to be blackmail. Or maybe he'd always known the truth, and made the decision to sacrifice Holly for Allaina. We'd never know for sure because Cotton was lost to us, and as I sat across from Gra'mère she wondered aloud if

the Redfield womb churned out poisonous milk. I couldn't answer
that for her or myself, but when I slept that night with the most
imperfect woman of my life at my side, I did not dream; there was
just too much in my waking life to haunt me. I'd been determined,
since I arrived back in Oakland, to place the detritus of my life
everywhere but where it belonged: right at my own feet. It made
me feel like a fool to see it plain. So much bravado, so many ex-
cuses, so much noise, and not a single fucking clue.

I made a vow as I drifted off. I wouldn't leave, I wouldn't
run, in body or spirit, until I'd overturned every stone in my life
and found the answer to every question that had ever plagued
me, even the ones I did not want to hear.

—————

The next day we heard through the grapevine that Yolanda had
gone into labor upon hearing the news of Emmet's death. He'd
been found in the San Leandro warehouse, along with Orieux, by
a cleaning crew. Holly called me at Sonny's, and the two of us left
in my El Camino to pick him up at the Tombs where he'd spent
the night in custody. Lamb had worked overtime to get Holly out
on bail, and his legal maneuvering had been aided by the creep
show of cons that made up Dutch's camp. Allaina had turned on
Silas, Tina on Dutch, and Mrs. Ritchie on them all. A statement
from Cotton, who'd surrounded himself with high-priced
lawyers, absolved Holly of all involvement in Ivy's murder but he
hadn't been cleared of anything else.

"We should have brought him clothes." Sonny was in the
driver's seat as we watched Holly come through the metal doors
of the county jail. "We should have brought him something
clean."

She was right, but it would have been a superficial fix. He was out of lockup but he wasn't free. There was a debt to be paid, and whether the sentence was handed down in a legal arena or the more vicious arena of the streets, we would all pay for the lives lost. We'd contributed through blindness, bullets, and greed to the circus act of Oakland crime, and even if we tendered our payment in flesh and blood it would never be enough.

Rain pounded the pavement as the late afternoon sun made its final descent over Alta Bates Hospital. Holly, showered and changed but still bruised, held a bouquet of flowers in his bandaged hand as he asked a nurse for Yolanda Landry's room number. I walked beside him, groggy and guilty, my arm in a sling and cement in my heart as we searched the bright corridors for Yolanda. We found her with the door open and the baby in her lap.

"Hey, lady." Holly stepped into the room with the flowers leading the way. He dropped them on the bed and placed his hand on her shoulder. He kissed the top of her head. She reached up to weave her fingers through his damaged ones. If it pained him he didn't make it evident.

He looked down at the baby wrapped tight in a blue blanket. "Got yourself a boy, huh?" His smile was strained. "What's his name?"

"Does it matter?" she asked. Her body jerked with fresh tears and Holly caught the baby before he tumbled off her lap. He handed him off to me, and I made do with my good arm as Yolanda continued to cry. Outside, the sky did the same. Holly's shoulders shook with his own grief and I looked away from them both.

What had he said to me just the night before? That he'd chosen this life when it looked beautiful. Standing in the wreckage I wondered when that had been.

Was it the first time Billy rolled up with a brand-new car, the sun at his back, and a pocket full of cash? And had it been less than gorgeous when he'd carried Billy's casket a mere four years later?

Or was it beautiful the first time he realized that his new-found power and fortune erased the memories of his mother's neglect? And had it been less so when he realized that the memories were seared into stone?

Could it have possibly been the moment when he realized that Cissy was all his? And did it disappear when she lay battered and close to death because of the life he'd chosen to live?

My guess was that it was the most beautiful when it was only a dream, before it became the tangible reality of an angry, displaced boy.

Did any of it matter?

Not really, and not to the wolf who watched from his corner, ready to take his place at the table, and thankful, yet again, for the feast he was offered. His eyes fell to Emmet's son and he smiled. I held on tight. The baby was asleep and I was grateful because I didn't know if I had what it took to look him in the eye. He was another sacrifice, you see. A Black boy without a father.

You know that story, right?

You've heard it.

It's a story so old it doesn't even break your heart anymore.

Acknowledgments

Now for the most important yet one of the hardest sections of a book to write. I dread the writing of the acknowledgments simply because I cringe at the thought of forgetting anyone who has made an important contribution to these pages, whether it be through their editorial, research, promotional, or agenting skills, a much needed smile, or words of support when Maceo and the Redfields proved to be their most elusive. So to any and everyone, including the many readers of *The Dying Ground* who took the time to e-mail me their thoughts and opinions—to all of you I say that my gratitude is immeasurable. Thank you.

Individually I would like to thank the following:

The Tramble women: Nicole, Nichelin, and Nichelia, the best cheerleaders a bloodline can buy.

My girlfriends, who become more beautiful and kind with each passing year: Dioni Perez, Stacy Green-Weiland, Angela Scott, Lori Buster-Price, Julie Larson-Jackson, and Christine Marino.

Daniele Spellman, who always has time for a talk, a hug, a meal, or a laugh.

Richard Abate, my agent at ICM. All agents should measure themselves against your greatness.

Alex Kohner, an extraordinary lawyer and, dare I say, friend.

Melody Guy, a wonderful editor and, more important, a patient editor.

Brian McLendon, for such an amazing job with *The Dying Ground*. Glad you're back.

John Mosley, who, once again, has provided me with an amazing amount of inspiration. Family doesn't have to be blood.

Robert Lawrence Clark: How can I ever thank you for all your hospitality?

Jeannie Mueller, my personal foreign-rights agent. Thank you.

Charles Murray: The circle was complete in 2003.

The Edward Albee Foundation, for the time and space for me to complete *The Last King*.

The Zora Neale Hurston/Richard Wright Foundation for its wonderful acknowledgment.

Friends of Chester Himes: Thanks for your support.

Nolan Coleman, Sr., Versie May, Kate Lee, Tia Maggini, Chastity Whitaker, Jebediah Reed, Karen Rupert, Courtney Toliver, Keith Adkins, Ace Atkins, Thumper, Steve Tollefson, Tamar Love-Grande, Peggy Hicks, Desiree Eien, Rico E. Anderson, Tabahani Book Club, Ladies of Color Turning Pages, SITNOL of Northern California, James M. Marshall, Amy Cheney, Philip Seelenbacher, Cody's on 4th Street, Robin Green at Sibanye, T. Greenwood, SZ'ers, Martha Laham, Catherine Patterson, and Kobe Beauregard, my Akita muse.

For research purposes I used the following titles: *Oakland:*

The Story of a City by Beth Bagwell, *Public Heroes, Private Felons: Athletes and Crimes Against Women* by Jeff Benedict, *Weather of the San Francisco Bay Region* by Harold Gilliam, and *Brotherman: The Odyssey of Black Men in America—An Anthology,* edited by Herb Boyd and Robert L. Allen.

And last but not least, I thank Judy Faye, my wild joker, who keeps us together with a smile and a strong hand. I couldn't love you more.

The Last King

A Reader's Guide

Nichelle D. Tramble

Reading Group Questions and Topics for Discussion

1. The Oakland of *The Last King* is a city possessed by drugs and those who profit from them. Nonetheless, we still see a city that retains a sense of community and manages to hold together through waves of violence and crime. Is the city dying? Does the author believe, as one of her characters says, that the younger generation is killing the city?

2. *The Last King* is a story of betrayal and loyalty—the ultimate betrayal of loved ones and the enduring loyalty of friends and family. At times, however, it seems as though betrayal and loyalty mix together. Does Cotton's blind loyalty contribute to his situation?

3. During his two years away, Maceo knew he owed something to the friends and family he left behind, Holly in particular. When does he finally repay the debt he owes?

4. Truths are often starkly revealed in situations of extreme danger. Explain why Maceo says that the only time his life felt real to him was when he was searching for his friend's killer and trying to save the life of the woman he loved.

5. Sonny and Maceo are both trying to avenge their friends. Are they also searching for redemption? Sonny characterizes the attraction she and Maceo share as "misfit love." Is their relationship about more than just expediency?

6. Maceo is haunted by death—the deaths of his parents, his friends, and even his own dreams. He tries to outrun his demons but can never truly escape them. Why? Is the wolf chasing him, or is he chasing it?

7. The author sets her story at the intersection of crime and professional sports, with a cast of characters ranging from ballers and dealers to whores and crack addicts. Do the easy money and fast living associated with both crime and basketball make them natural companions? How do the gangster element and NBA mystique flavor the story?

8. Cotton, Holly, and Maceo were each abandoned by their parents at early ages, and all still bear the scars into adulthood. Despite the similarity of their experiences, the three are quite different. Discuss the similarities and differences between the three characters.

9. Maceo says he considers himself a man, but not in front of Daddy Al. Has he grown up yet? As the patriarch of the

Redfield clan, what sway does Daddy Al have over the family?

10. The Redfields are tight-knit and fiercely protective of one another. How does Maceo violate their only rule—loyalty to the family?

11. Holly and Maceo have each developed scars in the time between *The Dying Ground,* the first Maceo Redfield novel, and *The Last King.* Discuss their evolution. What is in store for their future?

About the Author

NICHELLE D. TRAMBLE was born in Northern California. Her first novel, *The Dying Ground,* was shortlisted for the Zora Neale Hurston/ Richard Wright Foundation Debut Fiction Award. Tramble was also a Writer-in-Residence at the Edward J. Albee Foundation. The author currently resides in California, where she is at work on her next novel. Her website address is www.nichelletramble.com.